PATCHWORK

PATCHWORK

a novel by

KAREN OSBORN

Harcourt Brace Jovanovich, Publishers

San Diego   New York   London

HBJ

This is a work of fiction.
All the names, characters, organizations, and events
portrayed in this book are either the products
of the author's imagination or are used fictitiously
for verisimilitude. Any resemblance to any organization
or to any actual person, living or dead, is unintended.

Requests for permission to make copies of any part of
the work should be mailed to: Permissions Department,
Harcourt Brace Jovanovich, Publishers, 8th Floor,
Orlando, Florida 32887.

Library of Congress Cataloging-in-Publication Data
Osborn, Karen.
Patchwork/Karen Osborn.—1st ed.
p.   cm.
ISBN 0-15-171292-1
I. Title.
PS3565.S385P38   1991
813'.54—dc20   90-23878

Designed by Camilla Filancia
Printed in the United States of America
First edition   A B C D E

FOR MIKE

I would like to thank
Jane Gelfman for all the support
she gave me during
the writing of this book
and the people of
South Carolina's Piedmont region
who helped me to understand life
in the cotton mill towns.

Part 1

1930 – 1934

Chapter 1

ROSE'S STORY

IT WAS OVER a hundred degrees in the mill. All morning my head spun with the clack of spindles and the whoosh of threads that slipped between my fingers. They became long, thin lines of twisting whiteness, "devil hairs" we called them when they got tangled. Cotton dust stuck to my face and hair. It hung above, a billowy ceiling. I remember Annabelle's weight pressing down until my feet barely fit into my house slippers. When the floor shook from the banging of looms downstairs, I knew I'd fall into the threads crossing back and forth in front of me. They flew in my face. The spindles they wound onto jumped up and down. I kept thinking when they tangled my thick fingers could never set them straight.

Edward and me had kept from having a family long as we could, to save for this piece of land just outside town. We told ourselves we'd live on it someday. The mill houses were small, cheap, but you could fix them up pretty. Edward was two years younger than me, but he already made good money. Someday he wanted to have a farm like his mother and father did when he was little, wanted to have a few cows and a horse. I needed cloth for baby blankets and gowns. I was in the middle of thinking about this baby blanket I'd make, all fine and soft along the edges, when the whistle blew and there was Lily in the dust grabbing my hand, saying to follow her outside for a smoke. I could see she had on a new blouse under her apron, a pretty one. Lily never looked tired.

Outside, sitting against the wall, I felt the whole building shaking and knew it was alive, not just with all the people working and breathing cotton but with them machines and all their parts moving up and down and sideways and the cotton that was changing the way it was each minute. The boys were dumping baskets of dirty-looking raw cotton into the bins in the yard. I was just thinking how hot they must be with lifting them, when Lily starts in about Charles. Lily was married just a year, after all the time she spent running around with different mill boys. Already I sensed Charles was all trouble.

"Acts like a dang rooster half the time," she said, lighting a cigarette. Then she told about going down to Martin's, where Charles had been playing music. I had heard Edward talk about Martin's. It was a rough place, back of a house where they even served liquor. But Lily is like that, never been a bit afraid to go anywhere. She said how she got dressed up and went down there, but Charles was too busy crowing to notice her. "Got them hens pecking around him thicker than if he got the only comb in town, and he puffs his chest out and has to say you know what to each one. Lord only knows what he does nights when I'm not there." She blew smoke out real slow and ground the end of the cigarette into the dirt. "Jumps the whole bunch of them and tells them to go home and sit on their eggs."

I tried not to laugh. Lily had a crazy way of talking, and me pregnant too. When she said she'd got a dandy rooster who wanted her to sit on his eggs, I asked who was it. Lily shook another cigarette out of the package, saying how she'd keep them eggs warm. Then we both were laughing so hard we fell over, holding our sides. Branches twisted against the sky, and I wanted to follow their pattern the rest of my life, so much plainer and easier to see than the thin threads crossing each other. That's when the pain started, making me lean back against the wall.

"Is it your labor?" Lily kept asking me. But I was just seven months pregnant and couldn't believe I'd have the baby so soon. When the pain left, I felt same as ever. Lily run to get Edward, joking about how I just didn't want to go back and work in that heat, which was true.

I had the baby in no time after we reached the house. The boss man at the mill sent a doctor over, and when I saw the look on his face, I wished he hadn't come. I could hold every bit of her in one of my hands, and she was made perfect, like those porcelain dolls that close their eyes when you lay them down. I heard him in the kitchen with Edward, saying he didn't "give a nickel for that child's life" but to keep it dry and fed and out of drafts. I saw the quick look he give before he left, like he wished the baby been born dead so he didn't have to think about coming back. Edward's eyes were flat when he came inside, telling me he couldn't see someone who would die, telling me he would not take the chance I had to by holding it.

"We can have another one," he told me. I couldn't say nothing.

If it weren't for Helen and the others I never could have nursed the tiny thing. Helen and them come over just after they got done at the mill. Must have skipped supper or let their men and young'uns eat old bread and beans. They was holding these bundles of cloth, all tied up.

"Where's the baby?" they were saying when Edward let them into the bedroom. He had to switch on the light so they could make us out. I pulled back the covers, letting the baby's head show. She was sleeping, and besides, I didn't want none of them to see she was so tiny.

But nothing stops Helen. She pulled back that blanket to get a good look. "It's so tiny," she breathed out. "Look at it."

And they all did, crowding around until all I seen were their faces hanging over us.

"Doctor and Edward think it won't live long," I told them, pulling the blanket back in place.

Matty turned away to spit into her handkerchief. "Doctors just men, and men don't know nothing about babies," she says when she gets done with spitting. Matty worked the looms now and again, just like a man would. All those men around her on the looms, and she never would take no back talk. If one of them touched her, even bumped her by accident, she'd kick him in the shins. "My sister-in-law had one about that size," she says to me, "and it grew. Every time we turned around it was growing, until it got bigger than the others its same age. A good baby too. Never did cry. It could be soaked with being wet and not cry." She looked around to see if we believed her. Even I was nodding my head. Matty had a way of telling things true. "Johnney. That's the one I mean. He's up to here now." She held her hand out beside her waist. "You can't tell nothing from their size."

Lizzy and Darla untied their bundles and started hunting through the baby clothes and blankets that were folded up inside. "Here's one's not too big," says Lizzy.

"I got some that'll do, with a tuck here and there," says Darla. "Where's your sewing basket, Rose? I'll set right here and fix them."

I pointed to where it set on the dresser, and she pulled the rocker up to the light and started sewing.

By the time they finished untying stuff, you never had seen so many baby gowns and tiny shirts, all soft and worn, diapers and baby blankets — most everything handmade. Some of them gowns had shiny pieces of ribbon drawn through them. And Helen gave a hat and sweater and the booties she made for her first one.

When Annie started her crying, I turned on my side to try and get her to eat. "Ain't got much of a suck," I told them. "Can't hardly feel her."

"Try putting a little sugar in her mouth first," says Lizzy. "That'll get her going. Where do you keep it?" she asks me. She was through the door before I could say a thing, hollering that she'd find it on her own. When she come back, her fingertip was all white with sugar. "Let me see her," she said, turning the baby around.

"Now don't go giving her too much," says Matty. "She'll expect Rose to taste that sweet." We all start to laughing while Lizzy's rubbing her finger inside the baby's mouth. When Annie opens her mouth for more, Lizzy turns her towards me, and she starts sucking.

"Does feel better," I told her. "I'll just have to keep the sugar bowl in here, right beside my bed, from now on."

We all started laughing again and didn't quit until we saw how late it was. When they were gone, I called Edward to find a drawer space for all them baby things. "Looks like you got yourself a bundle," he says, clearing a space. He walked over to the bed, slow, and sat down next to me. Annie was sleeping, curled up like a little package.

"She'll be okay," I told him. "She'll get bigger."

He put his arm around me, shaking his head. "Don't know," he told me.

That Saturday in the afternoon while I was sleeping, a few of them come by with breads and cookies, beans with thick pieces of ham in them. Then Sunday, right after church gets out, Esther, who works beside me in the spinning room since we was girls, brings over a baby bed, a pot full of meat stew, and a cake. "I got to get back to my girls," she hollers from the kitchen. She's got two — one that's four years now and one that just learned to walk. "Just heat up the stew."

All afternoon I was smelling them breads, cookies, cake, and that meat stew warming my kitchen.

I GOT MY STRENGTH back fast and for weeks carried Annie in a sling I made with a scrap of cloth. Sometimes I tucked her inside my dress. She seemed to like it best like that, close to me. Her weight was less than being pregnant. If she kicked or turned in her sleep, my body moved with her like I still carried her inside. When she woke she looked up at me with those quiet eyes. I think she knew just what was in my head.

Sometimes Edward asked to carry her to the window and show her how summer was all green and blue and growing. But then he give her back real quick, like why show her summer when she'd never taste it for herself. But Annabelle kept on growing. When the window colors changed to oranges and browns, she got too heavy to be in the sling all day, so I had to set her on a blanket. She giggled each time I picked her up.

It was in Edward's mother's mind to help us out, and she come over to sit with Annie while I went back up to the mill. Inside with that shaking and banging, the smell and sticky feel of cotton everywhere, and what with me sore from having all that milk, there was little else I could think on but how Annabelle was growing. You can't always believe those doctors; sometimes you got to listen to what's in your heart like it's Jesus speaking to you, which is really just what I always been taught.

Every few minutes I looked up from the flying threads just long enough to see was it near breaktime. When the whistle started blowing, I run outside, my milk dripping everywhere, mixing with all that sweat, but I never cared. I was looking for Edward's mother to come down the road, bent over with carrying Annie, moving slow. Nelly was nursing hers too, and we'd watch together, then sit on a piece of grass beside the gate or on wood crates if the ground was cold. We held them to the tittie, like Nelly'd say, until they were sleeping and their grannies could carry them home.

Some days a boss man would walk by us, real close like. "Can't you women be decent? Ain't you got a scrap of cloth to put over you?" he'd tell us, shaking his head but all the time looking.

"Why bother?" I says to one of them. "Just a bunch of women looking, besides you." After that he act like he don't see us.

But the best thing about the fall was the change in Edward. He come out each afternoon to walk me to the gate, giving me play pretties he'd made from spools and such. When it snowed for the first time that winter he took Annie to the window and pointed, saying, "Look, even the sky is white," just like that, like it was a kind of miracle.

THE JULY that Annie turned two, Edward got this raise for becoming a loom fixer and told me to stay home. I was getting big already with our second one. I spent most of the day watching Annie and keeping the house clean and decorated with curtains and pictures from magazines and a calendar I cut out and pasted to frames.

I had put Annie down for a nap one morning when Mama rode up in the old wagon filled with corn and tubs of beans and okra. We was planning on putting up soup. First I had to fetch the tomatoes from a garden I'd planted out back. Mama must have noticed how the weight of that baby slowed me down, because she followed, saying she'd carry them to the porch. They was warm and ripe and splitting in the sun.

We sat down, shucking corn and snapping beans. The sounds we made felt like the rhythm inside me that I'd hear if I shut my eyes and listened real hard. Mama started talking about Juney. At first I didn't even hear, something about some boy she was with, getting ice cream. I let her voice fill me up too and started a rhyme in my head: "One potato, two potato, three potato, four . . ."

"I hate to even see Lillian come by now," Mama said. The beans snapped between her fingers. "Afraid she'll get to talking to Juney."

I looked her straight in the eye, which being as how she's my mother I ain't done much. "Mama," I told her, "Lily is married now."

"Well, look at that boy she married. And what kinda wedding is it with nobody there?" She picked up an ear of corn and pulled off the husk with one quick jerk. "Even your daddy and me had a wedding. That ain't no marriage. Soon she'll have all those boys hanging around her again, working in that mill like she does. Every lowlife in town hangs out around there."

I kept snapping beans, slow and even, letting them make up their own rhythm. Mama always was good at reading the future for Lily. But I didn't let on about that. What made me mad was seeing how she'd kept it against us for working at the mill, when she pushed us to start working there herself. First time I'd seen that, but it'd been in my face a long time. "Did you forget how she started working there?" I asked her. I was sitting stiff in my chair, and neither one of us was snapping beans or shucking any corn. "We was out of school before we was June's age, working to help out you and Daddy." I had to say it, her bragging about Juney going to school and

her boyfriends. Since Mama and Daddy's farm was between the mill and town, Juney went to the big high
school in town, where the rich kids went. Mama tried to
make her all kind of fancy dresses to wear, and Juney
always had to have her hair done up. I worked hard and
was proud of me and Edward. But I shouldn't have said
nothing.

Mama got up quick, saying she was going home. I
told her to stay; then I had to add something about Lily,
because I'm not like Lily but I think I can see why she
acts like she does. "I just wish you'd let Lily be. I got
lucky with marrying Edward, but it's hard working like
that, twelve hours a day and in the heat too, standing on
a hard floor, watching threads, same thing every day.
There ain't much time for courting and marriage. Lily
just wanted some fun in life."

"Fun," Mama broke in. "That's why I don't want her
coming around Juney, giving her fool ideas about what
fun is."

"It's not fair comparing them like that," I said, picking up a bean and breaking it in two just for the sound.
"June came later, after Fredrick and Benjy and all.
Everything's been different for her. Me and Lily — " And
I stopped there, because suddenly I could see it too clear,
and I knew more than I wanted to. Mama had put Lily
and me to work back before I could even remember, taking us out of school early in spring to pull plows and help
with planting. I was cleaning the house and cooking and

barely could reach the stove, while Mama helped Daddy or took care of Benjy and Fredrick. The Christmas after Fredrick and Benjy died, Mama was pregnant with June. Most Christmases we got candy sticks and oranges in the stockings we pinned up. We'd cut a hole in the oranges and suck out the juice with the candy stick, making it real sweet. Lily and me hung our stockings up, but in the morning they were empty. At first I thought it was some kind of mistake, but when I saw it weren't I just couldn't help it, I sat on the floor and cried. Finally Daddy pulled me outside, said to hush before he made me. "But I do everything you and Mama tell me," I said, which was true.

He got sad-looking and sat down with me. "That's not it," he told me. "It's just we got so little for the cotton this year, and with what happened to your brothers . . ." Maybe he stopped there, or I just couldn't remember no more.

I used to treat Juney almost like my own, rocking her, changing her clothes, but now I remembered the dolls she got each year under the tree and thought how the money for them must have come from me and Lily's earnings.

Annie was crying, and I heard Mama get up, sliding the metal tub across the porch boards, saying, "I'll get her. You stay put." My fingers started snapping beans, moving quick like without me even thinking. I told myself how much Mama had slowed down since Daddy's death and how it wasn't right for me to upset her. When she sat down to rock Annie, it filled the dark places in me.

THAT FALL, about midafternoon, I had both An-nie and the baby — Benjy we called him — asleep when June come up to the house with a cake Mama had made. I put on coffee for us to have with it, seeing how it was getting cool now that summer was gone, and set out plates and napkins for the cake, trying to make the table look pretty. That's when she told me about James wanting a spring wedding. I knew Mama wanted her to wait until next year, but I have learned one thing, that most people don't take to advice once they got their mind set on something, especially when it's marriage. I made that mistake with Lily, and I knew I would not make it again, so I kept my mouth closed.

"James is working with his daddy now, and he needs a wife." She hurried the words like I would try to stop her, but I just set there. "I'll be finished with high school by then." She fingered the spoon I'd set in front of her.

I nodded and started slicing the cake. June'd be get-ting what she always wanted — living in her own house in town, married to somebody rich, far away from the mill. I guess it was envy, but all I could think was how she'd get left standing by the altar once his mama found out where Juney lived and how her mama and daddy was cotton dirt farmers and her two sisters worked in the mill ever since they could reach the spindles and carry a bucket lunch.

"Besides," she kept on, "if I don't marry him soon, there's others that would. After all, his daddy owns the bank." She walked over to the window, turned towards me, all the time running her fingers along the edge of that spoon like it was something precious. "But I don't have much to worry about. Like Missy told me, there aren't many girls prettier than me at the high school."

The dresses June wore were shorter than I would have put on. They showed her legs. This one came in at the waist and was tied with a shiny little belt. She liked a full skirt.

The knife slid through the cake real easy. Since I was trying to cut the pieces even, I didn't know Lily was at the door until she knocked. I'd been weeks without seeing her, and she was so pretty standing there in the door-frame, smiling the way she did sometimes that made her face all lit up. I run over to hug her, then stepped back to look at her dress, which showed her legs more than June's and was right out of one of them fashion maga-zines. Her face all made up too under a new hat. Next to her, June and me looked plain, but especially me after having Annie and Benjy.

"Had to see how you was doing with two babies," Lily told me, holding my hands. "I still look up from my spindle thinking you'll be standing there," which was probably true, as we'd worked together like that for more

than ten years. She started telling me about the mill ladies and how two of them had to quit because they were
having babies, how one lady had lost hers and almost on
the mill floor. Now they were making the pregnant ones
quit, so you had to hide it as long as you could. There
was talk of making all the women quit. Each day more
men lined up looking for work.

Then Lily saw June. She dropped my hands and just
stood there looking. It'd been over three months since
they seen each other. June seemed nervous and maybe
jealous too. Lily had always been so pretty, but I guess I
was used to it. After a minute of standing there, Lily
reached out for June's hands. June kept hers to herself.
"I hear there's gonna be another wedding," Lily says finally. "Well, I hope he's handsome."

Everybody sat down. I put a piece of cake and cup
of coffee in front of Lily, and thinking on making con-
versation, I said, "How's Charles?" Just soon as those
words jumped loose, though, I was sorry. Lydia, who
works at the mill, had told me last week that he was
staying out all night sometimes now, playing in every back
room in town.

"Oh, he's just fine, real fine," Lily said, taking off her
hat and laying it careful-like on the table as she sat down.
"I guess you heard — the whole town seems to know our
business." She laughed. "When he comes home I'm so
glad to see him, I forget it all. I oughta leave him."

I could see June getting red around the ears and taking a long, careful time to eat her cake. So I said, "Leaving your husband is a terrible thing. I don't believe I could do it, even if I was you," trying to sound sympathetic.

It didn't help none. "No, you don't understand," she said fast, her dark eyes darting all over my face. "It's not the talk or even what it'd do to Mama, though Lord knows I don't mean to hurt her."

June finished her cake, got up quick, and went in the next room. I heard her picking up Annie. "I guess I shouldn't talk that way in front of virgin ears," says Lily, taking a small bite of cake and pushing the plate away. "She might learn something about marriage."

"Oh, stop, Lily," I blurted without thinking. "Not everybody gets married goes crazy." I stopped short and come over to Lily, saying, "I'm sorry, honey. I didn't mean — "

But she cut me off, pushing away the hands I'd put on her shoulders. "You're right," she said. "I am crazy. I keep telling myself to leave before it gets worse. But then he walks in the house, puts his arms around me . . ."

I felt my face go red. I never was pulled to Edward like that. I mean, I loved him, but I could see how Charles got Lily wound up so tight the little threads were about to split.

"Truth is," Lily started again, "I ain't seen him in over four days now. I keep thinking about where he is and who he's with. I still joke, calling him a rooster who's got too much juice, and laugh in his face, calling them whores when he tells me their names, because I know that makes him maddest. Then I can tell myself he's doing it just to make me jealous, to keep me on his string." She stopped for a second, looking, I guess, at the surprise on my face. "I shouldn't be going on like this. I ain't told nobody. This is the longest he's been gone."

I went up behind her, not knowing what to say, and started smoothing back her hair, all thick and dark like sweet chestnuts. "You know I don't understand it all, you and him," I told her, "but anytime you want to come by . . ."

When she stood up, my hands hung loose and empty in the air. "Thanks, honey," she said. "I better get now. Edward'll be home soon, and you gotta put supper on. Maybe by the time I walk home, Charles'll be there." She was already opening the door.

"Come back soon, now," I told her, "anytime. If he's not there tonight, come back for supper."

She said okay and to say bye to Juney for her. I watched her through the window becoming a misty blur in the evening light and tried to think hard on how a man like Charles, who was handsome enough but had a wild, mean streak in him that anybody could see, got her to marry him and then stay with him while he went out on her.

June came back in the kitchen carrying Benjy, saying she guessed she better get home too, that Mama'd be keeping supper. Then she asked was Lily okay.

"I hope so," I said. "Charles ain't been coming home."

June had to start in about what Mama thinks. "I don't see why she married him," she says. "Mama says he's no good, says everybody knows it. I don't know why Lily did it. Mama thinks it was to spite her."

I took the baby. Annie was playing on the floor with spoons. "Mama thinks everything Lily does is to spite her," I told Juney. "Who knows why Lily married him. Maybe not even Lily. I guess she loves him, and she can't help that."

Next June started in about James, saying how she loved him because he was so good to her and respected her. She touched the bright new necklace she had on, saying how he gives her things. Lily is prettier than anybody I ever seen except in magazines, but that don't always help around men. One summer when we was picking, I remember Daddy taking Lily into the barn and switching her legs with a stick after the men he'd hired to help pick kept stopping work to whistle every time she pulled up her skirt to step over a cotton bush or untangle her threads from the stickers. "Well, sometimes things change after you marry," I started to tell Juney, but she was on the floor saying bye to Annie. She slipped out the door, probably thinking about marrying James and the nice house they'd get on the other side of town and maybe even seeing how she'd fix it up. She was walking away real fast before I could tell her different.

When Edward came home the kitchen was warm and Annie was sitting up at the table watching me pour cornmeal batter slow into the skillet. I always let her clean the bowl afterwards with her finger. Edward threw Benjy in the air until he giggled, then put his arm around my waist, said he'd clean up for supper, and I told myself it was all okay — Lily going crazy, June all happy and marrying somebody rich, my two babies, this kitchen that is almost too small for us, and Edward, who's always sweaty when he comes home but hugs me anyways, saying how he loves my corn bread. I even told myself it was okay I was gaining all this weight after having two babies. I set the table with my best white napkins and a bowl of sweet chestnuts to celebrate.

Chapter 2

*L*ILY'S STORY

IT WAS MORNING when I rolled over to Charles's side of the bed, felt how cold it was, and knew he hadn't come in all night. I told myself I needed to get up and fill the stove with coal, but since it was Sunday I crawled back to my warm place on the bed and crept deeper under the quilt. Lying there, my mind went loose over everything, like unwinding a thread that has lots of colors. I could follow the way we gone, but I couldn't see my way out.

His hair was yellow as the maple leaves we walked through that first fall. I know how he must have planned it ahead — stopping like he did after we passed that church, turning me to him, and kissing me on the mouth. Then he put his hands under my blouse, his nails deep in the skin on my back when he pressed me to him. Not saying anything, he pulled me behind the church to the graveyard and unbuttoned my blouse. When I looked into his face, I saw a smile just waiting to come out. He pushed me to the ground. "Not here," I said in a whisper, but he just mumbled something out of the corner of his mouth about the dead not caring, all the time sliding off my panties. When he lifted my skirt, his hands didn't even shake, he was so sure, like he'd done it every day. He didn't fumble none, like the other mill boys I went with. When the damp got in my clothes, I let him come across that wide space I always got spun around myself even back when I was little and sat on Daddy's lap or told secrets with Rose.

When I met him the summer before at one of them mill dances, I was wearing a dress of that shiny rayon, cut short-like so just anybody could see the shape of my legs. We danced around the floor, and then he was pushing me out the door into the sticky night. His voice harsh as the rasp of locusts, he leaned out of the darkness, saying how we needed to go for a walk, pressing my arm like he'd make me say yes. I looked straight in his face and laughed, called him crazy, told him I didn't even know his name.

"It's Charles," he told me. "Charles Stone." Maybe it was his looks, and he was something to look at even in work clothes, or maybe I just felt the quick hum of summer's last heat, but I reached right up and kissed him on the mouth. Then I ran inside.

Later I heard him start a fight over nothing but pushing and shoving. The other boys were calling him crazy, trying to make him quit. I heard his sharp laugh and saw him after in the dark doorway peering in at me dancing with one of the Ingsley brothers, grinning like the fight and me and the whole dance was some kind of joke he thought of.

We got married that next spring. For weeks Charles come home early every evening and pulled me away from the kitchen where I stood trying to think on what to make for supper. He pulled me away into the bedroom, saying I was supper enough. He always made me laugh. Later we fried bacon for sandwiches and cut into fresh tomatoes. Some nights we'd go on down to Martin's or some other place where Charles would be playing music. He'd sing the one he wrote for me. Everybody'd be talking about how someday he'd get known.

We had to share an outdoor privy, hardly did ever get to take a real bath. One Sunday morning he set the big old tub on our kitchen floor, filled it with water he heated on the stove. He poured in some sweet-smelling stuff he bought to make bubbles, pulled my nightgown off over my head, took off his own clothes, and we both got in. Even had some kind of drink he made with liquor in real glasses. Said it was our "private Sunday worship service." When we got hungry for breakfast, he jumped out of the tub, didn't even wrap a towel round his hips, stood at the stove like that frying our eggs.

When he lost the mill job, he got to hanging around,

staying out late, after my shift work was done. First time, I asked where he been and didn't let up until he told me. "Been to see a few friends," he said finally, and he opened the icebox and took a long swallow of tea straight from the pitcher. That's when I went and sat on the porch steps, my lips pressed together so tight like I'd bite off the tears. But he come out, walking soft-like. I heard him pulling a chair from behind me and felt him reach out and touch my hair. He called me honey, saying, "You're the prettiest thing I ever seen, and I want you; it scares me how much I want you. But I guess it's easy, your being here and all."

Charles always did like excitement, couldn't stand to be knowing how each day would go. "Marriage is too regular for you," I spat back, trying to stand up, but he pushed me back down.

His face was all drawn up, and I knew I weren't no joke to him anymore. "When we're lying in there," he said, "and I can't get enough fast enough, I see your face afterwards and you're happy, like you're thinking about starting supper or a dress you want to put on. It makes me crazy." I guess I get his meaning. I always got something to keep back, even with Charles.

I turned away and moved down the steps. "So you thought you'd spend some of that wanting on one of them whores you used to go with," I told him. His heavy shoes hit the boards when he walked into the house.

Later I crawled into bed, thinking he'd be asleep, but

he weren't. He wanted something too. He kept telling me, "I don't want to go out on you, but it's the only way I got to hold something back, something of myself."

And I know that's what makes me want him so bad. Each day I got to hold my breath because there's no way of knowing what he'll do. And no matter how many ways he loves me, there's always part of him I can't reach. That morning when I woke up, he was gone. I got out of bed, fried me an egg. When he came in I didn't say a word. I looked at him, but I didn't let myself see him.

THE NIGHT I walked to Rose's house, it was dark, but that didn't scare me none; the worst done already happened. At first I thought the surprise on her face was just at seeing me standing there in the night and after not seeing me for more than a couple weeks, but later I seen that it was my face, all swollen and colored from Charles's fists. I tried to tell Rose what happened, how Charles come home for supper with some talk about last night and where I'd been, when he was out all night so how'd he know, and about how I was married but that didn't mean I weren't no whore. He said he found the necklace, the one Mr. Tolland give me, held it out in his rough hand, saying he was gonna sell it. I tried to grab it from him, saying he wouldn't sell nothing of mine. But he was pushing me down, saying who did I think I was, having a necklace someone else give me. I tried to tell him, "I got you, and that's all I want."

"That's right, you got me," he said. "I'll show you how much of me you got." Then he was on me and I couldn't get him off.

I guess my story come out wrong. All Rose kept asking was who was Mr. Tolland, which was not important as there was nothing between us, but the necklace was pretty.

Edward had disappeared into the next room, getting ready for bed. Rose whispered for me to stay on with them, and she warmed up water and got a gown of hers for me to put on. Later that night, when I was laying on the sofa bed, I hear them whispering, Edward asking how long I'm planning on staying, telling Rose that I have to go back and how Charles is my husband. Edward never did know me much. Rose starts crying, saying how he saw what Charles done, but Edward's voice was real clear. He said, "You know your sister. She's been asking for this sort of trouble all her life," which sounded just like something my daddy would say.

All night I kept seeing Charles playing his guitar or grinning over me when we was laying on the bed, and the look in his eyes that says he might do anything, didn't matter how crazy or wild. I figured I'd go back after he begged me.

Rose got her way. The next morning she tells me I can stay on as long as I need to. Seems like that winter I got lost in them turning spindles; the threads twisted in long thin lines, crossing each other up like they was the thoughts running around in my head. And Charles never did beg me. All day I hear the mill women laughing with each other, pretending like they're putting a little spider in the other one's apron pocket or trying to trip each other up. They're careful not to say nothing to me.

At night, after me and Rose got the kitchen clean, I walked alone, even if the air were a wet chill and Rose telling me not to go out. When I couldn't stay away I'd look for Charles at the rooms he rented or in one of them back rooms where there was liquor drinking. He'd be sitting in a circle of smoke, the only handsome thing in the room, his face set in hard lines like a man who wasn't afraid to pull out a pistol or start a fight or grab some pretty lady, carry her off.

While we loved each other on the bed I'd see myself turning round and round in a spiral like them threads make, his easy grin everywhere I looked. If I stayed on with him, coming back after work to cook his meals, I'd spiral down tighter until I'd wake up in the dark or early light to see he hadn't come home or until he come home late, too drunk to make love. He'd lay on top of me and pin my arms to my sides. Sometimes he'd fall asleep like that and I'd know I done reached the tight point of the spiral. I'd go back to Rose's in the morning.

At the divorce hearing he was quiet, what with Rose telling about them bruises on my face and how my arm had to be set before I could go back to work, and me saying how many nights he slept out.

Chapter 3

ROSE'S STORY

I RODE MATTY'S MULE out to Mama's when I heard. Mama's neighbor had carried me the news and stayed on with the babies. Walking up to the square frame house, I couldn't see how it had held us all. I opened the door to the kitchen with its wooden plank table and then peered into the dark bedroom where all us kids used to sleep. The house was so cold I could tell there hadn't been no fire made. Then I see June all curled up in the armchair in the living room, holding her wedding dress. "She finished it for me last night," she told me, "sewed on the last lace before she laid down."

I walked over and took that dress, which was all wrinkled. "No sense in ruining it," I told her, hanging it up. Putting my arm around her, I walked her into the kitchen. "Wash your face, now. You'll feel better," I said to her. She looked like she been crying all morning.

"Tenderhearted," Daddy always called her. I took plenty of blame for June's mischief, let Mama think I broke a pitcher or got into the sweets, since June would mope around for days after one whipping, but I couldn't keep this from her. I was drying her face, and June was crying into the towel. I had to get hard to keep from crying myself. "Mama's been sickly ever since Daddy died," I said to us both. "It was her time, and she went sleeping and peaceful. Let her go. Tomorrow you start your own family with James."

"She stayed up late sewing the lace on. Just like when she was making that quilt for you and she'd stay up half the night." A few weeks ago, Mama'd brought the quilt by. She'd sewn together small pieces of cloth she'd cut from mill scraps I gave her into a star pattern, smaller stars opening up into larger stars. "Around the World," it was called. Before she died, she'd planned to make one for Lily and June.

"I went in there this morning to tell her I'd seen how she finished the dress so lovely," June said, still crying into that towel, "and she was there on the bed. At first I thought she was asleep, but she was so cold." June was shaking now. "Remember how when we were little she'd curl up with us in one of the trundle beds and read from the school reader with us, making up the words she didn't know?"

"June." I took her shoulders. "I loved Mama too. But we knew she was sickly."

"I wanted James to take me away from these small rooms crowded with old furniture and from all that dirt Daddy dug in, but I thought Mama would come live with us. I don't want a family of my own. I want our family back, the way it was before Daddy fell from the barn and took sick, when we crowded around this table and Uncle Ben would come out to help Daddy. The house was full of warm smells of baked ham and sweet potatoes, and all of us together around the table. After supper Mama would put off the dishes to sit with me, or I'd go out with Uncle Ben and get a ride on his horse."

June was the baby back then. All of us crowded around that little table, with the food disappearing in a few minutes, Daddy and Uncle Ben fighting over the harvest money Uncle Ben would lose at cards. I tried to say all this to June, but she threw the crumpled towel at me and turned away, saying, "You're trying to ruin it for me, blacken everything I have."

"I only want you to see both sides and let go of all this," I told her. "James has got a smart head on him, and his family's got money. He'll make a fine husband." She sat down at the table and stopped crying. "And he's been good to you," I went on. "Takes you into town all the time, gives you all kind of presents, and doesn't care where you come from. Not many boys from town would do like that. You're graduated from high school now," I told her, "and about to marry a good husband."

Juney stuck out her chin in a pout. She never could

admit how poor Mama and Daddy were and how much above her James was. But when I asked her if she could help me with Mama, she said yes. So I filled the wash-basin at the pump and picked out some linens. Back in the bedroom, I laid out Mama's Sunday dress and her newest underclothes. With all the wrinkles, Mama's face was like a web. I thought how I'd go back to my own house later to get some lotion to soften the skin. She shouldn't meet Daddy, I thought, looking like an old woman.

June brought the basin back with the water warm, so I knew she had a fire going. My fingers were so cold I ripped the sleeve of Mama's nightgown trying to pull her hand through. I had to get June to help me with lifting her up so we could pull the gown over her head, and it ripped again, a long tear that ran the whole length, making a noise that filled the room. I had just turned Mama over so I could roll up the sheets and put on fresh linens, when I saw June, shaky and white as Mama, backing out the door, mumbling something about more clothes she was getting. I let her go even though now I had to make up the bed by myself and not let Mama fall.

When June got back I had on the fresh linens. Mama was so thin and pale she looked like a young girl against the sheets, if you didn't look at her face. I was washing her with a cloth, taking my time and thinking how this was the last I'd get to touch her. When Fredrick and Benjamin died I helped Mama and Daddy. Benjy was so little he fit right in the washbasin, and Mama screamed when Daddy held his head under to wash his hair. "It don't matter now, Evey," he kept telling her. But she cried until he helped her into the other room and told me to finish.

June was sitting in a chair next to the bed, holding Mama's hand. I told her about this scented soap I was using that I'd brought from the house, how it smelled sweeter than the lard soap Mama made. June didn't move at all, not even to blink. "I thought we'd wrap her hair up in those fancy knots, the way Mama did sometimes on Sundays," I said to her, thinking it'd help to get her talking. But she nodded like she was having a dream that I wasn't part of. That's always been June's way, living in some kind of storybook. I kept hoping for her sake that James was real and not just somebody she dreamed up. "Go on to the kitchen, if you want, while I finish," I told her, trying to make it sound nice. I was wishing Lily was there to help, but she was at the mill. I put the cloth in the basin and wrung it out, trying to think about all the good Mama did in this world.

We had the funeral that evening. It was simple but real nice, with hymn singing and the preacher talking about how Mama's life was pure and good, how she was walking with God. Mama's brothers and Edward lowered the coffin in the ground next to Daddy and Benjy and Fredrick. As they was filling in the hole and the preacher was blessing her soul, Lily came walking up, in a bright green dress cut too short, without a hat, and her face made up too. I could hear people whispering. Before anyone could tell her to leave, I reached for her hand and pulled her to me. We stood there with our arms around each other and me feeling how sad I was inside.

All this time June was at the back with James and his mother, who held the clasp of her fur coat with her hand and looked down on all of us. When James got to the house that afternoon and June showed him the dress, sobbing about how she couldn't marry him, he looked straight at me, saying it was my fault, I didn't have no business expecting June to help get Mama ready, how I been against their wedding all along, which was not true.

But they married the next day anyhow. June was real quiet the whole time, looking like a storybook princess in the dress Mama had finished, her eyes lost like she was still dreaming. I stood up with her, and a few others were there, but there weren't no reception. The house was fancy, just like June said, but they hadn't gone to no trouble, didn't even have flowers. James's mother made us all leave soon as the ceremony was done, like it weren't a real wedding. Me and Edward said goodbye polite as we could. I was thinking how worn out we must look — Edward in his one suit he's got for Sundays and me in my flower-print dress. I'd washed and ironed it good, but the pattern looks rubbed off in some places. There weren't many to say goodbye to — James's sister and her husband, his aunt, a few cousins, and his grandmother. June's girlfriend Missy weren't even there. And Edward and me were the only family there for June. James had told us ahead of time Lily couldn't enter their house.

I DIDN'T SEE none of June after the wedding, but I heard plenty, as Izzy, who works in spinning with me, has a son who works at the grocery in town, and he hears everything. June had bought all kind of cloth for curtains and some rugs and furniture to fill her house with. The ladies who come by the grocery said how she'd made her house cheap looking. I'd seen the house from the outside. It was on a real nice street near the downtown, with all kind of trees along the road. It was red brick. Not real big or fancy, but the kind of house people live in who got good-paying jobs at the bank or hospital or law offices. I couldn't see it in my mind as cheap, no matter what kind of curtains June put up. Some folks will say next to anything out of meanness. That's what I told myself when Izzy said how them town ladies wouldn't invite June to their lunches even if she did marry Mr. Cutler's son.

The same day Izzy tells me this I seen Missy. She was working in the spinning room, stringing threads through a feeder so they'd come out straight. Never was a worser job. You got to stand in one place all day just watching for crossed threads and broken ones as they come through the feeder and get wound onto a roller so we can use them on the looms. When you spot a tangle or a broke one, you got to quick thread it right again or knot it before it wraps onto the roller. I was on break, walking to the bathroom, when I seen her standing in front of the feeder, squinting at the moving threads.

"What are you doing in the mill?" I asked her. Missy lived close to town on a farm near the one Mama and Daddy had owned, the farm we had to sell to pay the back taxes after Mama died. She and June both got to go to the school in town. Missy was a year behind June, and she always made sure never to miss any classes during planting time. Here she was in the mill, and she hadn't even graduated yet.

"Daddy took sick," she tells me. "I had to get some kind of job."

I shook my head. "Are you quitting school or what?" I was yelling on account of the noise from the feeder turning.

"I'll have to. Ma's home taking care of Daddy."

"Have you seen June?" I shout. "This ain't no place for you. Maybe James can find you work in town. You got more schooling than most that works here."

Just then a broke thread came up near the feeder. Missy tried to knot it again quick as she could, but it slipped out and she had to cut off the machine before the broke one wound on the roller.

"I went by June's house last week," she says while she's tying another knot.

But the feeder being off didn't help the noise much

with all them other machines going, and I had to ask her,
"When did you say?"

"Last week," she says again. "June wouldn't let me
through the front door. Said she was busy." I couldn't
see Missy's face, just her hands.

That's when the floor man comes by, telling Missy
she needs to quit talking and pay attention, how the machine getting cut off costs them money. I got back to my
place real quick, even forgot about going to the bathroom.

Her telling me that was why I was so surprised when
June sent me a note in the mail saying she and James
would be glad to come to dinner. I was proud I could
make out the writing myself, since I had to ask Edward
to help write the note asking them.

That Sunday after church they drove their car up into
the yard. It was the first I'd seen of it, and I was wishing
later they'd offer to take us all for a ride. From the kitchen
window I watched James in a dark blue suit that was
brand-new looking get out and walk around and open
June's door. Just like having a motion picture to watch
in my backyard, I thought. June had on a lacy dress that
gathered around her shoulders and hung loose to her hips.
It made me wonder was she pregnant. Still she looked
like a picture in a magazine, and the beads on her necklace flashed real bright in the sun.

Before I could stop Lily, she goes running out the
door to meet them. I hadn't told June that Lily was com-

ing to dinner and never had a way to tell her Lily was thinking on marriage again. Forrest Treherne was a boss man up at the mill, and nervous as I was to have him in my house, I was more scared of what June and James would think.

"Juney," I could hear Lily calling. And I saw for the first time how shiny Lily's red satiny dress was, how short it was cut, and how white her bare shoulders were under the thin straps.

June's face tightened into what might be a smile on somebody else. Ever since she started high school she's hated the name Juney.

"Come meet my friend," says Lily, grabbing June's limp hand and pulling her around the house to the front door, where Forrest sat in the living room.

Not more than five minutes later, June comes into the kitchen, pushing her curled hair back from her face, looking all undone. "What's Lily doing here, and with a man?" she says first thing, without even saying hello after all this time.

"Lily's had a hard time," I told her, "in case you been too busy to notice." I was mad that she hadn't even took notice of me and all the food I was worrying over for dinner. "Be glad she's finding her happiness."

"Finding happiness at our expense," says June, the red in her face showing right through the powder. "The divorce was bad enough. When my friends in town asked about it, I didn't know what to say. James tells his associates we're not really related." She was sounding like

James did, using them big words, only her mouth stumbled over them.

"Well, you talk to her, then." I bit at the words, and the dinner knives made a heavy sound when I laid them on the table.

Just then Edward came in with the baby and Annie, who runs right up to June, holding a fistful of dandelions. A child can take the anger out of just about anybody. "For dinner," she says. "I picked them, pretty."

"They are pretty," June tells her, bending down to pat her head. "I've brought some roses for your hallway and one for you to put next to your bed. They come from the rosebushes in our yard, beautiful rosebushes. Come with me. We'll get them from the car." Then she gives me a look to let me know she won't forget what I done, inviting Lily out here. From the door I seen her smile at Edward like she pities him marrying me since I ain't got no more sense than to treat Lily like a sister.

I took out my best serving dishes, the ones Mama give me, with the fine little flowers all along the edges. "Let her treat me and Lily like she never seen us," I whispered. "Her and her fancy house." But then I seen her and Annie in the yard, and all them roses — yellow and pink. There was more than June could hold in her arms, and I watched her wrap a bunch of them in paper and give them to Annie to carry. Pink and yellow, my favorite colors for roses, colors that whisper from their vases, letting me know it's okay to rest or even to daydream a little.

Seeing them roses set all around the house made me forget to worry about Lily and Forrest and what June and James would think. All through dinner I was just tasting how tender the roast was on my tongue and how buttery and flaky the biscuits were. But when everybody was about finished with the apple pies I'd spent Saturday baking and when we were drinking our coffee, Lily decides to speak up.

"I hope you'll all be as happy as I am when you hear this news," she says. The coffee starts sticking in my throat. Much as I swallowed, I couldn't make it all go down. "Mr. Treherne has asked me to marry him, and I said yes."

The only sound was Edward and James stirring more sugar in their coffee. Mr. Treherne got red in the face, and it was sad to see a boss man get that worked up.

"I mean to do right for Lily," he said. I could tell he was shaking somewhere inside. "I love her and I respect her. I know things haven't gone right for her in the past, but that's over with. It'll be a proper marriage. Lily won't have to work no more, and maybe we can start a family." His nose turned the color of a beet, and I wished he'd quit sounding all undone. "I hope you all will take that into consideration. Your approval sure means a lot to Lily."

I couldn't look nowhere but into my coffee, waiting on June or James to say something. That's when I heard June. She starts to laughing, giggling really. "I guess a wedding is a whole lot better than a divorce," she says.

When I got strong enough to look up, I seen James

frowning at her like she was a little crazy. And I guess we all thought that at first, except maybe Lily, who was grinning like the cat that swallowed what it'd been chasing all day.

The men went out on the porch, Edward shaking his head but acting real polite and asking did the other ones want a smoke.

I had just started to get my table cleared off, stacking my good plates real careful by the sink, when Lily comes up, puts her arms around me and June, who was standing next to me about to pour more coffee. "We're marrying in November," she says, "and I want you both to stand up with me."

I nearly dropped one of my good plates when June started to laughing again. "My baby's due in the winter." She was choked with her laughing. "I'll have to watch it all sitting down."

"When was you gonna tell us?" I ask her. "After it was born and part way grown?" But really I was happy she'd said it and that all three of us were hugging. The sound of our laughing got bigger and bigger until it filled up the kitchen and I felt sure we'd wake the babies sleeping in the back room. But I didn't care who we waked up. We weren't together like that, the three of us, since before Daddy died, since way back before Lily and me started at the mill.

"I don't care if you're bigger than a cow," says Lily, kissing June. "I want you next to me. I'm doing it all backwards anyway. Mama always did say I'd go wrong for sure, hanging around the mill. Maybe I'm finally gonna do right from it. And I want you there with me when I do."

June didn't answer yes to her. But she never said no neither.

THAT NIGHT, lying in bed with Edward, feeling how the sheets were all worn to a softness and hearing Annie and Benjy's quiet even breathing spread all through the house, I let my mind go loose and didn't worry on nothing. That's when Edward had to start in about the stretch-out.

"They're putting clocks on all the looms," he says. "It ain't right. I much as told Forrest so today. The weavers don't even get a break to sit down and drink a Coke no more." He tells how Avery and Matt are ready to break their clocks or find another mill. "It's hard on us loom fixers too," he says. "We got way more looms to warp and keep running. If something's not fixed right they put my name on it and I got to answer to that boss man McClayer. Now, Forrest ain't half bad. A man can talk to him and he'll listen. But McClayer just stands there with his notepad, writing down what he calls 'the incident.' Then he shuts that pad, clicking his mouth, and says, 'It'll have to come out of your pay.' Before you can think enough to blink your eyes, you're watching the back of that white coat he's always wearing. He's got his notepad out again and is writing up some other poor guy."

Edward is usually short on words, but once he got started seems like he couldn't stop them from falling out. "Ain't fun anymore," he said, and told how they don't have time for talking or joking, though Avery did cover the back of somebody's spindle with grease, which Edward said they laughed about all afternoon. Some days Edward don't get home for dinner, things is moving so fast.

"There's talk of protesting," says Edward, turning over on his back so he's watching the ceiling and not me. "Matt and some of the weavers might walk out."

I get up onto my elbows and look down on his face. Even in the dark, with just the street lights coming through the curtains, I can make out the set lines of his jaw. "Don't you be talking no walkout," I tell him. "They might tell us to move on, and where we gonna go with two babies?"

He don't move. Not one muscle on his face changed. I lay back down into the worn sheets, let sleep cover me.

Later that same week Matt and Avery come here after supper. They sit with Edward on the porch until the mill's night whistle blows. I lay in bed, wrapped up inside their thick mumbling. When Edward come crawling under the covers, I ask him what he's planning. I can hardly make myself whisper. "Nothing," he tells me. "I told Matt and Avery they better not walk out. Forrest says any who do will lose their jobs. Stretch-out's gonna stay."

$\mathcal{L}$ILY'S STORY

ALL SUMMER Forrest and me talked about the wedding, until pretty soon I could see it'd be the biggest thing to happen in Ash Hill all year. I quit working in July. Forrest tried to tell me to keep on until after the wedding, but he let me have my way. "I need time to make my dress and all," I told him. Besides, I was about to burn up in that hot mill. I guess them girls will miss not having anyone to treat bad.

Forrest was older and not much to look at the way Charles was, but I knew he'd do about anything for me, and I didn't feel all turned around inside the way Charles made me feel. I had done pretty good at stopping myself every time I started thinking on Charles, when I went shopping to get lace for the dress Rose was helping me make and saw him across the street. When I didn't wave or nothing, he come over just the same. He had his sleeves rolled up, and his arms and face and neck was dark from the sun. I went shaky inside with how much I wanted to follow him home and fall into bed with him.

First thing he tells me is how he's got this real good job with a builder. He pointed at a torn-up-looking building down the road, saying they was putting up a motion picture place. "It's real steady work and pays good," he said. "I been wanting to come out to your sister's and let you know. Just weren't sure how she'd take it." He was grinning like nothing bad had ever happened between us and we could have fun again.

I said how that was real good about the job. He looked at me serious-like and said maybe we could try it again.

I was meaning to tell him the truth about Forrest and me, but all I could do was smile at him and try and look real pretty. Then he had my hand and we was walking up and down all kind of streets, past stores and houses with kids playing in the yards and women hanging out their laundry, all the time Charles talking about his job and how he missed me. I wasn't thinking about nothing except his voice, all thick and sweet, like running water, and the shape he made walking next to me.

When we got to his room, he shut the door, and I felt his mouth over mine, slow and hot like the afternoon was. He was pulling my blouse out of my skirt, and I slid under him like something real thick pours, slow and even, his hand all warm on my stomach. When I opened my eyes we were on the bed.

Afterwards I came to about what I had done and got up quick, saying how none of this was right and I was gonna be married in a few weeks. Charles just looked all undone and sit down on the bed, saying, "Damn. You got over me quick," and how all it took was some other man talking me into his bed. I stood there staring at him, half undressed, wondering how he could say all this. When he tried to pull me back onto the bed, saying how we'd talk about it later and he had this real good job and all, I pulled loose while I still could and backed out the door, all the time trying to fasten my blouse up. Charles had sat up on the bed, his shirt undone, showing his fine-looking chest. The look on his face said he couldn't believe I'd walk out. I ran the whole way back to where I'd left Forrest's car, hoping the wind would come rushing on me and blow away Charles's smell. Forrest and Rose would be waiting on me, and I couldn't let either of them know.

MR. SAYERS SAID we had to have the wedding at his house, he wouldn't hear any different. Mr. Sayers owns the mill and lives up on the hill, looking over all of the mill town, in a big house, white columns on the porch. Forrest been managing the mill for him for years, Mr. Sayers saying they're like brothers. He's all the time calling Forrest up to his house, sitting him down with a lemonade in a rocker on that porch of his, giving Forrest all kind of advice. But then he has them big, fancy ballroom dances and Forrest don't get asked.

When Forrest asks if I care if we have the wedding there, I tell him I won't hear any different. Mr. Sayers's wife had the ballroom decorated. There was even a fancy chandelier hanging there. I kept thinking how all its lights and all them flowers everywhere were for me, and how Charles never could give me all this.

I told Forrest I wanted the biggest wedding Ash Hill ever seen. Most everyone from town and the mill was there. About every ten minutes I stuck my head out the door where me and Rose and June were fixing ourselves up, so I could see who was standing in the hallway. When I spotted Mrs. Cutler, on her husband's arm, her little dark eyes darting everywhere like she'd miss something, I would have stepped out and told her how her kind ain't allowed in fancy mansions like this one. But Rose was behind me, tugging at my sleeve, giving me a look that says "watch out" and "don't cause no trouble" all at once.

"It wouldn't do for nobody to see the bride yet," she said, leaning against the door so it shut. "Bad luck."

I guess I know what kind of luck I run into with getting a big wedding and everybody staring until their faces turned green at me walking down the aisle, pretty as a movie-star bride, prettier than any bride they'd ever seen or would see in Ash Hill. As I walked in, I could hear the mill ladies, sitting at the back in their sack dresses that hid how big they got from having babies, saying how Forrest worked so hard for every penny and how that's all I wanted. I wouldn't hide that I was glad to get what he give me. They said Charles's name and how I married one for looks and one for money. Made me laugh. "When this one end in divorce," Cheryle, who used to work with me, says, "she'll have to move to the next state to get her another one." I knew I'd prove them wrong on that. I wouldn't be working no more, and Forrest promised me a big fancy house and horses to raise if I wanted. I weren't thinking on divorce.

At the altar, I looked right into Forrest's eyes, like me and my fancy gown was all for him. It made me even more full of myself the way he blushed.

They did the reception on what Mr. Sayers called "the lawn." I swelled up inside near to laughing when I saw how most everyone from town had showed up and how they had to toast my wedding. They might not have gobbled down all them cakes and cookies and breads if they'd knowed how Rose baked most of the food in that little kitchen of hers, the house so hot all week that she kept complaining her babies couldn't sleep none.

Forrest and me was talking to Mr. Adkins, a lawyer from town, and them two businessmen — I just can't keep ahold of their names. I had to pinch myself to keep from grinning when Forrest has to say "excuse me" so he can help break up a fight started between mill boys and them from town. Was Forrest who invited all them mill people, saying that's who we worked with. Not me no more.

I walked real slow-like, with my head high as it would go, to the patio, where they had a band and people was dancing. Town boys dancing with mill girls, hoping they'd get something from them the town girls wouldn't give. A flower garden full of mums — all kinds of colors — grew along the walkway. I snapped a purple one off and spun it around with my fingers, seeing how bright and bold it was in the sun. Then I let it fall to the ground and didn't look down when I felt it under my feet.

More and more people was dancing. Rose got Edward out there. I saw him stumble, looking too stiff in the suit Forrest give him. Anybody could tell it weren't made for him. But I smiled real big at them, and Rose, much as she looked like just another mill hand in the fancy dress she made herself, looked good to me.

I finished off another glass of punch, and all the colors from the spinning dresses went together with the blue from the sky like some bright twisting thread. Then, inside them colors, I hear June squealing, "I love to dance." When she starts giggling she can't stop, and James has to hold her up.

"You're making a fool of yourself again," I hear him hiss, just like a viper. "A real spectacle."

But June just laughs bigger. "That's what I am, a crazy little fool, and everybody already knows it. Ask Mrs. Farmer." She waves at a dried-up prune of a lady who's dressed like she's got money, old money. Mrs. Farmer points her nose up further in the air, keeps in step with her husband, who owns part in the railroad goes through this town. "I can't even hold a teacup right, can I?" June is trying to stumble towards Mrs. Farmer, and James has his arm around her waist, big as it is, and pulls her towards a bench.

"Sit," I hear him say, like she's some kind of dog. I never have been one much for girlfriends, but Rose and June is my sisters, and ain't nobody can talk to my sister like she's a dog.

"Come on, honey," I say to June, helping her up, giving James my eye. "Let's find a nice chair for you to sit in."

She grins up at me and keeps trying to fall. "My baby's kicking again," she says loud enough so she's telling everybody. "Wants us to dance some more."

I wrap her arms around my neck and we do a few turns. James has walked off all red-faced. By the time I get her in the shade next to the house, she's got her eyes shut, near sleeping. "James, I love my James," she's whispering as I let her slump down into the big cushiony chair. Even set her feet up for her.

"James don't give a hoot for you," I tell her. "Least when you're drunk. Guess you didn't know about that punch." I got Forrest to pour some liquor in it. First time I ever seen June with liquor in her. She was right funny snoring away in that chair, belly hanging out of her new, fancy dress. I covered her up from all them staring ladies.

When I found Forrest, he was drinking punch, talking to them mill ladies, telling them about the house he was building me up the hill from the mill town — a big house with two real bathrooms and space outside for the horses I wanted. "It'll take a while to get finished," he was telling them. "Until then we'll stay out at my rooms. It'll be crowded, but I want Lily to have her own house, not move into one built for someone else." He was so pleased and proud with his planning that I could have kissed him.

I could see those fat hens' feathers rise up while they shriveled inside their baggy dresses. They was thinking of the houses the mill let them live in for cheap, with their three narrow rooms. Some of them didn't have no yards and had to share a privy and their water. They was thinking about how living right had got them those houses that weren't even theirs and how I'd lived all wrong and look what I got.

"Right now," I told them, "I'd like to dance with my husband." I took Forrest's arm, and even though he was stepping on my feet I didn't let on that he weren't the grandest dancer. I learned how to do that way back — act one way on the outside and let myself have whatever was true on the inside. I'd come home late and Daddy'd believe how sorry I was to make him and Mama worry, even though Mama seemed to see through whatever I said. Forrest blushed at every smile I give him, and he squeezed my waist tighter and tighter. When I let my eyes get all wide and soft, he whispered how lucky he was to have me to love him, when really I wouldn't mind sleeping in his bed but there were others I'd rather be in.

When I saw some of them mill ladies still watching, I pulled Forrest over to the edge of the lawn, wrapped my arms around his neck, and kissed him slow on the mouth. Then he put his mouth to my ear and, stumbling on the words, whispered how he wanted me. Our courting had been real respectable.

"You won't have long to wait," I told him. He pulled away, winked at me, and asked could we stop dancing so he could save his strength for tonight. I had to laugh out loud at him thinking about how much strength it would take to deal with me. But I said that'd be fine and let him walk over to get me some more punch.

It weren't until most everyone was leaving I saw June again. She was just then trying to get up out of the chair I set her in. Rubbing her pregnant belly like a country girl. Guess she forgot all that schooling she had in town. And she was singing in that soft voice she gets, real pretty. "Bye, baby bunting, Daddy's gone a-hunting, to find a little rabbit skin to wrap his baby bunting in. Daddy, Daddy, where's my baby's daddy?" she calls out.

James comes up behind her. "Get your jacket on, June," he tells her, fitting the fine linen jacket over her shoulders. "We're leaving." He's been at the bar, drinking with some of the other town folks. Hard liquor. They shut down the place Charles used to sing at. Said there was liquor being sold. Then they come here, drink more than they can hold.

"You get enough refreshment?" I call out to him.

Forrest is having our bags put in the car. We're driving all the way to Atlanta tonight so we can stay in a big hotel.

James's face gets all drawn in. He don't reply.

"You got such a fine daddy," June's cooing away at that baby, rubbing a circle on her belly again. "He'll buy you all sorts of pretty things and dress you up fine."

James pulls her to her feet. "Come on, June." As he's pushing her towards the drive, I see Rose stop cleaning the cake table and reach out and pat June's hand between hers with that look she's got saying everything will be all right, you just wait and see. I look at June, who's stumbling against the rich, angry husband she's got, and know it won't.

Chapter 5

ROSE'S STORY

ALL OF JANUARY freezing rain fell until everything was slick and full of glittering. Then the snow piled up. The mill stayed open mostly, except when the electricity was out, and Edward had to go out in that weather and work on the lines. I knew it was dangerous. While the babies slept, I'd sit by the window getting chilled until Edward come home. He'd drink the hot coffee I give him and let me take off his wet boots and thaw his feet slow in a pan of warm water.

For weeks I did not leave the house, as it was too much to wrap both babies up in blankets. Some afternoons, Helen waved at me from her window. Once she run over while her little one was sleeping, just to see was I okay. All day Annie runs on the slick linoleum, until I know she will fall against the stove I must keep hot. But seems like since she lived after being born so early, nothing hurts her.

I heard that June had her baby, that it was a girl.
None of us knew what a hard time of it she had until
much later, when I went to talk to the doctor to try and
find out what happened and if there weren't something
he could do about it all. With the weather so bad, I never
got out to see June. I didn't go up that way much anyhow, as I always felt the funny looks I got when I walked
to that part of town. But I did think about her and how
she must be lonely in that house in town, even if it was
made up fancy with new furniture and all. Least I had
Helen and the others to stop in after I had my babies.
And when Dorothy had her boy that December, we all
went by even though it was cold and there was snow on
the ground. I brought a sweater and hat and little boo-
tees all knit out of wool. I would have saved them for
June's baby, but I knew it would have all kind of clothes
to wear. I could see how it'd be, with James's mother
there all the time, like I knew she would be, telling June
how to take care of a baby.

All January I watched the snow swirl over the windows and thought when it finally thawed I would go out
and plant something, even if the ground was nothing but
mud, even if it did freeze again.

Then the end of February come. By ten in the morning the sky was the blue of a robin's egg. Already I could
hear the dripping outside of ice and snow melting. It was
the first thaw, and I was thinking how I would dress the
babies in the sweaters I made them and take them outside to see the world was still there, when I hear this car

engine cut off in the driveway. First thing I think is something's happened to Edward and they come to tell me. But soon as I think this I hear a baby crying and see James get out carrying it, not even wrapped in a blanket against the air. His mother is standing behind him when I open the door, her mouth closed tight like the metal grip on the purse she always carries. The cold from the doorway seems to get in my throat, but I take the baby from James and wrap it up in the towel I'm holding, thinking how James ain't got no sense when it comes to babies. Then the question the cold put there comes out, and I ask where she is.

"In the hospital. Put away, where she belongs," James's mother says, folding her arms tight in front of her. "She tried to kill Silvia. James walked in on her. Lord knows what would have happened if he hadn't come home early. She was about to put her own baby in water she'd just boiled in the kettle."

James stared straight ahead, past me, past the baby he'd handed over. "I never saw how crazy she was before this. She was crying hysterically when I took the baby."

"Said she was giving it a bath," his mother goes on. "I tried and tried to teach that girl how to care for a baby, but she couldn't even remember how to boil baby bottles. It must be bred into you people, not to understand cleanliness." I could see her eyes, just like a bird's, quick and dark, looking around my kitchen at the peeling linoleum covered with the scrambled eggs Annie'd dropped at breakfast and the dirty walls we didn't have the money to paint or paper.

I heard the scraping sound of James's feet against the floor. He looked down at his shoes, and when he looked back up at me there was something new in his eyes, like he was sad about it all, and my heart skipped a little, thinking how he still might love her. "The night Silvia was born," he told me, "I thought I'd lost her. There was a lot of bleeding. Afterwards we tried to care for her. The doctor said she was all right. It's been nearly two months now."

Behind them I could see the sky, a brilliant dome that stretched over us all, fragile as glass. I heard myself saying, "You should have told me she was having trouble. I could have helped."

When James spoke I almost looked to see that the sky hadn't cracked into pieces. "She had Mother's help," he said, glancing at his mother, who nodded. "The baby's almost two months old. Some nights when I'd get home she wasn't even dressed. Piles of magazines and clothes everywhere. I couldn't find a chair to sit in. If it wasn't for Mother we never would have had a decent meal."

"James," I said, whispering it, trying to make the softness come back into his face, "you loved her. I know it. When they buried Mama and you got so mad at me and stood at the graveyard with your arm around June like you wouldn't let nothing bad touch her, ever, that was your way of loving her. I could tell it. And you loved her for who she was. You didn't care nothing then about her background."

I saw a warm place in his eyes. "I did love her," he said. "Even after the baby was born and everything got so hard. I — "

But Mrs. Cutler stepped forward. "You and your family," she said, pointing a finger at me, "tricked him into the marriage. You held back everything about June and how sick she was, sick in the mind." Her finger was long and bony. The stone in her ring was bigger than the dried beans I shelled out, and it flashed in the sun. "My son has a future ahead of him. Who knows what kind she was running with from the mill where you all work before James married her. I tried to tell him you people can't be trusted to live decently. The child doesn't even look like him."

"Where did you take her?" I could feel my throat closing. "What hospital?"

"State. In Columbia. Mother came with me. We drove all night to take her there. Had to tie her up." James was looking at the floor, pulling at his finger. Then I saw it was his ring he was turning. "Nothing she said made any sense. The doctor there had to give her a shot to make her shut up. They had restraints, and they have the proper treatments there. We were assured. Though I don't know how much can be done . . ." His voice got real soft.

"It's up to you to raise the child," Mrs. Cutler said, so loud the baby started to cry. I jiggled it a little to get it to hush. All that kept me from shaking was holding it. Behind me I felt Annie and Benjy sitting under the kitchen table. "After all," she went on, "the baby's your sister's, and Lord only knows who the father is. I intend to see that the marriage is annulled."

I looked at the baby, but all I could think about was June locked up somewhere strange and how marrying James had made her so happy. "What will they do to her?" I asked James. "She's only just turned twenty."

He looked at the floor. Never said nothing.

"James, let's go." Mrs. Cutler pulled at his sleeve. "I want to get this marriage cleared up first thing. I'm sorry for your family, Rose," she told me, "but you should have let my son know before the marriage about June's problem."

I watched them back out the door and drive quickly away. All I could think was that I'd go to Columbia and find the hospital. When I looked down at the baby, sleeping in my arms like she'll never wake, my breasts ached with how little milk I got left. Sometimes when Benjy is hungry I make sweet pudding and feed it to him on my fingers. I will go empty from how much these babies need. Then I remember how Mama would get a baby goat and put a nipple on a jar for it to suck on, and I start dressing Annie and Benjy so we can all go out to the store for some of them nipples and more milk.

Later, when Edward came home, Annie was sitting in the rocker, feeding June's baby with the bottle I made. "June's baby?" he asked right off. I nodded. Then he wanted to know where June was.

"Columbia," I said, and told him all of it, how James had took her to the state hospital after June tried to kill the baby, how he acted like the baby weren't even his. I could feel all that had happened rising up in my face, but I was so scared Edward would say I had to give the baby up that I didn't let it show.

Edward turned to me with eyes that said nothing. He took off his coat and went to look at the baby. When he come back to the stove, the steam from the potatoes I was cooking was so thick we couldn't hardly see each other. But I knew the look on his face when I heard him. "We don't need this child," he told me. "It's up to James and his mother to raise her. Looks just like him, same nose and eyes. Don't see how he can't claim her."

"I know," I said, pouring the potatoes into the sink, letting the steam cover me. "But I can't just turn out my own sister's child. James doesn't want her, and she'd probably just end up in some home."

"What about the two you already got?" he asked. "How you gonna take care of Annie and two babies? You gonna nurse them both?"

"I got two, don't I?" I told him, and saw how he grinned a little. I moved back from the sink so he could wash up. Then I showed him how June's baby liked that store-bought bottle. "And I want us to go to Columbia," I said to him. "June's just twenty. She'll be okay here with me, and she could help."

That's when he said he'd call the hospital but that sometimes a person might seem all right but the bad part of their mind is just sitting there waiting to come out. I kept quiet, putting the cut-up chicken in a heavy skillet, and it made me feel better that I didn't have to think about the supper I was fixing; it just come out right by itself.

I was up most of the night with Silvia. She sucked down whole jars of milk, then cried like it had all run out of her and she was empty inside. For months it went on like that, me falling asleep in the rocker with June's baby thrashing in my arms. Then all day, me moving slow, like daylight was the dream I was having. I knew it was hard on Annie and Benjy and Edward, but when Edward told me I give too much, I said how if this baby was all I could have of June, I'd keep her. He never did call Columbia. I could tell how everyone had forgot June, except me and Lily. We wrote to the hospital and waited weeks for their letter. When it came, it was just two sentences saying she was undergoing treatment.

Part 2

1942 - 1944

Chapter 6

LILY'S STORY

I BEEN AT old Mr. Franklin's for a good part of the afternoon, lifting the harnesses and reins off the hooks, rubbing my hands over the saddles, feeling how their leather bends under my fingers. I'd stacked up some brushes, a blanket, and a new hunting rifle for Forrest. He hunts dove, deer, ducks, even rabbit sometimes, and likes it when I buy him something special. Old Mr. Franklin, just grinning at me from the counter, tells me to take my time. When the men come in they act too polite, excusing themselves every time they talk loud or laugh. Most of them are old, with the young ones gone off to the war. Still I like coming here, knowing they jump at the sight of me.

I had a few things stacked up, when I looked out and saw him leaning against the door, watching. It was more than six years he'd been gone. I remembered right off how it was when he left, me wanting him to stay and him saying there weren't nothing here to hold him. I hit him in the face, however I could. He gripped my arms until they bruised. The last thing I heard was his voice, a loud hiss, saying he couldn't stand to see me run home to Forrest no more and asking how did it feel not to be getting everything I wanted. After the door closed behind him, I sat in his empty room so long Forrest grabbed me when I got home and pushed me up against the kitchen wall. When he seen the bruises on my arms, he slapped me, saying how I deserved what I get.

I stood there watching Charles through the reins that hung from the ceiling, all this going through my head. A slow grin spread over his face. I thought how I'd pay for the blanket, the rifle, the brushes, then go on home without saying a word. I'd had me some fun since he been gone. I'd get what I wanted in an hour or so, then be home to cook supper. Now, with the men gone overseas, Forrest was easier. He quit sitting guard every evening and had started going out himself some, helping with the draft and all. Sometimes he took me to bed early to get his in.

I carried my things to the register, walking real slow and smiling sweet at Mr. Franklin while he rung them up. I took my bag and walked to the car, started it up, and drove off. I didn't even look to see if Charles was watching.

An hour later I'm driving back into town. Soon as I

see him loafing on the sidewalk, I pull over. He slides in, says the name of the boardinghouse he's staying at. When we got there I followed him to his room, neither one of us saying anything. Inside, he looked me over. I was older, near forty, but I'd kept my shape. I had on a stylish skirt, green, cut so it showed my hips. You could see my slip through the blouse. Charles smiled, said I hadn't changed none.

The next week I go by Charles's to give him the money he needs and stay on until suppertime. As I walked into his room, he was undressing me, his mouth heavy and sweet. I don't think to say no. Later we talk about all the places he saw traveling and how the war's made things hard but not near so bad as during the Depression. He says they could start drafting the older men like him soon, and he doesn't want to go. Then he jokes, calling me White Lily and Lily of the Valley, like I was a pure virgin. Then we get all worked up again, lying there with hardly any clothes on. I started things, running my hands everywhere. He takes it from me slow, not like Forrest, who thinks I can't get nothing out of it all except the baby he wants to give me.

I get home and Forrest is wanting to know where I been. When I say nothing, he slaps my face. I take a long look into his eyes, and he slaps me again, saying how I got to answer. I raise my face up higher, stare until he walks out and the car starts up.

Some nights he comes home late, says he's been at

the draft board helping to pick who they'll send. "Go," I tell him, "fight for your country," but he says they want him here, running the mill, making socks and hospital sheets. "You're making socks," I tell him, "making socks like a grandmother, while the real men is fighting."

He tells me I got to help out, says they need hands at the mill to get production up for the war effort. "You're experienced, Lily," he says. "You could really help us win this war."

"I didn't get married to keep working in a mill," I tell him. Turning up the radio, he sits downstairs trying to hear what battles they're fighting, with his face knotted up half the night.

With most of my boyfriends gone and Forrest all bent up about the war, Charles is the only one can give me any fun. "War's a joke," he says when the radio news of it comes on. "I ain't got no use fighting for nobody but me. Ain't gonna get my head blowed off. This here's all that needs to get blowed off," he says, pointing at his thang rising up between us.

One Monday morning when Forrest is at the mill, the doorbell rings before I finish my coffee. I'd been eating sweet rolls and thinking on the day, how I'd go into town later, visit Charles like I promised him, then maybe stop on the way home and buy me a new hat. Since the war started, it was hard to find much of anything new, but I'd heard how there was a store downtown that got some new hats in, just like the ones they show sometimes in those city stores.

When I pulled open the heavy door, there was Rose, dressed like it was Sunday, holding her youngest by the hand. Hardly nobody comes to my door in the morning, least of all Rose, who tells me to visit her anytime but won't walk on up to my house. I let them in and had them sit in the parlor, seeing they was all dressed up. Rose sat down on the edge of the couch, real proper, and told Becky to sit still and not touch anything. I got some pretty little things Forrest likes to give me spread out on the tables. I brought the child a piece of sweet roll to keep her happy and asked Rose what was on her mind.

"It's about the mill school closing up," she said, and coughed a little, raising up her hand to her mouth.

"I got no say about that," I told her real quick, getting out of my chair to hunt a smoke. I would have preferred a pinch right then, but we were in the parlor. "It come from up top. They were having trouble keeping teachers with the war on."

"That weren't it." She was waving me away with her hand. "I want mine to go still. To the school in town, that is." She looked down at her hands, that were folded in her lap now. "I got no way to get them there and back."

I couldn't help laughing, even forgot to light my cigarette. Rose has got four, counting that one of June's. Becky's not school age yet, and the rest is too smart as it is. "Those kids don't need no more schooling. Soon enough they'll be working at the mill. You want to send them off to town so they can meet somebody, end up like June?

Let them have a little fun. What do they need with proper grammar and arithmetic?"

"I don't want them at the mill that soon. And the kind of fun they'd have, they'd just be into trouble." Her voice got soft, and then she quit talking and was fiddling with the handle on the purse she held. I could see where the threads had worn on it even from where I was sitting.

"Okay," I said, smiling, letting her think I'd seen it her way. "What do you want me to do?"

Her face got pinched up, and she scooted over on the couch so she could reach out and squeeze my hand. "Lily, you got to help me. Give me use of your car to get them there and back. It's six miles. Remember when we was little and Daddy used to bring the wagon with blankets if a storm come up, meet us partway? We'd huddle together on the floorboards and shut our eyes so we couldn't see if the water was too high to cross?" Her eyes got full of tears. "I'll pay you what I can, really I will. I wouldn't beg, but I got nobody else can help me."

"What's Edward say?" I pulled back a little from her. I seen how he shook his head and let the door slam behind him as he backed out if I was there on a visit when he come home.

"He don't even know I'm here." Now she was crying, soft-like and into her hands. Becky crammed the rest of the sweet roll in her mouth and climbed up into her mama's lap. "He wants the mill to let the little ones work again, says Benjy and Annie and Silvie is old enough.

Says they need more workers with the war on. We had an awful fight about it. But I just know he'll change his mind when he sees I can get them to the town school." She squeezed my hand hard. "He's got to, Lily. Please help me."

I had planned on saying no. I'd been studying on what she'd ask of me, and I wasn't about to give up my car every day or drive down like one of them mothers in their checkered aprons. But I got to thinking about Rose doing something against Edward, against what most of the mill town'd be doing, and I put down my cigarette and was pulling Rose to her feet, saying how we got to learn her how to drive.

"Right now?" She tried to sit back down.

"Why not? Come on." I had to pull her out of the house, Becky following after us real slow and whining for her mama. "Rose, you get in that driver's seat and I'll direct you." I had to laugh at her hiking up her good Sunday dress to get in.

Rose passed her hands real slow over the wheel. They were shaking, but her face was lit up. She yelled at Becky to quit whining and sit on the porch. Becky commenced to holler, but when I slammed the car door and went around to get in, she sat down on the top step, sucking her thumb. "You start this thing by turning the knob and pushing on the pedal," I said, and had to grab the dashboard when we lurched ahead. Rose was screaming and laughing all at once. I just grinned.

She drove around the circle in front of my house at least ten times. More than once we went off into the yard, and I thought how Forrest would be out there that evening patching up the marks. When she put on the brake we both near went through the window.

Rose called Becky to come get in with us, and it was all Becky could do to keep that sullen look from sliding off her face, she was so proud to sit on the seat between us. I had Rose drive down the road a piece, then turn around, which weren't easy, and drive back. Mr. Hawkins passed us in his truck loaded up with cotton for the mill and had to run off the side of the road to keep from hitting us. I laughed so hard I wasn't watching as we went by the drive, and told Rose to turn too late. She ran straight into the ditch. We had to flag down a mill truck and get the boys to pull her out.

All that week we practice until she gets good. Once school starts, she walks up to my house on the hill overlooking the mill town to get the car in the mornings. Then I drive up for them in the afternoons. I make them children sit on the car seat like it was a bench on Sunday. If they start jumping or talking I tell them Forrest will beat the pants off them. He'd never touch them except to put candy in their hands, but they believe me.

Everyone knows I am driving about town to do a good turn for my sister. And Forrest likes me helping out with the children. He quits telling me to come down to the mill. On my way to the school, I can stop over to see Charles without Forrest ever knowing.

Then it is late November, near Thanksgiving time. Usually I stop to see Charles before I go to the school, but today I stopped by Mr. Turner's like I promised, as he is sweet on me. He had a pretty blouse covered with hand-done lace, and all wrapped up too. But that means I have to stop at Charles's on the way back from town to give him the money he needs. I pull up in front of the house he stays at and tell them kids if I hear one sound from them I'll get Uncle Forrest to beat them until they fall over dead. And if one of them gets out of the car, I'll drive off and leave them to find their own way.

It was cold and wet out. Charles ain't got but a little laundry heater, his room about the same as being outside. He was waiting on me in bed under the blanket. "Come on under." He pulled off the blanket a little, and I seen he was under there naked. "Come on in and get some." He was smiling real big. I took off most my clothes before I thought about the window that looked out onto the road and how the curtains weren't pulled. But as I crawled in with him I told myself the room was dark and them kids dumb.

"That's right," he was saying. "Just slide under me. I got hard as a pipe thinking on your pretty self."

We stayed at it for a good long time. When Charles finished, I remembered them kids. "I gotta run, quick," I told him, jumping out, pulling my slip over my head.

"What's your hurry?" His voice was low, like honeysuckle'd sound if it could. I reached for my dress as he switched on the light.

"Turn that off. Them kids is out there in the car." I threw the dress over my head as I said this. Charles didn't move.

"I just want to see you." He was trying to pull me back in bed.

I stepped over to the bed and reached for the lamp, but Charles grabbed my arm, bending it back. "Leave it," he growled at me. "I got a right to look at all I want of you."

I stepped into my shoes and left the door open behind me, not thinking he'd get out of bed to close it before switching the light. Some days I swear to myself I will quit Charles. When Forrest beats me, Charles says I could come stay with him anytime. Me having to work in the mill just to eat don't mean nothing to him.

I got in the car, and them kids never said a word. I could hear them shivering the whole way. Next morning Rose comes to the house, shaking like a dried husk the wind got hold of. Annie and Benjy went to Edward with all they seen, and Edward has said no more taking his kids to school. "I don't care what he says, Lily. I'm taking them in today," she says, and doesn't ask me if what Annie says she seen, parked in front of Charles's, is true or not.

"Go ahead," I tell her, "drive them in." As long

as she is going against what Edward has said, I won't stop her.

She takes the keys out of my hand and is gone. Rose don't think what her kids talking means for me. I'll go to Charles's when Rose gets back, stay there until school lets out. If I'm gonna get roughed up, I may's well have me some fun for it.

When me and Forrest first got stuck together, Forrest would carry me to bed, saying I was a new bride, and be all clumsy and gentle with me. After supper was over, he'd tell the mill talk, me laughing, carrying on, or walk out to the field and watch the horses. If I was riding them, he'd sit on the fence and holler at me, "Go on, Lily. Jump her."

I had to sell the horses. He says it ain't right, with rationing and everybody working hard, for me to be out riding them for pleasure. Since we ain't had no kids, he wants me down at the mill. He's having to run it days and nights to keep up.

I don't see the others as something against him. I ain't looking to leave him.

When he come home, I was putting up my coat. Hadn't started supper. "Where you been today?" he asks me.

Edward must have told him what them kids seen. But Forrest won't come out and say he knows.

I smile. "Where you pray I weren't," I tell him, closing the closet door. "With whoever you don't want me to be with." I get up and walk towards the kitchen to get supper on. "And I stayed there a good long time." I say that last as I walk past him.

His hand come out like a snake striking. I don't see it, only hear the slap, feel the side of my face go numb with tingling. "Who is he?" My shoulders soften under his grip. "Tell me who it is, Lily." My back hits the wall, and I slide down to the floor.

When I close my eyes the blackness comes between us. I hear his heavy steps and the door slamming. I open them, get to my feet, look at the rack and see one of his guns missing. Maybe he went hunting, I tell myself.

When Forrest comes back, he eats the wieners I cooked, even said how they tasted good, which was his way of letting things pass.

Some nights, even if he don't ask, I tell him I been under the best there is. His hands are tired when they strike out at me. They fall like the heavy wings of a bird shot from the sky.

All month Forrest and me fight, him saying how I ain't got no respect for him, going to town the way I do. He says he'll drag me to church Sunday morning, let the preacher shout some sense into my head. All night he waits on me to say "I'm sorry." "It's sinful, Lily," he says, like he will save me from hellfire. I ain't got time to think about what's after this lifetime. I ain't interested in preachers' notions.

Sunday morning I expect Forrest to drag me awake, tell me to dress fancy for church so he can parade me in

for them mill workers to point at, but when I wake I see
his bed is empty, the sheets cold. His shotgun's missing
from the rack, and I know he's gone off hunting squirrel,
rabbit, whatever he can bring down. There's a powder-
ing of snow on the ground. He'll be able to follow their
tracks, trap them in the little cross of his sight. "Go on,"
I told him last week when he said the ground was just
right. "You can pretend you're hunting Japs or Nazis,
just like all the boys who is so young they got to stay
home with their mamas."

It's midday before I get my breakfast. I'm sitting at
the table, a cup of fresh coffee in my hand, turning the
pages of one of them ladies' magazines, when he comes
through the door holding out two rabbits on a string.
"Look here, Lily," he calls to me, lifting them high. "Look
what I got us for dinner."

"Get them out of my house," I tell him. "Just 'cause
shooting some little animals makes you think you're the
man you ain't don't mean I got to skin and cook them."
I looked down at my magazine. They was showing a new
way to fix up your hair, pulled back with barrettes. I
hear Forrest stomping down the hall, the door's thud. I
got enough ration cards for cut-up meat to last this week.
I don't need to be fooling with no rabbits.

Chapter 7

ROSE'S STORY

WHEN I READ June's postcards about how her
new husband owns all these buildings in Florida, what
she says gets all mixed up with what I know about him
being in that hospital for drinking. Edward says it's part
of her sickness, but I keep thinking she's got a good part
of it right and the rest is just hoping and wishing. "That's
what prayers are, most times," I say to Edward. "Like
last winter when I kept asking the Lord for enough money
so we wouldn't have to give up our land and could still
get that new coal heater we need, and then you got that
money."

"Weren't because of no prayer." Edward laughed. "I
worked all those double shifts when they had to get them
hospital sheets out for the war. I was due that money."

"The Lord has mysterious ways, that's what the
preacher man tells. How do you know what made you

fall into them extra nights? What made the hospitals need extra sheets at that very time?"

Edward set down his coffee and put out the cigarette he was smoking, then with one stretched-out hand pulled me to him so he could put his arms around me without having to stand up. The children were asleep. "Next you'll say the war is Providence, then you'll have to argue your preacher." I tried to push apart his hands, that were folded on my waist.

"I don't set much by your preacher's notions, but I do go to church with you every Sunday, and Wednesday nights too, you got to admit." He hurried the words, pulling me closer. "Seems like, whatever's true about Providence — and you and me know nothing about the truth there, so seems like whichever's true — June is more believing in what she ain't got rather than praying for what she wants the Lord to give her." He patted my stomach like he was proud of his figuring.

This time I pulled back his hands and took his coffee cup from the table. "If we don't know nothing about Providence from down here, what do we know about June? She might have married him, and maybe he does own them buildings. How do we know, when it's way down in Florida?" I was wiping out the cup with the cloth hard as I could.

"I know June, that's how. She ran off with him from that hospital they both were in. Somebody like her ain't in this world."

"Maybe what's not in this world is real too, just as real as the rest of it."

Edward got up to leave the room. "Next you'll be saying the war's made up. They'll have to lock you in too."

"Don't you ever hear nothing that preacher says? Heaven's just as real as earth is. You can't see it, but it's there. Same could be true for prayers and dreams. Maybe June sees things different, that's all."

I got quiet, hearing how strange I sounded. Edward shrugged his shoulders, walked into the next room. I heard the click as he turned on the radio, then the low humming of voices, and knew without looking he was leaning forward in the chair, hunched over the voice box like each word it said about the war was all that mattered. In my mind, I said a prayer over and over: "Let it be true for her, Lord, let it be true."

EACH DAY Annie comes home crying to be back in her own mill school. "Carol Anne's mama doesn't make her go," she tells me again and again. "She's waiting on the mill to open the mill school again or get a bus to take all the mill kids to the town school."

"Maybe the mill school will open again next fall," I tell her. "Until then you go to the school in town and be glad that you're going." I always wished Mama and Daddy didn't take me out before I learned much reading and writing.

But Annie sits on the porch most of the afternoon, sulking. "Help me with this laundry," or "Haul me some coal from the bin," I holler to her, just to keep her busy.

One day she gets home late, after Lily drops off the others.

"She had to stay after," Benjy tells me, but he don't know why. "Aunt Lily said she wouldn't wait on trouble-makers."

Least two hours later, she comes in, dragging her feet, and me waiting on her to keep Becky while I take Edward his supper, since he has to stay for the second.

"If you was misbehaving I'll take care of you when I get back," I tell her, picking up the wide wooden spoon I use. "Right now you see that Becky comes to no harm."

That night after supper she tells me how the teacher kept her after since she can't multiply right. I can punish her, she says, but she wants to start at the mill soon as she can, rather than go to school in town.

"We got to learn everything by heart, like all about Europe and names of rocks. I can't read most of the words, and my writing's no good." She says the town girls call her dumb, and she wants to see if Edward can find her a job.

"You're too young," I tell her. "Don't know what you're asking." Then, even though I never could read much, I tell her to get her books. "Bring them in here, on the table," I holler as she goes to find them.

We start with her reader. I get her to say the lesson

out loud and help her guess at the words she don't know. When we open the science book, the words get long and strange looking, but we talk about the pictures of plants drawn like they was up close, with little arrows pointing from them.

When Silvia comes in to say good night she reads a whole page out loud and only has to stop once. I can't figure how she knows all this. We light the lamp and sit there making out words, Silvia saying the long ones. After a while my eyes stop and the words get strung together like lightning bugs when the night's thick with them or tiny white buttons on the edge of a shirt front. Annie and me and Benjy all lay there quiet listening to Silvia, her voice clear and pure as a bell, sounding each word out.

EACH EVENING when Silvia comes home, she does her homework. She gets good marks from the teachers even though the school in town is harder than the mill school and we heard some got moved back a grade or more. But most of the time, some kind of story's going round in her head, like with June. I just want to make sure it's the right one.

Last winter she come to me wanting to know could she get a bike for Benjy. None of my kids ever could buy for each other. "Santa will bring him something," I tell her. "You don't worry none about it." I get something for each one of them and put it under the tree. But a bike, I couldn't afford no bike.

"I figured out there's no Santa," Silvia said, which showed sense. "And Benjy wants a bike. I've seen him watching the boys ride them home after school."

The child has a heart for Benjy. I had to let her start school a year early, she was crying after him so. "Suppose I say okay? Where you gonna get a bike?"

"I will," she tells me. "I can find one."

When I told Edward, he says, "Don't let her get to dreaming like June. Believing her own make-believe won't get a bike."

But believing must have helped her some, because two weeks later she takes me out to the shed, saying she's got something hid. Snow was flying thick as cotton in the spinning room. I wrapped up good and followed her out. Sure enough, she had a bike out there. Old, I could tell, but painted red, white, and blue, with a little flag on the handlebars. One of them teachers gave it to her and even found her the paint to make it pretty.

"You want to put it under the tree like it's from Santa?" she asked me. I almost cried. Sometimes I wonder if the Lord's got something special planned for her after she had such a hard time of it early on.

"We'll put it under the tree but write out a tag, 'With help from Silvia,' " I told her. "Benjy'll sure be thankful to have a sister who loves him."

She smiled and hugged my neck. She's always been the one to hug and kiss me and her daddy, even though she's not ours. I thank the Lord she has such a good heart. I tell Helen and Lacy what she done. They can't believe how good she is. Even Edward can't help loving her like his own.

It weren't until she was eight I told her she weren't mine. She had opened my Bible to the family tree, and I snatched it away before she could see how some of the lines were crossed up and names marked out. Silvia is too smart, not like Annabelle, who takes whatever I tell her and folds it away with her prayerbook pictures to study. Silvia was the one figured out Lily was seeing boyfriends, even before they seen Charles like that. When the baby I had before Becky was born dead, the others played outside all day like they couldn't hear my cries, but she kept coming to the door, wanting to know was I okay. Later she come at me with all kind of questions, like why wasn't I fat no more and did the doctor being here mean somebody died.

She wanted to know right off why I took away the Bible. "You didn't want me to see that?" she kept asking, like I hurt her. Thinking that she'd guess it someday, I told her. It was my weakness not to tell her it all, but just that she was adopted, that we took her in when she was a baby, that we love her like our own. She seemed to like the idea. I told myself how all young girls get these romantic notions and she was just making up stories about her real parents for fun. There were so many wrongdoings all tangled up. I didn't think my keeping the whole truth would be one more knot in the snarl.

When she was nine I took her to the bank to meet James. He sat across from us at a big fancy desk, a stack of important-looking papers in front of him. He smiled real polite. "Rose, how good to see you. It's been a long time," he said, but didn't stand up to greet me. "What can I do for you?"

"Just wanted you to meet Silvia, here. She just turned nine." We was standing by the door, Silvia's hand tightening on mine as she looked around the room at the big paintings and the thick curtains that were made of a tapestry. Then she fixed her eyes on James, and I saw him go a little red around the ears. Except for that, she could have been anybody.

"I've got a little girl who's just a few years younger than you," he said.

"Do they look alike?" I asked him without thinking. I came believing it was only right he took an interest in her. The office was real quiet. I could hear a fan cut on somewhere. James rustled a few papers.

Then he look me straight in the eyes. "Not much at all, really," he said. "My little girl's got brown hair like mine." Silvia had June's hair, yellow as feed corn. He looked at Silvia real serious. "Do you go to school?"

She stepped back, pulled at my hand to go. "Yes, sir," she told him. "It be starting up soon."

"It will be starting," he corrected her, smiling. "Now, isn't that how they taught you in school?"

Silvia nodded. She usually talks real good too. James

scared her. "We'll be going now," I said. "Say 'bye' to Mr. Cutler, Silvia."

James stood up and for the first time smiled like we was friends. "Now, you tell my secretary to give you a piece of candy before you go, Silvia. You tell her I said so." He held out his opened hand like he held a gift in it.

Silvia nodded and backed out as I pulled the heavy door closed behind us. I had to remind her to ask for her candy. "Can I take two?" she asked the secretary: "One for me and one for my brother?"

"Well, I guess," the secretary told her, holding out the bowl full of hard candy drops. "But just two," she added, snapping the lid back on as soon as Silvia got her pieces out.

We was still standing there, me waiting for James to come out after all and make right by her. It weren't his money I wanted for Silvia, just some words about how he liked her or that she should come back to see him.

The secretary looked up from the typing she'd gone back to. "Did you want something else? Do you need to open an account or buy some bonds?"

I shook my head. "We'll be going on now," I said as we walked out the door.

James was part of my reason for telling Silvia we didn't know who her real parents were but that I was almost sure they was dead. I was afeared she'd go in to see James and he'd throw her out, or worse, act like she meant nothing to him, just another mill kid wanting candy.

Edward said I was crazy telling her part truth, part lie, said I shouldn't have said nothing. He never did understand Silvia, and said she couldn't think good because she weren't like Annabelle, who could cook a chicken up same as me by the time she was ten. "Half truth is better than no truth," I told him. He was shaking his head, walking out the door.

THE DAY Edward told me about the mill school opening again, it got over a hundred. I'd turned the young ones outside, said to stay in the shade, and put Becky in the swing with a baby doll I made from an old pair of socks when she turned four. After setting the swing to rocking, I told her if she got out, the yard might burn her bare feet. Standing at the window, I could hear her telling the baby doll to stay put.

With nobody but me inside, I fired up the stove like I had to. I'd been to the garden early and got okra and corn, what hadn't burned up, and tomatoes for slicing. I'd bought the ham pieces the day before.

By the time I heard the whistle, the house was about to pop open. "Doorknob near left a hole in my hand," says Edward, coming in. "This place is worse than the mill. What are you doing in here?" He sat down, wiping his face with the rag he carried.

"Cooking your dinner," I told him, and poured boiling water off the corn, my eyes shut tight against the heat.

"We'll have to eat it outside with the critters."

Becky came through the door and started bawling. "Poor child," Edward said. "The heat burst like opening a furnace door in her face. Follow me, Becky. We'll wait outside for your mama to bring us dinner." Which is how we had ourselves a picnic in the yard, all spread out on a blanket like a holiday, only the hot food didn't taste near as good with the sun.

All that made the news about the school opening in the fall seem extra special. I welcomed it like if a breeze had started to blow against my cheek. Edward told how they saw not enough mill children was going into town. Said the mill would double up on classes and look for some extra teachers.

Annie was eating corn and grinning. "Do you hear, Mama? We don't have to go to town no more." So excited she couldn't hardly swallow.

"You don't have to be driving that car of Lily's no more. Now, the high school kids will still go to town, but they'll have a bus and ride together," Edward said, eating his third ear of corn. He was eyeing me over the cob.

"I'm glad," I told him. "Make it easier on me," and I shook my head at all the food he tried to pass.

"Weren't right, you driving that fancy car through town." He pushed away his plate like we was at the table. "I like mine staying put. They got no business going into town." He stood up, and I couldn't see his face for the sun. "I got to get back now. If I'm late, don't keep supper. Just save me something." Most days he don't even get home for dinner no more. War's made the stretch-out worse.

As the children ran off towards the river, I stacked the empty plates. "Don't get in that water," I called after them. "I don't care how hot it gets." I knew if I was going to get Edward to build us that farmhouse out on our piece of land, I better make him start soon, before he decided he belonged nowhere else but here.

ONCE THE MILL SCHOOL got going again I didn't see Lily much, only heard from Lacy that she was going out to town most days. "That sister of yours has got Mr. Treherne wrapped around her finger too tight," says Lacy. "He is too good to her. She ought to be helping out with the war effort like the rest of us." I get busy with the house and my kids and don't care what I hear. Half of it don't seem real.

I nearly jumped, the morning I heard her voice through the kitchen door. "Got some of them biscuits for a crazy married lady?" she called out at me just as I was wiping my table clean from breakfast. What Lily come to tell me was less real seeming than the rest. She sat down, and I give her the biscuits. Becky was still at the table, spreading jelly with her fingers, licking them clean. "Charles come into some money. Don't ask me how." She laughed real big. "He's leaving town. I guess I might go with him."

I poured her coffee, set the cup in the saucer, and heard it rattle as I carried it to her place and set it down. "You done spilled half the cup," Lily says, and laughs.

"I don't know what you got to laugh at," I told her. "You must be half crazy to tell me something like that, and in front of Becky too. You are crazy if you tell him you'll go." I sent Becky to her room to play, turned my back on Lily, and started my dishes. Before it was over I'd broke one of my best plates.

Lily sat at the table, calm as ever, with a slight smile in her eyes, spreading jam on the biscuits. "Can't hardly get out of my own house anymore. Forrest has me bring him his dinner; guess he likes to see the others gawk at me. Then he gets back early for supper, only goes out to check on the mill or help out at the draft board. Expects me to be cooking the whole time for him too." I heard the knife clatter as she set it down. "Might as well be closed up in the mill all day. Can't see out neither way."

"You go with Charles, how it gonna be different, having to go where he says and when he says. If that money's not legal, he might get caught. Think how free you'll be in a jail cell somewhere." That's when I dropped my good plate, turned back to the sink so fast it hit against the porcelain. "Now look what I done," I said, bending down to get the pieces. "Got so upset over all you been saying." My hands shook so I couldn't hold on to all the pieces.

Lily laughed before she got off the chair to help me. "It's me that'll get in prison, not you." She handed me a small piece she dug out from under the counter.

"That's all of them, I think. Maybe I can glue them." Becky had come into the kitchen, stood watching me try to fit the pieces together.

"Rose, I'll get you another plate. We'll go into town when you get the dishes done and look for one with the same pattern. We can take Becky for a Coke." Lily had sat back down in front of her biscuits. She was still smiling. "Besides, I promised to stop by Charles's. He ain't working today. Said he'd be there all morning."

"I ain't going near Charles's place, and besides, they don't keep those patterns in town. I'll glue it together. You'll hardly know."

"Suit yourself," she said, and took a long drink of coffee. "I still don't know what's got you all tied up."

"Go on, Becky," I said without turning from the counter. "Go back to the bedroom to play."

"I'm scared back there," she said in a little voice.

I spun around to tell her to mind, but when I saw her face the words left me. I hunted a little blackboard for her to draw on. "You can sit on the couch by the window," I said, handing it to her. I wiped my hands and left the dishes to dry by themselves so I could sit down at the table across from Lily. "How can you think of running off with Charles? Who's he got to run from anyways?" I asked her.

"The draft board tried to get him. He says he ain't going."

"Lily, Forrest is on that draft board, and this town don't think much of you. With him in a fit about your leaving, you'll end up in jail too."

Lily laughed the long, loud laugh she got. I heard Becky run to the bedroom. Then, stretching back in the chair like to get comfortable, Lily said, "Just what I need. A sister to tell me the truth." She reached down into one of the beaded bags she carries to pull out her cigarette case. I got back up and went to the sink, took up my towel, and started drying them dishes. Behind me I heard the clicks of her case opening and shutting, then the match brushing against the box. "I'm getting old, Rose. Got to have some fun while I still can. You just pretend I ain't come here, ain't said nothing to you. Most of the time I don't tell nobody what's in my head. You don't know half of what I do."

I set the spoons in their place in the drawer, then the forks, lining them up straight. "I guess I don't want to know the truth about what you done or might do. Not nothing against the law." I kept my back turned.

"Truth!" Lily laughed again. "Most times, Lily don't even know the truth about Lily. Why you think you should?" I turned around, saw her grind out the cigarette on her plate and open the case for a new one, all in one motion, smooth, unthinking, like when I stir flour and milk for biscuits and pour it out into the pan every morning.

"Some nights," she said, "I might even like Forrest enough to sleep in his bed wearing them lacy nightgowns he buys for me. I think I'll stay on, even if it does mean being where Forrest wants. Then the house closes in, until nothing makes me free of it. I start thinking how running with Charles would feel, with every day different than the one before it, how I would never know nothing for sure. And Charles needs me with him like Forrest never could."

I must have stood there looking for a few minutes. When I thought to say something, Lily'd finished her smoking and was standing up to leave. Helen was at the door with a pie she'd brought me for the mending I done for her. Her mouth was wide open with seeing Lily in my kitchen. I kept trying to find the right words as Lily was waving and slipping out the door.

IT WAS SPRING, and a month or two after Lily's visit, when I seen June standing on the road that runs in front of the house. At first I couldn't tell who it was. She had on a dress that was way too big and more worn out than most of mine, and her hair was cut all funny. Her sweater was too small to button all the way. She'd set a paper bag down beside her. Even from the window I could see she was pregnant.

Wiping my hands dry on my apron, I stepped out on the porch. With the war on, sometimes women come through town looking for a sister or cousin. They might have lost a husband to the war and not have nowhere to go. I waved at her. "Can I help you with something?" I yelled.

Then I seen her eyes, all soft and blue, looking like the sky spread over a cornfield, and I knew it was her. Neither one of us said anything when I came running down to the road, but I couldn't stop smoothing her hair with my hands. It felt coarse and ragged under my fingers, and big as she was around the middle, her arms was skinny.

I took her bag. "You must be tired," I whispered, scared she'd disappear like a dream I was having. "Come on inside. Get you some breakfast."

Just then Annie steps out on the porch, yells, "Mama, you want me to dress Becky? Benjy and Silvia already went down to the river to play."

"Yes," I yelled back, glancing at June to see if she heard the name right.

Her face turned all warm with her smile. "You named one after mine," she said, her eyes deep into me. And I guessed then that she thought hers was somewhere else, with James and his folks or adopted by some stranger.

When we got inside, I sat her down at the table and fried up ham strips, eggs, poured her coffee and warmed a few biscuits. She sat there quiet with all that time between us, and I had to talk fast to fill up the empty spaces. "I guess you know from them cards I wrote you that I got four young'uns now." I counted Silvia as my own. "They're all in school, except for Becky. She's my baby. Annie's got just a few more years until she graduates." I flipped the eggs over. "In a couple more years she'll be riding the bus to high school in town. Can't believe how grown up she's getting." Then I stopped my talking and served up June's food. Last time she seen Annie, Annie was just a baby. The room got big with how much time had went by.

Setting that plate in front of June, all full with the steaming food, chased away them empty spaces the years had set there. It could have been any morning she stopped in to visit.

But then Annie and Becky came into the kitchen. "Say hi to your Aunt June," I told them, and they stopped, Annie just staring.

"Last time I saw you, you were a tiny thing, smaller than Becky," June said real friendly-like to Annie. "I used to bring you flowers. We'd put them in a little glass beside your bed and you'd say how they made the whole room sweet so then you didn't mind lying down for your nap."

Annie nodded, her mouth dropped open like she didn't remember none of what June said and wouldn't care to if she could. "Well, I'll take Becky outside to play now," she says, backing out the door.

Soon as I look back at June, I see how the tears is pouring from her eyes, like they'll never quit, and her not even bothering to wipe them. I wrung the dish towel in my hands. "These kids of mine don't know how to act polite," I said.

"That bus ride took all day and night," June said,

like she was talking to the kitchen walls, the tears still streaming. "All those men in uniforms. I told the bus driver I was going to stay with my family."

"Come on now," I said to her. "Try to stop crying so you can eat. The food's almost cold." I gave her a hankie to wipe her face and smoothed back her hair.

When I sat down across from her, there was just the sound of her eating. I was remembering her postcards. Some said Jerry was her husband. "You said Jerry left Florida too. Is he waiting on you somewhere?" I kept trying to get her to look up from her plate at me. "I mean, it was real good of him to let you come all this way, especially seeing how you are." I nodded towards her waist, that was tight against her dress. "Where is he, June?" I asked finally when she wouldn't look up.

"He got sent overseas," she said, but I was afeared she was lying, trying to make me think good of her. "You know, he's in the army now. He's got a whole box of medals they've given him. He's a captain."

"Must have been hard on him," I said, laying the dish towel careful-like over the back of a chair, "leaving a wife who's gonna have a baby."

"Yes," she says, like all she was saying was the truth, and ate the last piece of ham strip. "But when his country needed him, he had to go."

I carried her plate to the sink, dipped it in the warm soapy water. I could hear Edward's voice in my head, asking where we'd get the money to keep June with us, and her expecting. When I turned from the sink I had a cup in my hand I was rubbing dry with the towel. "Is your husband sending you anything?" I asked her, watching the cup turn white and shiny. "I mean, is he sending you any of his pay or something you can live on while you wait for him?"

June got up and walked to the door. She touched the screen, turned, and looked right at me. "Yes," she said. "A letter should get here any day. I gave him your address before he left."

It was something I could tell to Edward. "As long as he's doing right by you," I said, slipping my arm around her.

Everything was still. The empty tire swing swayed back and forth, the mud under it sunken with prints where the kids had run. Already my kitchen felt warm and heavy. I stood behind June with my arms around her shoulders.

Each morning after Annie, Benjy, and Silvia left for school, June sat on the porch rocker. I watched her through the window while the sink filled with water, as I wiped each plate clean, then rubbed it with a towel until it shined. I watched her rocking and looking out over her stomach, over the grass that gets too thin, and over the tomato garden. If it was a clear morning, the mountains came out to let us know there's more than the mill town whistle blowing.

When I finish with my kitchen and step outside, I hear that she is singing to herself about a child that's lost its mama. I lean against the porch rail, let my eyes fill with tears, thinking that it's for Silvia's good I keep her, for Silvia's good I ain't said nothing.

Then I bring June inside and rub her hands if they're cold, fix her another slice of ham, more biscuits. Becky plays with her doll. Helen and Lacy, most all the others, are working the first, so no one comes by for a visit. June smiles and eats, tells me he'll be a strong baby. Says again how Jerry will be back for her when the war's over. I know her time will be soon, but when I try to think on it each thought gets tangled with the next one and pretty soon I'm telling June how I'll go with her to Florida and Edward how we'll send her to Jerry's people to wait. Then I get out my baby clothes to mend and take all morning to find the cradle Edward done stored in the shed. I can still go back to the mill, I tell myself, and it ain't so crowded with June on the couch. At dinner Edward watches June patting herself, the way that comes natural to most women when they're waiting to have a baby. He stands up too quick and before I can offer more food is out of sight, the kitchen door rattling on its hinges.

Chapter 8

SILVIA'S STORY

WHEN MAMA'S NOT WATCHING I take off running to the river near our house. Benjy is behind me, his breath coming in short puffs, his feet pounding the hard clay. Most often there are others down here, boys Benjy tells to let me play or he won't. But today the river is quiet and so still when I stir it up it settles before I pull the stick out. I find a moss-covered rock to sit on and watch how the river makes patterns of the rest of the world, patterns that are always shifting because the water's moving. Near the bank where the water's shallow, the sky's all broken up by rocks. I lean over, touch the water with my toe so the lines change.

Benjy brings down a couple of long sticks, says he's making us fishing lines and we can sit here on the cool of the bank dangling them into the water. I take a stick, hang it down the way he does.

"Good," he says. "Now we're running from Japs, hiding out. This is all we got to eat — fish — which means we got to catch something. Then we'll make a fire to cook it, only we have to keep it from smoking, or the Japs might see us."

"We're in France," I tell him, "or maybe England."

"No." He shakes his head. "We're in the South Pacific."

This is how I like the river best, with just me and Benjy down here making up whatever story suits us. I stand up, pull my stick back hard. "It's a big one!" I yell, falling backwards. He rushes over, holds my hand with the stick up in the air, triumphant. If the other boys were here, they wouldn't let me be the one to catch it.

Benjy holds his hand out like he's got a line between his fingers. "It's not only big, Silvia, but it's a trout. Now we'll eat for sure tonight."

He hands me the fish and I hold it up to the sunlight, seeing how the scales glitter like coins. Already Benjy is gathering sticks for the fire. "We don't have matches," he says. "You start rubbing sticks together for starting it."

Again I am the one who gets to save us. Not like at home, where if somebody has to mail a parcel or pick up our ration book, Annie's in charge. I pick up two sticks smoothed by the way the water has washed over them and begin to rub them together carefully, slowly. When Benjy has finished building his pile he walks over to me, says what a fine flame is jumping between my hands. He helps me shield it as we walk to the pile of sticks and dried leaves, helps me light the fire that will feed us.

I SEE THE STORM CLOUDS, hear the broken shutter bang in the wind, and watch the man on horse-back come slowly up the hill, around him the storm gathering. Miss Gearson is calling my name. She says it twice, tells me to come out of my daydreaming and name a poem that Mr. Poe wrote. " 'The Raven,' " I tell her, standing up to give the answer. When she smiles I know to sit down again.

I like the desks with their pencil boxes and the black-boards all shiny. I like Miss Gearson, who makes me stay late to tell me I am smart but I have to learn concentra-tion. But most of all I like the books lined up on Miss Gearson's shelf, the ones she lets us take home to read by signing a little card. "Just one," she tells me when I see two I want to read together. She laughs and says I'll still get them all read by vacation time.

In geography class there's a globe at the front of the room, by Mrs. Miller's desk. I close my eyes and make it spin. When it stops I touch the world with my finger. I open my eyes, read the name. "That's where I'll go when I'm grown," I tell myself. Once I asked Mrs. Miller about South America, and she showed me some pictures of mountains that grew beside a clear blue ocean and women who carried baskets on their heads. When I told

Mama I want to go to Brazil, she said I'm not to worry about anything but doing good in school.

Benjy says school's okay because I'm there. When Benjy has to stay in to work more arithmetic problems, I sit by myself on the curb of the sidewalk, eat the biscuits and jelly Mama sends with me for recess, and begin a book about Africa, where elephants and tigers live. But I look up when I feel them standing there, Isabelle and Minnie. "Bastard," Isabelle says. "That's what my mother says you are."

She stands there smiling at me like knowing all that makes her grown up and important. Minnie giggles into her hand. I say my name, three times in a row as if it's a spell. Isabelle grabs Minnie, whose mouth is hanging wide enough to catch birds. "Come on," says Isabelle. "Let's get away from her. She's weird."

I wait until they're gone to tell myself the story about the man and woman riding the train through town. They have traveled to foreign countries. Their clothes are handsome. The woman wears a wide hat and a necklace given to her on her marriage day. The baby she holds is dressed in a fine white lace gown. They play with the baby, making sweet sounds over it. Then I see the train go off the rails and begin to swerve. The window is open, and Mama stands outside the train holding out her arms, promising to love it as her own. The woman cries as she lowers the baby. The train is pulled by its own speed onto the bridge before it swerves completely off the tracks.

When the lunch bell rings, I cram the rest of my biscuit in my mouth and walk down the hall that throbs with boys and girls. When I get home, I'll ask Mama to see the christening gown.

AUNT JUNE is having a baby. I like to sit near her while I do my homework. When I finish my arithmetic problems, she tells me all the special things about Florida, like that palm trees and oranges grow there. "The beaches are pure white with sand, and there was a banana tree growing in the backyard. When I got hungry, I'd get Jerry to pick one for me." Sometimes she puts my hand to her wide stomach and I feel something moving under the skin. "That's the baby kicking," she tells me, "trying to get out." I ask Mama how Aunt June got to have a baby, what she had to do to get it to grow in there. Mama says someday I'll know.

Aunt June tells us anything we ask her. She explains about her husband who is overseas and about how the baby will be born soon. Benjy wants to know all the time about her husband, who is fighting the war. "How'd he get to go?" he asks. "He must be in Europe," Benjy says when she tells him she doesn't know what country he's stationed in. "Probably France. I bet he's fighting Nazis."

"I would love to go to France," I tell them. "Paris, France."

"Yes, he's in France," she says. "He's been flying one of those new planes they've developed."

Benjy's eyes are big and clear, like windows that have just been washed or the round mirrors on Aunt Lily's car. "A bomber. That's what I want to fly. I'll sign up soon as I can."

Later when we're getting ready for bed, I call him "Pilot Benjamin" and poke him between the ribs. I run around the room with my arms out and make the plane noise.

"Quit," he tells me, and leaves the room. When he comes back he brings me a biscuit covered with jam, so I know he's not mad.

I WAS WALKING HOME from school when I felt Benjy behind me. "Come on," he whispered, brushing up against me, and we were running through the yards, past Mrs. Harper, who was hanging out laundry, and almost ran into Mrs. Gibson, who had her baby on her hip. "Where you kids running off to?" she yelled. "Watch where you're going. I'm gonna tell your ma." I turned around. "I'll tell your ma on you," she yelled again.

By the time I caught Benjy he was at the edge of town. "This is the Stidwell place," I said. "Stinks." Daddy said it was a good thing the Stidwells had moved out, because they didn't know how to live right, always leaving their trash in the yard, letting their children wear ripped pants to school. "Let's get out of here," I called to Benjy, but he was already inside.

I opened the door real slow. The Stidwells had been

gone a few days, but I guess the mill didn't have time to get the house cleaned up yet. Something scurried into the dark part of the room when I cracked the door open. I squinted, saw it was a rat.

"Benjy, let's go," I called again. "I saw a rat, and besides, the Stidwells haven't been gone long. They might come back." Mr. Stidwell was a large man with a booming voice who chased the other kids from his yard with sticks.

"Naw," Benjy yelled from one of the bedrooms. "They went back to the mountains. Their boy got killed in the war."

I pushed open the door and crept inside. There were empty cans on the counter, the metal all jagged where they'd been cut open. In the corner, newspapers were stacked, a few rags balled up on the top of the pile. Somebody'd saved the labels from the cans, peeled them real careful and pressed them. They didn't have an indoor privy like we do now, and somebody'd gone on the kitchen floor. I called Benjy again, told him it stank in here. That's when he came out of the back bedroom with a puppy in his hand. "Johnny told me last week that their dog had puppies. All of them's dead but this one."

Except for its eyes and nose, that were moving, the puppy lay limp in Benjy's hands. "Looks almost dead," I said, reaching out to touch it. It was warm and soft, with big ears. "Daddy will never let you keep it. With the rationing we barely get enough food for us. Mama says if it weren't for the garden we made and her canning, we wouldn't get many vegetables this winter."

Benjy's face fell so deep I knew I had to help him. "You want me to leave it in this house to die?" he asked me. "I'll give it my food to eat if I have to."

"I guess we could keep it in the shed out back. That way when Mama sees it we can say it wandered over."

Benjy wrapped the puppy in his shirt, and we started back to our house. "Promise," he said to me, "promise that when I get to go over and fight, you'll watch out for it."

"When you go over to fight?" I asked him. "Daddy says the war will be over before then."

His face darkened as he bent over the puppy, and he wouldn't say anything to me the rest of the way back.

THEN IT'S SUMMER and school's out. The morning of the summer picnic, we all pack two baskets of sandwich bread, salads, and cake. Mama makes lemonade. Since they have the picnic on the yard near the mill, we walk, carrying the baskets. Almost every family in the mill town is walking, carrying food. The kids yell to each other and laugh. Annie runs ahead with her friends, but I walk slowly with Aunt June and help Benjy with the basket when he gets tired.

At the picnic, the tables are spread with checkered cloths. Someone has butchered a cow, so we can take as much meat as we want. Baskets of bread and rolls, green beans from the garden, sliced tomatoes, potato salad, even large round blocks of cheese, cover the tables. Jars of pickled beets, onions, bread-and-butter pickles, jams, and fruit spreads line up like colorful soldiers. The cakes and pies have their own table — apple, peach, strawberry, Mama's chocolate cake with the walnut cream icing. I look at Benjy and we grin at each other. I can't remember ever seeing this much food to choose from, and there's enough that we can eat all we want.

Benjy and I fill our plates and sit near Mama and Daddy's blanket while we eat. Annie is nearby with Carol Anne and some boys from school. When Benjy runs off she waves to me to come sit with them, but I'd rather lie on the blanket and watch Benjy run towards the baseball field, where they're setting up a game.

Later we all go down to watch, and the afternoon stretches out long and hot. When Benjy hits the ball his legs are quick as a deer's.

Annie waved at me again to come sit with her and her friends. Then she walked over, stood beside me. "Come on, Silvia," she said. "Quit staring at that silly game and come sit with us girls. We're talking about Billy and Steve and them while they're busy playing." She giggled.

Annie's got lots of friends. She's even got a boyfriend. "No," I told her. "I'm just going to sit with Daddy and watch Benjy play."

"Who cares about Benjy?" she said, but sat down with us for a minute. "We're having girl talk."

And I see how she fits in — learning to cook and sew, eating ice cream with the girls at the company store, talking about boys.

"No," I told her, since I knew I'd never fit right. "I'll just stay here."

"Always trying to go against things," she said, standing up. "That's your problem. And you spend too much time watching Benjy."

When she was gone, I shut my eyes to it all, tilted my face back, and let the sun whiten the whole inside of my head. I lay back against the seat like that a good while, until Mama saw me and made me get under some shade.

That night before bed I run through the brush, a swift deer, grasshoppers scattering, my hair like streamers in the wind. Alone in the bushes, I can't see the house, just sky, all rose-colored, and I hear the twigs snapping, grass swishing, the insects. Then Benjy is behind me. I know before I feel him touch my hand. When we run to the house, fireflies are everywhere. Later he tells me how one got in my hair and he saw my whole head light up. I am quick and burning. When we get back, Mama stands at the door with a switch, saying one more minute, if we got back one minute later. Inside, Benjy turns and grins.

The next morning it gets hot early. Benjy and I are at the river. We are gypsies, Indians, we are soldiers. Holding on above the thick knot of the rope, we fly over the river. Both banks are ours and the water itself, which is muddy from the drought. Then Benjy swings out by himself, drops into the water. When he stands the water barely reaches his shoulders. "Come in, Silvia," he calls. "It's fine."

Daddy and Mama have told us never to swim in the river. "That's how your daddy's little brother died," Mama told me once. "Got in a suck hole. They couldn't even find his body." When Mama sees us on the banks near the water, she cuts a willow branch and wears us out right there even if the neighbor boys are watching. I've touched the water with only my fingers, toes. The rope dangles near my hand. Benjy goes under, then stands further out to show me it's not too deep. I swing out over the water and as I fall watch the branches make triangles of the sky. When I hit, I laugh with surprise at the water's touch.

We climb out and swing over again and again, dropping into the cool, murky river. The muddy bottom does not frighten me. We are swimming naked, our clothes hung on the bushes to dry. At first I do not notice how we are with nothing covering us. It is like it was when we were younger on wash day, when Mama would fill the big tub and put us all in at once. I'd see how the skin hung down between Benjy's legs and it was all soft and different looking. Mama told us that made him a boy, which was why he got to wear pants and had his hair cut short.

We were Frenchmen fighting our way across the river,

when Benjy swims up behind me, puts his arms around my waist, and pulls me under with him. I feel his hands grip my belly and his soft part behind me moving in the water. We come up for air, laughing. I turn towards him, let him touch me wherever he wants. He moves his hand down my stomach, between my legs, and stops there, his smooth fingers cupped around me.

That's when I first see them, standing on the bank, real still, watching — three neighbor boys. They see me, that I've seen them, and one of them starts picking my clothes out of the bushes, the other two calling to Benjy, saying it's their turn. I have forgotten the rope swing, but one of them sees it and quickly swings out. Benjy and me are running through water, trying to get to the other bank, but the boy, Bryan, who tried to beat Benjy up last year, grabs me around the waist, pulls me under, grinding his body into mine like he wants a fight. Benjy is pushing him, telling him to go on, but Bryan's friends have swung out and they pull Benjy back.

Bryan pushes me away when he is done rubbing himself against me. I run towards the bank. When I climb out, the sun dries the drops of water on me, and I am cool in the noon heat. Benjy climbs out after me, wanting to know again and again if Bryan hurt me, saying he tried to stop him.

"I'm okay," I tell Benjy, looking straight at him so he'll hush about it. "But they ran off with my clothes. What'll I tell Mama?"

"Here, put these on." Benjy hands me his shorts, and all of a sudden I get embarrassed and put them on quick. He dresses in his underwear and shirt, then hands me a kerchief to tie on my chest. We run back to the house, hoping we can sneak in and change before Mama sees us, but she is standing in the yard calling us for dinner. Daddy's already home.

When she sees me, she jerks me aside, almost whispering, "Where are your clothes?"

"The boys, down at the river, they took them," I tell her, trying to get into the house, but she has me by the arm.

Daddy comes outside, stops Benjy as he goes up the steps. "What boys, Benjy? Who took your sister's clothes?"

Benjy gives him their names, and Daddy slaps him in the face, his hand making a long hard sound. "That's for not fighting them," he says, and goes back inside. I see Benjy run out of the yard and into the woods. I want to follow, but Mama is pulling me into the house, wanting to know where they hurt me.

"They didn't hurt me," I tell her. She says Daddy's going over after dinner to talk to Bryan's pa. I go to the other room to get away from their questions and dress for dinner.

When I come out, Benjy is at the table with Annabelle and Becky. I tap his shoulder when I walk by, to let him know I don't care about him not fighting more.

Chapter 9

LILY'S STORY

CAN'T BELIEVE who I'm seeing," I yelled out across Rose's kitchen when I first seen June standing there after all them years. Her hair was stringy and needed a cut in a bad way. And she was all swollen up. I stood there wondering did she give up her sour notions about what folks should and shouldn't wear and how a lady ought to look in all them years she had to think about what James done. I had on a shiny turquoise dress, cut low in the front, and had my hair pulled back with a pin the way I seen in a magazine. When I walked down the street, people looked.

"Juney has come back," I said, when she stood there open-mouthed, and gave her such a hug she gasped and grabbed hold of herself like she'd have that baby on Rose's kitchen floor.

I pushed her into a chair. "I am glad to see you come

back." I looked straight at her stomach, saw how it hung out from the rest of her. "Any man who'd go off and leave you must be crazy," I said, turning to face Rose, the question on my face waiting to be answered. But she just looked hard at the coffee water dripping through the ground-up beans and didn't say nothing.

"Fresh coffee smells so good," I told her, and sit at the table. "When's Becky start school?"

Rose was setting out the cups. "This fall," she says. "Becky's a quiet child. She'll do good. When school starts up for the fall, I'll be going back to work."

I shook my head, then twisted in my chair, looked June in the face, smiled. "And how you like being back?" I asked her.

But Rose has to go interfering. "Don't be asking June a lot of questions, now," she says, and starts setting the table with her good dishes like we're company. "June doesn't need to be wasting her breath."

"Lordy, Rose," I near exploded. "It's been ten years since I seen her. I got a right to some questions." I leaned close to June. I could smell her sweat. "How was Florida? Looks like you had yourself a good time." I couldn't help the laugh that come out.

June looked up from the tablecloth she been fingering, looked me straight in the face. "Florida is a wonderful place," she says, "with lots of brand-new buildings, sandy beaches — white as you can imagine next to all that blue — fancy hotels. And people there know how to act.

Everyone was friendly and had good manners." Once she got started, she couldn't quit. "As for my husband," she says, telling what I most wanted to hear about, "I guess you haven't heard, but he got called overseas suddenly to fight for his country. That's why I'm here, waiting on his return."

Just then, Rose sets down a plate of biscuits on the table. "Drink your coffee and eat all you want of them biscuits," she says. "Everything's good and hot."

I helped myself to that biscuit plate. "We're glad to have you back, whatever the reason," I told her. Then I cut open the steaming biscuit, spread it thick as I could with butter and blackberry jam. "I guess you know, Rose and me frown on your being sent to that place in Columbia. We tried our best at letter writing to get you out of there, but we never got much of an answer. Our writing ain't too good, I guess. Now you're here, I plan to see to it nobody sends you back there." I looked at her serious-like over the coffee cup I pressed to my lips. I meant every bit of it.

"Just can't quite see how it happened, to this day I can't imagine it — you getting locked up down there for years, after one day of being crazy." I leaned towards her with my eyes. "I want you to know I been down to that bank lots of times to give James a piece of what I got on my mind; got thrown out twice by them special bank police. You should have seen them customers fly when I yelled out about James's real wife being locked up crazy just because he didn't like her being from a poor mama and papa, and his own child being — "

I could have kept on a good while like that, but Rose has to put her foot in. "June don't need to hear all this," she says, standing up. "Leave her be if you can't talk nice to her." She takes a step, and it's towards me. "Can't you see her condition, Lily?" she asks like I'm some dumb country girl. "She don't need to hear that."

Never mind what I been needing to say. Rose sits down again. Then we all just sit. "Well, Juney," I say when the quiet starts to eat at me, "whatever happens, you know you got me to get you out of it."

June smiled at me, the same smile she had as a kid, like nothing could touch her. "Don't worry," she says. "Jerry will be back for me soon as the baby's born. And it'll be a boy like he wanted. I know it'll be a boy."

WHEN I SEE Charles now, he is swift, certain, a flame burning up each eye. He cannot stay in one place but is up as soon as we get done, stacking the few pots he owns and clothing, making piles of what to take with him and what to give away. He says he's got the money and is leaving soon.

He knows I'll be waiting on him. He'll come by on his way out, knock twice at my window. It'll be night, Forrest sleeping. Or I'll drive into town to get him. We'll take Forrest's car. I got a small bag in the closet all packed.

Charles don't say just when he's leaving. Says I'll know soon.

Every two weeks I give Rose a mailing envelope with money in it. "It's for June," I tell her each time. Rose takes the envelope, puts it in her bag, and tells me again how June will say it's from her husband, who is overseas fighting the war.

She shakes her head. "I try to get some truth out of her. If she would say what's true, she'd be okay. She could have this baby, take care of it, maybe even find her a nice job in a shop or something. She has her looks still, underneath being pregnant, and she talks real fine."

I got no use for what's true. I tell Forrest my only business in town was the shopping. When Charles asks if I'll leave with him, I say soon as I get enough put back; then all I got I give to June. Sometimes I forget which way the lies go and tell Charles what was meant for Forrest or one of the others. Then I know better than to come around.

"Stories," Rose said when she first told me about how June saying she had a husband weren't all true. "Strung together like that was a way to live your life and keep it threaded straight. They get twisted up with what's real; then nobody knows, not even her, how it should come out. I tried. Ain't nobody but her can untangle them."

I got myself spun in devil hairs so thick I don't care if I get out.

Then one day I decide to take June into town to buy

her a pair of good shoes, like somehow that'll make a difference, like life could make sense again. "You can't be walking everywhere in them house slippers," I told her when I seen her at Rose's. "You need you some regular shoes. Folks won't know what to think when they see you come shuffling."

"They got good shoes at the company store," Rose told me.

"I'm taking her to town," I said, "get something that's quality." Rose frowned. Rose don't know nothing about buying at a shop. Edward gets everything they need at the company store.

As I pulled out onto the road, with June next to me on the front seat, stomach almost rubbing against the dash, Rose yelled for me to "be careful." Don't let nobody from the bank see her was what she meant. I do have some sense. With her swollen out, now's not the time. He'd know that ain't no melon. I'm waiting until it breaks from the vine so I can get her to the beauty shop for a morning or maybe take her shopping to find a new dress. I know James. If I get her looking like a cultivated flower, he'll give her anything. His wife, no waist, no hips, no bust, no matter how expensive the dresses she puts on, just a sack full of woman.

June got all nerves in the car, opening and shutting her purse (the leather peeled back to show cardboard), taking off her slippers, putting them on. "Now, June," I said, "settle back. I been driving this thing long enough

I won't get us killed. We gonna go to the finest shop in town." Generally, I got no use for women. Not many can keep to their own business. But June and Rose is my only relations, not counting Forrest, which I mostly don't.

June was muttering something about how Jerry always give her the best. My laugh made her jump so sudden, thought she'd fall out of the car, that baby not seen the world or even Ash Hill yet. "Don't one of them give us his best. They only like to brag on it. Every single one of them keeps what's his for himself and tries to keep what's yours, except when it comes to babies. Then they claim they don't own nothing. That's why you got to wheedle it out of them." June looked up at me and grinned, just like when we was kids and I'd talk her into helping me pull a trick on Rose or hide something from Mama. Took me right back. I had to start thinking that June still ain't nothing but a kid, all this time. She can let herself get used up and not know it. I saw I had to stand up for her. "You watch me, June," I told her. "I'll help you get what's yours."

She was looking straight ahead, out the window, maybe enjoying the way the trees and sky flash by when the car's moving. "I've already got what's mine," she said, rubbing little circles on her stomach with the palm of her hand. "Nobody can take this from me. I plan to take good care of him." She smiled, not at me but at the window or whatever she saw there, maybe just herself looking back. I knew right then I had to get to James or Jerry, one. I could see how it'd sit for June in Ash Hill, baby squalling and her not having no man about.

It weren't until we got the shoes and was ready to start home that I got struck by it. June had took her time picking out a stylish pair of walking shoes. The price didn't bother me none, and I had to compliment her on her taste. We was walking to the car when I said, "How about ice cream before we go back?" June nodded, and we got two scoops of chocolate at the drugstore fountain. We sat at the counter. June had to hitch up all that weight to get on the stool. I could hear the whispering at the other end, where a few town ladies sat, one of them an old mill wife whose husband had got himself a job working in the mail house.

Then it hit me — she'd come stay with me and Forrest when the baby got born. All them hens clucking about me. This would start them cackling. Already I could see the faces popping wide with surprise. Later we'd say the father got killed in the war. And Forrest. I'd let him think it was for us, because I know how bad he wants one. Bound to let me go about anywhere, long as a baby's in the house. We got two more bedrooms. I thought how I'd put June in one and the other for the baby. Already I was thinking on the baby bed we'd get.

June was sleeping when we got back to Rose's, the car motor humming, sun coming through the window all on her until she looked warm and content. Just waiting,

I thought, for some man to take her in his arms and not let her out of them.

The next evening when Forrest gets home I'm upstairs hanging curtains to match the baby bed I got all set up. He comes up behind me, not saying nothing, just wrapping his arms around my waist, smiling real grateful like. And I know what he thinks, but I'll work him around to the truth later. Right now I feel all warmed up to him, and our bed is just down the hall. Forrest is not like most men, who will get you anywhere they can if you're purring. So I take his hand, lead him like a boy to the bedroom.

With the door closed, he takes me without asking, until I get all weak feeling in my stomach, my clothes falling everywhere, and I know I will do whatever he wants of me. But then he stops, pulls back, asks, "Is it all right? Will we hurt something?"

Everything I was wanting falls away. I shrug my shoulders, like I don't care. He stands up, says he was wrong and how we got to be careful. "No more driving for you," he says, smiling. I hadn't counted on this and almost tell him the truth about my planning for June. But he smiles so big, kisses my face. "We'll look for someone to keep the house up and cook," he says in a real soft, even tender voice. "You spend whatever you need."

Chapter 10

ROSE'S STORY

JUNE'S BABY was born middle of the night. I told Edward to call for the doctor that evening after supper, and June gave birth to it after eleven, not making a sound as it slipped into the doctor's hands. I saw it, a girl, all sleek and new, its face pinched, but eyes clear as heaven.

The doctor carried that baby out of the house, just like that, never let it leave his hands. "Let me hold it," I was calling after him. "Give it to June." I could hear her moaning behind me.

Edward stopped me at the door. "It's the best way," he said as the doctor pulled out onto the road.

"That's all we get of her?" I said as the yard went black. "June didn't get a look, doesn't even know it's a girl. At least let it nurse a day or two. How's it gonna live?"

"Doc's taking it to the hospital. He can get a good home for it. He's doing what's best here." I seen then how Edward had this all planned. I couldn't make myself look at him. "Doc said for you to put a tight brassiere on her so she loses her milk; said it might hurt some at first, but not too bad."

June's crying filled the house. I could hear one of mine stirring in the next room. Edward walked out into the yard. Ever since I came near bleeding to my death after Becky was born, he left me alone at night, said he was afraid for me to have another one. Until that night, I wanted him to ask for something from me; I'd get under the blankets and rub up so close he'd have to put his arms around me to keep comfortable. Now there was nothing I could ever think of wanting from him.

Me and June slept in Edward's and my bed that night, with me holding on to her like she was one of mine, still little and hurting. Next afternoon, milk fever set in, and I kept her in there to nurse her. Later I asked myself why I never told her about Silvia so she knew there was something that was hers. I told myself it was being used to seeing Silvia like my own. Maybe I got all caught up in wanting her for my own and being scared Silvia would want to be with her true mama. I kept shut about the truth and let June cry through her fever, with only my cool cloths to soothe her.

When Edward come home next evening with the doctor, I said how the fever was down, so he'd know he weren't needed. He went on in anyway. When he come out, June was with him, holding his arm, stumbling a little, but her face all smooth and sweet like a child's. "Would you pack up June's things?" the doctor says to me.

"I need a new paper sack, if you've got one," June says.

I went in the bedroom where her things were and had to close the door so I could think. Mostly I was praying on Lily being home. Lily wouldn't let him walk out leading June like a pet. "She's coming to my house," I could hear her saying. "Don't nobody get in my way." But Lily'd been gone more than two nights now, with Forrest hot as a poker and me knowing about Charles running from the draft and maybe stealing too. I been trying to forget, so I didn't let go about it to Edward.

I was thinking hard to find a way out for June, when I heard the crinkling noise paper makes and seen Silvia in the corner, reading. "What is it, Mama?" she asked me.

"You love your Aunt June, don't you, child?"

She nodded.

"You'd help her if she needed you to, wouldn't you?"

She nodded again, closing the book.

"Run to your Aunt Lily's house. If Uncle Forrest answers the door, leave a message for her to come here soon as she can. If Aunt Lily answers, tell her I said to come quick. Don't say no more. Can you do that?"

She got up, nodding her head again.

"If your daddy says anything to you, act like you can't hear him. Go quick and get back here."

When she slipped out, the door hardly opened. I found

a hatbox with a string I'd been saving, took the lid off it, and began to fold the few things June got. I took down two of my dresses from a few years back that I kept meaning to let out. They was good quality, sold at the mill store, not faded a bit. I got them folded up and set on top, when I heard Edward. "Where are you going? I ask you. Answer me." I heard the slap when he hit her and the smack of the screen door when Silvia ran out again.

I was staring at the bedroom door when Edward pushed it open. "You got her things packed? They're waiting on you in Doc's car." He didn't say nothing about Silvia.

"I ain't finished," I told him, and turned to the closet. I heard his heavy step behind me as he bent to pick up the hatbox.

"Looks finished to me," he said. "This here's all she'll need." He had to work at getting the box to close. I saw how the string was all caught inside.

"I'll get it," I said, taking it out of his hands.

"Just see you bring it soon. Doc's waiting." The door swung wide and closed like a gust got hold of it.

I never had to ask where she was going. I guess I knowed Edward wouldn't stand her staying too long. "Don't you let her get around Annie and Silvia. All I need is them getting the idea they can go out, let some boy have his way. She needs a husband to make her stop them fairy tales. I guess James did right getting clear of

her. Now he's got a proper wife." I had to listen to all
he said, and her my sister too.

In my top drawer I found a bar of scented soap Lily
gave me and a photograph she had made of us two. I
wrapped them both in a lace hankie, put them on top of
the dresses, and fit the lid on the box. When I carried it
out, Edward was on the porch. He'd cut on the light.
The sky was just now turning the clouds behind the mill
the soft deep color of plums. I could see where most
everyone on our street was out on their porches, looking to see why the doc's car was at our house. Edward
got the box from my hands, took it to the car, that
was already humming. I didn't wave or nothing when it
pulled out.

"He'll take her to the train station. They got somebody to watch her the whole way." The screen door clat-
tered shut behind him.

I sat on the porch with Silvia after the others had
gone to bed. She had run all the way to Lily's, but when
she knocked on the door, no one came, not even Forrest.
As I sat in the rocker, she curled up at my feet and asked
where they took June and would June be all right.

"All we can do is pray for her," I told Silvia. "She's
back in Columbia. Your daddy and the doc sent her there."

I got a hard place in me after what Edward done and
couldn't look at him without my face closing up tight,
like the morning glories that turn in on themselves and
shrivel up. He brought me some cloth from the mill store,

said to sew me something new, even got me some shoes like they been wearing in town with the short heels they calling pumps. "Where I got to go in these?" I asked, and laid them on the shelf, where the dirt wouldn't get them.

It was late summer. I was waiting to see where me and Edward would go when it got cold, to keep away from each other.

THE MILL WHISTLE had blowed and the kids had run off to play when Lily come banging on the door. June'd been gone a few weeks, each day slipping from under me until I broke the eggs into the skillet without counting, beat up potatoes and didn't feel my arm go sore. Edward came home on time saying he missed me, trying to peck my cheek. I saw him but didn't hear what he said. When he touched me, I turned away without looking. But Lily made me look close, like the sound of a gun going off makes you hear even what you're trying not to.

She was beat up the worst I ever seen, purple rising up out of her face and a dark stickiness where blood had dried up. One eye was swollen shut, but the tears still sprang out of it when I tried to wipe off the blood with a damp cloth.

"We gotta call the doctor out here," I told her.

"No," she said, flat.

"Who done it?"

"Forrest."

I heard how her voice was cracked and weak, then

pulled back her hair and saw the dark rings around her
neck. "He near killed you. When'd he do this?"

"Last night, late. He come to get me." She was gasping. "It hurts to say." She touched her neck with a finger
like making sure it was still there. I filled a washpan with
warm water, got another cloth, soap, thinking I'd wash
her off good, see how much damage there was, and pay
for a town doctor if I had to. When I pulled off her clothes,
she went stiff, then limp, like nothing could hurt her no
more. Her face and neck had got the worst, but there
was a purple stain spread out over one breast and smaller
bruises where she'd fallen.

After washing her good where the blood from her nose
had fallen, I rubbed her with liniment. She groaned a
little, didn't say nothing. I had her lying down on the
bed. When I got done, she slept. I kept the door shut
when the kids came in for dinner, so they never knew
she was there until that evening. When she woke up, I
gave her a cup of broth, some soft bread to chew.

"I got to go somewhere," she said after swallowing
the broth. "Where can I go, Rose?"

"Edward threw June out," I said, to warn her. "He
got the doctor to carry her to the train station. Sent her
back to Columbia. Signed the papers himself."

She laid back on the bed, shut her eyes. "Did she
have the baby?" she asked when she opened them again.

I nodded. "A girl. Never even got to hold it. Doctor
took that too. Milk fever set in the next day."

"I was gonna keep them at my house. Even got a

room fixed. Forrest thought" — she closed her eyes again — "Forrest thought it was ours I was planning for. I expect he knows now."

She was breathing slow and even, "sleep breaths" I always called them. "I guess I was making up two lives — one with Forrest and June and her baby, one running with Charles." She was coughing. "Both done ruint now. Looks like I ain't got me a life."

I thought sure she would choke. "Almost wish they'd send me down with June. The military police come for Charles. Said he was a deserter and a thief too, though they couldn't get proof of that. We was staying in an empty house about six hours' drive from here in the mountains. Must have followed us there. I took Forrest's car. Maybe he sent them." She was coughing again.

"Quiet now, Lily. Lie back and rest."

"Funny thing about it — me and Charles was fighting when they closed in. I wanted to go further north where we could stay somewhere nice and not be known. Charles had friends in Georgia, said he was headed that way. Except for me having the car, he might have left me. When they got me back, Forrest was waiting." She laid back, closed her eyes again. "Don't know what Charles'll get. I got life." She grinned at her own joke.

Edward come home early, said before he even saw her that Lily had better get home. "Go home?" I spun around. "Did you see her? Forrest almost killed her. How can she go home?" It was the most I'd said to him since he'd sent away June and her baby.

I thought how worn out he looked leaning up against the doorframe, his hands in the pockets of his overalls like there wasn't nothing he could do. He shook his head. "Lily done bought this one. I wouldn't have taken her back. When I get home again, have her gone." He let the door slam.

I remembered Becky sitting at the table. "What'd Aunt Lily buy, Mama? Where's she going?"

I smoothed her hair back, thought how it was long enough to pin up in pigtails. "I don't know, baby," I told her. "Lily don't even know."

Before Edward come back, I helped Lily dress and walked her back to her house, helped her upstairs and into her bed. On my way out I run into Forrest. He thanked me for bringing Lily home but told me to stay out of their business.

It was that night Edward come to me. I held on to the pillow like I was sleeping, but he rolled me over, facing him, whispering so low I couldn't make out the words. Took me a while to see what he wanted, he'd left me alone so long at night.

I never know why some things make me cry. Once I got started, seemed like I'd cry all night. Edward got all of me, somehow, in his arms, rocked me back and forth like when a baby's crying for no reason you can see. "Is it June and Lily?" he said after a while. "I know you can't help that they're your sisters."

I pulled back from him, leaned up against the pillows. "I'm not ashamed of them," I told him. "I'm ashamed of what you done. You got no feeling, taking away a new-born child, calling that doctor behind me, making Lily go back. Ever since we got married you been coming between me and them."

I could see his face in the little bit of light that come through the window and how it was getting wrinkles I could work my fingers into. "Some things got to get done," he said, reaching, looking for my hands in the dark. "Most times a woman's too weak to get them done; then the man's got to see to it. I thought it'd be easier on you, not knowing I'd talked to the doc about June. He's the one told me we ain't had no choice."

Edward lay back down, like to let his words settle. I got to thinking about choice and how June ain't had any when they drove her down there and how if she wanted to have that baby or didn't, she couldn't change nothing, how she couldn't keep James or Jerry, neither one, from walking away. Then I thought on Lily, how she always act like she had a choice, going just where she wanted, paying no mind to Forrest or even the law. But now it come out that she can't change nothing either. I saw how she was maybe more stuck than June. And I saw how maybe Edward was right and how I couldn't make no difference. We all had to do certain things that was in us. All the lives that had got twisted up inside me fell loose like when them devil hairs would get in a big tangle and I'd find the one string that done it. When I pull it the knot falls apart and the strings hang loose and straight.

I ain't turned much towards Edward for kissing and such. Seems like the Bible's against that, and most times it's not in me to do it. When I did that night I could feel how he was shaking under me, shivering like the room got cold. "Come here," I said. "Maybe I can make you warm."

He rolled me over, real careful-like, not shivering no more. I got warm inside all through my chest and stomach, down into my feet, and didn't care none when he finished quick and was asleep, his arm a weight across me.

The next morning I walked on up to the mill with Edward, Annie saying she'd see every one of them got to their first day of school. The ground was cool through my shoes. The whole way Edward was talking how he was proud to have me coming back and how maybe we could build us a house like we planned. I took the hand he offered when we climbed the steep hill to the mill gate.

I knew most of them that were walking through the gate, but it didn't seem right seeing them this early, the men's overalls still stiff from hanging on the lines, the young women wearing shorter dresses than I was used to, carrying their aprons.

Maybe with my own house I could keep things straight, I thought. The young ones would like living on a farm, could get them a few animals. Edward might get him some hunting dogs. I pictured the garden I'd make, with all that space.

When I get inside I can't hear nothing for the noise.

Forrest is talking; I see his lips moving. He sends me to the weaving room with a man I never seen. "Can't I work in the spinning room?" I yell out, but Forrest is already talking to someone else, looking at the papers held out to him.

The looms are larger than the ones I seen here before. They're lined up one on top of another, until there's little room to walk between them. Cloth for sheets and bandages for them boys overseas rolls onto the big rollers like it'll be going until the end of time. Already I know the clacking heddles and quick banging of the beaters will fill up my sleep.

The boss man shows me how I got to watch my looms, keep the batteries full of bobbins. He shows me which machines are mine. "We'll just give you eighty today, until you get used to the job," he says. When he leaves, I can't move fast enough. By the time I get to the looms, an empty shuttle's shooting across. It takes me too long to fit the bobbins in, and then I have to walk back for more. When I get back, there are three more wanting bobbins, and I haven't even gotten to the end of my row yet. I walk from loom to loom until the threads fly all directions, making different patterns, each one too crazy to follow.

That afternoon, the boss man takes me outside, tells me I got to work faster. He says there's clocks on them looms showing how much I get done. My clocks ain't showing that I done enough. "Everybody's got to keep up now," he tells me. "We got to keep production moving."

Before we go inside, he smiles and says he knows I'll do okay. And that afternoon seems like they quit emptying out so quick on me. The threads pull off the sleeves in long straight lines, moving up and down like they should. When I run back for more bobbins, I see Helen filling her apron. "They got you in here now," she says. "It's a better job, once you're used to it." I'm reading her lips.

I fold my apron over and fill it like she does.

"When do we get our break?" I ask her.

"Break?" She shakes her head, yells out, "No breaks."

I drop a bobbin, then realize I can't pick it up without spilling the ones in my apron. "No break?" I yell back.

"If you hurry and fill your batteries, you might get time for a Coke." She smiles at me before she runs off. I walk from loom to loom, pull out the empty spindles, fit the new ones in. When I get to the end of my row, I look up over the looms and wave at Helen. The shuttles fly across the moving warps, the pattern always changing, each thread in its place.

Part 3

---

1 9 4 9 – 1 9 5 1

$\mathcal{L}$ILY'S STORY

I DROVE the new red Mercury I had to beg from Forrest into town today. At the grocer's I got me some magazines, a bottle of Jergen's lotion, the kind that makes your hands kissing soft, and a few things that Forrest never brings home from the mill store — doughnuts, ice cream, little tins of sardines, and cigarettes. When he comes home that evening, I'm filling the icebox, stuffing the bread drawer. I got two whole cartons of cigarettes sitting on the table. "What are you doing?" he asks, leaning up against the doorframe. "Just leave the shopping to me." I hear his slow steps going up the stairs.

The fry pan I set the pork chop in is thick with grease. Soon it's splattering the walls, sticking to the ceiling. Twisting the lid off a can of beans, I think how Forrest would love the smell of this pork chop cooking. I dump the beans in the serving dish, put them on the table cold.

What Forrest don't know is I seen Charles today while I was sitting at a stop sign. He knocked on the window until I unrolled it. "I'm playing at Maxine's, that new club just outside town. Got me a room over the club. Come on out some night." I heard of Maxine's, just an old house for drinking and cards.

"You got your whore out there with you?" I ask him.

He closed his hands around the edge of the window. "You looking fine, Lily," he says. "We had us some good old times, didn't we?"

I left him standing on the street corner.

Before I get done eating, Forrest comes down. "From now on, I'll send out for the groceries." His steps are thick and slow when he goes back up the stairs.

SATURDAYS Forrest takes his shotgun down, stomps through the hallway in his boots. Before the door slams, I hear him counting out shells. Around suppertime he'll come back, carrying a few squirrels, rabbits, maybe quail. He ties them from the porch rails, telling me to skin them. They hang there until they rot. I have to go out the back way to keep away from their stink.

At night I lie awake in the room I made up for myself, listening to the jingle of rifle shells and the crack the gun makes when he takes it apart or snaps it back together again. In the morning it sits on its rack, gleaming with oil.

Except for me, the house stays empty all day. My

shoes echo. Dust gathers in the corners, hangs from the ceilings. Across the front of the house, windows look out on a hazelnut tree and smaller maples. I pull the sash, sit in the rectangle of light the window makes on the rug, and read the magazines I get in town, piling them on the floor when I'm through.

Forrest says them at the mill talk about me not joining the ladies' club. "You could work their bazaar," he tells me, and wants to know why I won't help out.

When I stand in front of the mirror I see my skin's gone gray as the hair around my face. I rub on powder, rouge, so thick my face can't be seen, just the red glimmer. I smile. The makeup doesn't crack. With my eyes colored, I look like a doll.

When Forrest comes home he calls me a whore. He eats the plate lunch and supper they got at the mill; says the house smells. The dishes pile up in the sink, on the counters and tables. I pull out a new pan from the cabinet each time I cook. Soon I'll have to quit cooking and eat like the rats do, nibbling on cheese and crackers.

Last night I fried me some bacon, grease spitting on the wall, smoke curling through the rooms. Forrest went out on the porch, muttering about how they'd have to get the place condemned after having me live in it. I cracked me an egg, fried it up in all that grease, put it between two slices of store-bought bread.

Some nights, I turn on the television set we got and watch Sid Caesar and Milton Berle. Forrest likes to watch the fights. But he mostly stays in his bedroom with the door locked. When he's gone I wander in there, see the neat row of shoes in his closet, the ironed clothes on the hangers, the blanket pulled tight across the bed. I could dump the stacks of folded pajamas from their drawer and pull the suits down one by one. Sometimes I wish his fists still fell on me.

Finally I drove out to Maxine's. It was afternoon, bright, the leaves just falling off the trees enough so it was easy to see things. She was in the yard, hanging laundry. Looks like that's why he's got her, I thought, to do his cleaning. When she pinned up a plaid flannel with long sleeves, I remembered how his shirts always smelled of him even when they just come from the wash.

She was hanging up the last thing in her basket, a pair of pants, when Charles came outside, stood behind her, and reached around to grab her titties. "Quit!" she squealed. From the road I could hear his chuckle as he walked back to the house. That's when I seen all of her. She turned to the road, staring off beyond me at something, maybe at the way the sky was so empty, before she bent to pick up the basket and carry it inside. She had on a worn-out-looking cotton dress that buttoned up the front, and her hair hung all uneven on her shoulders. She was young. I could tell just by the way she stood there with one hand on her hip, even though I couldn't see if her face was pretty. She had long quick steps when she walked to the house.

Driving home, I thought about stopping by one evening to hear him play and if he'd get rid of her for a
while, or maybe she'd stay, sulking in the corner. I bent
down the mirror and looked into my face. The sun was
right behind me, coming in through the back window,
showing how much of my hair was going gray. I could
get me a rinse like they use now, but my mouth and eyes
still keep them lines no matter how much makeup I cake
on. The gray was coming through where the rouge had
worn off.

I look back at the road just in time to keep from driving into a ditch. When I drive through town I don't stop
at the drugstore to buy a rinse or more makeup, don't
stop nowhere. I tell myself I'll fry up a ham piece when
I get home and open a can of beans.

When Forrest comes home, after supper at the mill,
he kicks the clothes that lie in the hall out of his way.
I'm sitting at the table in the dining room. I've started
using the good china. It all piles up the same in the kitchen.
Just as I'm fixing to bite into a thick slice of ham, he
grabs me by the hair, pulls me out of my chair, and pushes
me into the kitchen. "Pick up those dishes," he says, "all
of them."

I lie on the linoleum floor, tracing my finger along
the outline his feet make in the dust. He comes back in
with a wet dishcloth, forces my fingers around it. "Scrub,"
he yells at me. My fingers go limp. "Scrub the floor," he
yells louder, and fits his big hand over mine, pushing it

back and forth. "Clean the damn floor!" When he kicks me I make myself into a ball against the wall.

That night, late, I go out on the porch. Two rabbits hang by their hind legs from the upper rail. The faint smell of rotting meat floats down from them. I've got the sharp kitchen knife. When I cut the strings, they fall, small, soft, their eyes dark buttons. I make a cut, fit the knife in between fur and flesh, peel back the skin so that the darkening meat shows. Their smell gets in my head. By the porch light, I can't see too good and cut meat off with the skin. The rabbits are stiff, like they'll be forever in the middle of a jump. "I know what it's like when you can't run," I tell them as the skin pulls off, tattered but whole. I'll feed the meat to Forrest's dogs, leave the soft limp skins on the seat of his car. Maybe with the skins taken off he can see them better.

All the next evening I wait for Forrest to say something about them skins. But he eats a late supper quiet-like, then climbs the stairs to his room. That night Forrest's dogs were barking again. I climbed out of bed, pulled on a dress, even took out my good shoes and coat, walked to the porch. It was a clear night like we get in the fall. The sky was streaked with stars, but I didn't need to sit there admiring them. I knew, soon as my hand touched the doorknob, I'd drive out to Maxine's. It was Saturday; Charles would be playing until late. I wouldn't have to stop the car, just drive by, see what kind of a crowd they got.

The dogs' barking got louder as I reached the car.

Just as I was opening the door I feel him behind me. "Where you going, Lily?" Like a heavy paw, his hand lay on my shoulder.

"Nowhere," I said, stepping towards the house, leaving the car door to hang open. My legs was beginning to shake from the cold. His fingers dug into me.

"Just a minute." He stepped up behind me, smelling of tobacco. "You was going off to see Charles, wasn't you?" My face turned hot where his breath touched it. "Even though he's got him a new girlfriend, you just can't stay away." He took my arm, twisted me around until his face was inches from mine. "You lost your looks early, didn't you? Not so pretty, like you used to be." I stumbled. He was lumbering behind me, pushing me towards the house. "Funny thing is I still want you."

Behind me, on the steps, his shape got bigger. I could hear his heavy breathing. "You ain't got no right locking your door to me every night." The sound he let out as he threw me on the bed was a growl. "You're gonna give me what I want."

His body hung over me; I could see his teeth in the dark. He let his trousers fall off and lifted my dress. "Ain't even got the decency to wear stockings. You're a slut, Lily. An old whore who only looks good when the make-up's thick."

He shoved into me so hard I let out a cry. "I bet you and Charles used to do it like animals all afternoon." His hand clawed at my ear.

When he got done he rolled over, the bed creaking

under his heaviness. I stood up quick as I could and run to my room.

It takes me so long to get to sleep, I wake up late. Forrest is gone. I can tell by the hollow sound the floor makes when I step out of bed. I put on a housecoat, go downstairs. His rifle's missing. Maybe he'll bring down something big, I think. It'll take him all week to haul it back.

When he does get home, he's got nothing. I hear him set the rifle on its rack. I'm in the kitchen, staring out the window at the pasture I used to keep my horses in, when he comes up behind me, pats my back like he wants to touch me. "How come you didn't stay last night?" he asked me. "I didn't mean to hurt you. No reason to run off like that."

I turn around. "Didn't know you wanted me to stay," I tell him, and reach my hands up behind his neck. I rub his head in the back a little. "Just got to tell me when you want me to stay."

He's got his hands on my hips, like he don't know where else to put them. "Do you mean it, Lily?" He pats me, looks at the floor.

"Sure." I kiss his cheek. There's a trap waiting in all this for me to set, I'm telling myself.

Chapter 12

ROSE'S STORY

ME AND EDWARD rode out in the old Ford to look at the house. The wooden beams stood empty of walls or a floor. He'd got help from some of the men at the mill getting the framework up, and Benjy worked on it too. A few evenings a week and Saturdays they come out, with Silvia tagging along to carry nails or whatever to them. I tell her to go to one of them club meetings for young ladies or to the social at the church with Annie, but I guess none of us can stay away from the house now it's started. I been driving out there myself, just to see how it's sitting and name the flower bushes I'll put in — lilac, mock orange, bougainvillea — around the front porch.

When we get back, Helen wants me to can the last of the tomatoes with her. We spent yesterday picking everything we could before the first frost. Edward carries the tub of tomatoes I got on the porch over to Helen's, saying not to worry about supper, they'll make sandwiches. Helen's got her big pot on the stove, and she's already skinning tomatoes. She tells me how Mr. Hanson's in the hospital with emphysema and his wife's saying it's on account of working in the mill all this time. "She went down to the main office to try and get compensation," Helen says. "Told them he was sick from breathing cotton dust."

"Did she get anything?" I was running water over the tomatoes that filled her sink.

"What do you think?" Helen laughed a little.

"No real proof that cotton dust will hurt you," I say, carrying a few tomatoes to the stove. After we dip them in boiling water the skins peel off real easy. "Edward says that stuff about it being dangerous is made up."

"Seems like they should give him a little something." The knife Helen used to cut out the stems slipped from her hands, skid across the floor. I stooped to get it. "My hands is so tired I can't keep a knife in them," she told me.

After we got the tomato jars in the cooker, I stood at her kitchen door. With the windows lit up I could see into my house. Edward was at the table, reading the paper. Becky had the ironing board set up, fixing to press her church dress. For twenty years now we'd been living in that little square of light.

Helen was telling about the preacher's wife, who was in Georgia visiting her daughter, who had a new baby.

Helen never does ask me about the house we're building. Don't neither one of us seem to think about me moving. As Edward went to the sink, I remembered how he'd put his arm around my waist when we stood next to the new house that afternoon. "We'll fix you a pretty window to look out when you wash dishes," he'd said.

But the next week Edward says we're out of money and got to wait until next spring to put the walls up. "The roof will keep it from the weather," he tells me, but I keep seeing the snow all over my kitchen, squirrels and mice making their nests in my closets. "I want a kitchen big enough for a table that all of us can eat on," I tell him, "and three bedrooms so Benjy can have his own and don't have to sleep on a cot in the living room." He's too big to be sleeping with the girls, and there ain't but two bedrooms here. When it gets cold, at least he's got a warm place by the oil heater. In the girls' room, they can see their breath.

When I get done work, I'm too tired to worry on it all. I got to run to keep up, them beaters banging so loud I can't hear my own mind telling me which way to move or how to thread the spindle so the cloth comes out right. Soon as I get one loom filled with spools, another one's empty. If the clock stops turning, the boss man sees how long it takes me. There ain't hardly a way to get a break, even for lunch. When I can, I hurry to get my batteries filled, then run to the water room for five or ten minutes. Helen and Matty try to get done too so we can all sit on the bench that's got four holes cut in it and talk. Some days it's the only time we sit down.

Matty pulls a pinch of snuff from her apron the way the old-timey people do. When she has to ask me four or five times if I can help out at the church social, she yells, "Are you deaf?"

"My head's just too full up," I tell her.

She nods. I guess she sees what I mean. If the looms ain't banging, them threads is flying. They cross over each other going faster than I can see. The cloth could be turning onto the roller knotted up or smooth as fine silk, the batteries might be full of spindles or empty, no way for me to know.

After I get my batteries caught up, Mr. Cramer tells me to work with one of the weavers, Matty or Thomas, who shows me how to watch for breaks and tie up the threads. I been using weaver's knots since I started in the spinning room, but I ain't never had to tie them this fast. The knots slip off Matty's fingers so quick I don't see them. "You gotta be able to tie sixty of these a minute," she tells me. After I get them all tied, she shows me how to lean over the threads and pull the beater back into place. "Wear a sleeveless blouse tomorrow," she says, "so your sleeves won't be in the way." Since my arms aren't strong enough, I have to pull back on the beater three times before it's in place. "You'll get better at it," Matty tells me.

Then Mr. Cramer gives me twenty of my own looms. "You won't be filling that many batteries today," he tells me. "We're using thicker threads." The knots slip off my fingers quicker and quicker. I try to mark any mistakes I see. Thomas hollers over about my fingers being in knots, just to kid me, but when a warp gets all tangled up with a few broken threads, it takes me so long to get them straight that I miss another loom's broken thread and can't find the end to tie it up. That's when I hear Matty yelling, "Fire!" and turn to see the loom next to me in flames. I seen them burn like this before when they get too hot, and the weaver always puts it out. I reach for the bucket of water on top of the loom. Just as I am throwing it on the flames, I hear Edward behind me. The water's falling real slow and I can't hear his words, but his hand grabs my arm. When we are by the door, I see the sparks. Matty and Thomas have run out too.

"You can't dump water on a burning loom," Edward is telling me. "That water's for cooling the crosspiece if it gets too hot. You could have been electrocuted." Gerald and Jimmy, both loom fixers, are using fire extinguishers to get the flames out. Edward goes back to his work, but I see him watching me over his shoulder. Mr. Cramer comes over to say how the loom burning wasn't my fault and that it's too dry in the room. Steam pours out of the pipes above us. It's already so hot and humid I could wring out my blouse. And here it is almost December.

The next morning, I'm back to filling batteries, and nobody says anything about weaving to me.

Soon after all this, Forrest called me out to tell me I

been moved back to the spinning room. I didn't say nothing, just stood with the battery I was loading and looked him in the eye. He started shifting his feet back and forth, looking sideways like he might be checking on a weaver. "I been here a long time, Forrest," I said to him. "Why they moving me back?"

He shrugged. "Nothing I can do about it, Rose. Mr. Cramer says you aren't keeping up." He looked over my shoulder. "We thought about making you a weaver, but we've got to keep things moving in here." I was rubbing the knots on my fingers. "Spinning room isn't that bad. There'll be a slight cut in pay, but the work will be easier on you."

"Same thing," I told him. "I'll be on my feet all day, still tying threads." I was thinking of the money. We wanted to get our house done the next summer, but Edward said we didn't have the money.

Forrest folded his arms across his chest. Ever since the war he's been wearing a fancy shirt and tie to work, with pants that didn't look like they come from the company store. He was supervisor over everything now. "There won't be as much pressure over there. Everything moves a little slower. You won't be pushed so much to keep up. The work's not as heavy."

"You ain't fooling me. I know the kind you got over there, the ones just starting out and the ones can't settle down and work nowhere. And the old ones. You saying I'm old?"

"I'm not saying anything, Rose." Forrest took a paper

from his clipboard, give it to me, then tucked the board under his arm like he's finished. "That's the notice telling you when to start your new job. Call my office if you have any questions."

Two days later I'm in the spinning room, learning my job from another boss man, who wears the same kind of tie as Forrest. Hundreds of spindles whirling so fast I can't hardly see them. The boss man shows me all the new ways they got of making threads, says everything's automatic, more than a thousand threads twisting onto the spindles. I got to walk between the rows and tie the threads together when one breaks. Walking back and forth, all them threads moving, makes me dizzy.

During the break I get me a Coke and sit at a table by myself, listen to the trash the girls talk about their men. The room gets so full of smoke I go back to my place before I need to. Now I'm in a different building I won't see Edward no more or Matty or Nelly or Helen or Lacy or any of them. "You'll have a job here doing something long as you want one," Forrest said, like that makes it okay for them to put me in the spinning room after the years I give.

In my sleep, the threads turn too fast. I walk back to the control room. Nobody's there. The threads are running by themselves, going whichever way they want.

MOST DAYS when I get off work, the house is empty. Benjy and Silvia are off somewhere, and Becky stays after school for Girl Scouts or Young Homemakers.

Dirty breakfast dishes still on the counter, jackets and books piled on the table, and I got to start supper.

One afternoon Becky gets home late, after Young Homemakers Club. I'm just off work, standing at the sink, the big cooker full of grease and three other pans on the counter.

"Mama, can I bake me some brownies in the oven?" she asks.

"What you need brownies for? The social or something?"

"No, ma'am. I need to practice. Mrs. Tribble says I do."

"Practice what?" I still hadn't looked up.

"The modern way of baking I just learned."

I looked right at her, said, "You can practice on these dishes," and give her the wet dishrag.

I always do my own dishes. But as I stirred the stew, I watched her fill the sink with hot water and soap. "You need some rubber gloves," she tells me, "to keep your hands from getting chapped by the dishwater." My back was bent over the stove. But it's like I got eyes in the other side of my head. Becky sets the clean dishes on the table, dripping wet.

"Get them dripping pans off my table," I yelled without turning around.

"There's nowhere to put them while I finish washing," she says.

That's when I began to holler about the years it's taking to get the new house built. I work on my feet all day and come home to a kitchen too small to cook supper and wash dishes in. And Becky always telling me what some Girl Scout leader says. She stands there, her mouth wide open, wiping the cooker with a soapy cloth. I turned my back, set the table, heard Edward come in, and called everyone to supper.

"We got to use the sewing room at Homemakers today," Becky tells us at the supper table. "They got some new electric machines, and the mill gives us all the cloth we need."

"Be a sewing machine operator when you grow up," I tell her. "Make good money. And not near the noise in them places there is in the mill."

Then she has to start in about Mrs. Tribble. "Mrs. Tribble says to serve dinner rolls in a basket, with a napkin to keep them warm."

"Quit sounding off to your mother," says Edward, and she quits her talking.

After supper the kids and Edward have all gone off. Just when I get the last of my pots scrubbed, there's Annie at the door, John Lee tucked under her arm. Her face is full of what's happened between her and Billy, and before she opens her mouth to tell me, I can guess, since Carol Anne's mama hollered to me when I was leaving the mill this afternoon to let me know how Mr. Travis at the company store wouldn't give Annie no more credit to buy on. "Wouldn't even let her have milk for the baby's bottles," Gladys says. "Not until Billy paid on the bill they owe." Weren't like that when I had my babies. Company store helped you out if you needed something. Now they got high prices, won't let us that live in the mill houses buy nowhere else, and they cancel your credit when you get to owing too much. It's hard on them like Billy, who's just starting at the mill and don't make much.

Annie comes right in and I take the baby. He's buttoned up in the wool sweater I made him. "You had supper?" When she shakes her head, I get out what's left of the chicken we ate and fix her a plate.

"This is the last of John Lee's bottles." She takes it out of her bag, hands it to me. "Mr. Travis says no more credit, and when I told Billy how he had to pay on the bill this week, he walks out, leaving me to try and find some kind of food for John Lee."

I set the plate down, push her into a chair so she'll hush and eat. Annie and Billy couldn't wait to get married. Soon as they got graduated, had to get the preacher. Billy started at the mill, then they had John Lee. And the mill don't help out no more by giving them a house cheap to live in.

"I told Carol Anne and May what Mr. Travis done, and they said the mill would just as soon watch us starve than give us more credit or Billy a raise."

I was sitting at the table, feeding John Lee. He was almost done sucking, falling asleep there in my arms, the milk running out the side of his mouth. All full of milk and sleepy and warm, he didn't know about none of what his mama was talking. "I'll tell Edward to give you what you need," I said, still looking at John Lee.

MOST DAYS, I work straight through dinner, so it was evening before I get the letter from June's doctor in Columbia. I let it sit on the table while I took out my eggs and cheese and some milk and started the noodles for macaroni. The whole time I was opening wrappers and stirring the cheese in, it watched me. It watched me slice the butter to melt on top. When I got the pan in the oven and my sweet 'taters going, I sat down at the table to open it.

Since Edward was picking up the kids from school to take them with him out to the house soon as he got off work, I was left alone to try and sound out the doctor's writing. I couldn't get all the words, but one question stood out clear: "How did June kill her first child?" I knew then how deep James's evil gone and saw why June never asked me if Silvia was her daughter. James had it put on her papers that she killed her baby. And I kept the lie going, thinking maybe they told her the baby got adopted by somebody far away or that James's family kept her.

I put the letter in my top drawer under a pile of hankies in the back and got down to ask God's forgiveness for not helping June. "There's too many lies piled up now, Lord," I told him. "Looks like the truth just twist things more." I could see June coming back to claim Silvia, and Edward not standing for that. "If you'd give me a sign, Lord, that the truth would be the one strand that'd pull the whole snarl loose, I'd make Edward call that doctor and I'd tell everything to Silvia. I'd even take her to the bank, make James tell her who he was."

I waited on my knees until I heard Edward and the kids come in. Nothing but the smell of my supper cooking came near me. It was like the Lord turned away, the sight of all them lies making Him sick. I thought about Silvia or Benjy or Annabelle or Becky having to suffer for all we done. When we twist our lives up in knots, our children's threads get caught too, a boy drowns or a grandchild's born mindless. In the Book it says your own will pay for your sins.

I'd been kneeling so long I couldn't hardly stand. The whole time I'm serving up supper, I feel how weak my legs are, how little strength I got to hold me up.

THE NEXT DAY was Saturday, and we was fixing to drive out to the house, when Lily called. "Forrest got himself killed hunting" was all she said.

Edward wouldn't talk on the drive over. His fingers wrapped tight around the wheel until what he'd said so many times, "Lily's not right in her head," buzzed in my ears. But when we stopped in front of the house, the sheriff was already there and had sent a boy out to look at the trail of blood Forrest'd left when he was dragging himself to the house. They'd covered him with a blanket, an army blanket, probably left over from the war.

While the sheriff's men skirted the woods, looking for hunters, I kept trying to comfort Lily, but she just wanted to sit on the porch smoking cigarettes. "Why don't you go inside, Mrs. Treherne," the sheriff said to her, but she didn't answer, only pulled her sweater tighter.

She had on a dress, stockings too. When I asked where she'd been planning on going, she said, "Nowhere." She told the sheriff, who come over to write down her story, how Forrest had left that morning with his good rifle. "He was gone when I get up," she said.

The sheriff raised one eyebrow. "Then you hadn't seen him since last night?" he asks her.

"He goes out hunting early most Saturday mornings. I knew he'd gone because I heard the dogs barking when he let them loose and his rifle was gone off the rack." The cigarette hardly left her lips.

"Where'd he usually go?"

"Most times, up in them woods." She pointed behind their house. "I never did go with him. Don't care for killing things." She blew the smoke at him.

"And you didn't hear any shots, ma'am?" While she was grinding her cigarette into the porch floor, she shook her head. Edward give me a look like he thought she was lying. I was praying he wouldn't say nothing to the sheriff.

"Did he say anything before he died?" the sheriff asked, staring at her foot.

"By the time I found him he'd quit breathing. He was lying there where you saw him." Lily lit another cigarette.

After they left with his body, I told Edward to go on, that I'd stay with Lily awhile. "Don't worry about me none," she said. "I'm used to being here alone."

"Why don't you come back with us," I said to her, "have some supper, and Edward will run you on home later?" We'd gone into the house. It'd been more than two years since I been by to see Lily, but I'd heard how she quit cleaning and wore the same clothes for days. I expected to see dishes piled all over the sink and a dirty floor, but the house looked real clean, dishes drying in the rack, the windows shining in the winter sun. The fry pan from breakfast had been washed out. It sat on the stove, with a few beads of water still clinging to it.

"Won't you come with us?" I said again, turning to Lily, who was putting out her cigarette in the sink.

"Naw." She looked at me, carried her cigarette to the trash. "You go on. I'll see you tomorrow morning at the funeral." Edward honked the horn. I knew he'd be telling how she had some hand in Forrest's death, and I wouldn't know what to think was true. Lily had lit another cigarette and was knocking the ashes into an empty can. I couldn't find a way to hug her before I left.

Chapter 13

LILY'S STORY

I HAD FORREST laid out in a simple box, and I didn't allow no viewing. "I'll go to church now and then," Forrest would say. "I'll pray, but I won't look at a person when he's dead."

Rose came over before the funeral, wanting to know why I wasn't having a viewing. "It looks bad," she told me. "Looks like you can't wait to get him in ground, like you got no fear of the Lord."

I was laying out the dress I would wear to the funeral. It was navy blue with a scoop neck, made of shiny rayon material that fit tight over my hips. "What do you think? Black just never was my color." I picked out a string of pearls. "Maybe these will help dress it up."

"The Lord could strike you down for that." She was walking towards me, real careful, like she didn't want to get hit if He did.

I stepped out of her way and walked to my closet to pick out some navy shoes. "Pumps or high heels?" I ask, taking out a couple of pairs. "Or I got these with the open toes." The shoe's fine leather was soft under my fingers.

When I looked up, Rose stood in the middle of the room, her mouth dropped open like she'd forgot how to close it. "The Lord lays down certain things for us to do," she said finally. Fingering her purse, she looked down, then straight at me. "This will all come back to you," she said.

Laughing under my breath, I picked up the shoes. "That's some strange notion you got about having to do certain things." I stood up, looked at Rose. She had sat down on the bed, clutching her purse in front of her to keep from getting tainted. "I always done what I wanted." I set my dress shoes with the open toes on the floor near the dress. "These will do just fine."

"Look what you got, acting that way." She was talking between her teeth. "You were married all these years to someone you didn't love, carrying on with somebody else, who was nothing but trouble. You got no friends." She stopped, bent her head down until I didn't have to see her face. When she looked back up at me, her eyes was watery. "I just want to help. If you could find a way to live the Lord's way . . . He's punishing you now for not following Him."

I sat at my dressing table, sprayed on a little scent,

started to put my face on. In the mirror I could see Rose dabbing at her eyes with a hankie. "You think you got it all figured, don't you?" I asked her. My skin turned a creamy beige. I painted my cheeks a deep pink. "You think I got what I deserved out of life because I didn't follow some preacher's teachings." Over my eyebrows I drew thin lines. "I always done what I wanted, and I always got what I wanted. Sometimes I might have wanted the wrong thing or not seen what all come with what I wanted, but the Lord ain't got nothing to do with it." I colored my eyelids a deep blue. "Only thing is now I'd like to have a pretty little navy bag with beads on it to go with my dress, and I ain't got enough time to run into town and look for one."

As I painted a dark red smile on my mouth, I heard her get off the bed. She was a shadow moving across my mirror. Her slow steps went down the stairs. I hardly heard the front door shut behind her.

Even though Forrest hardly ever went to church, it was full for his funeral. Most every one of them from the mill came. When I walked into the church, I could hear the older ones, the women, calling me a painted whore. Gladys, who used to work next to me years ago when we both worked under Forrest, said out loud that she thought I'd killed Forrest. She had iron-colored hair and was too big to fit into a good dress anymore. Letting my hips sway, I walked on up to the first bench. When I sat down, one of the men Forrest worked with leaned

forward to say he was sorry for my loss. I smiled, held
out my hand to him, said how much I appreciated his
concern.

The veil on the little hat I wore put just enough shadow
over my face. I didn't spoil my lipstick none by smoking
a cigarette. If Forrest coulda seen me, he'd have been in
love all over again. It'd been a long time since I dressed
up for him.

I didn't see Rose until the burial. When she looked at
me, I winked from under my veil. I stayed until they
shoveled every last bit of cold, wet dirt back into that
hole. The preacher kept asking did I want him to drive
back to the house with me. I shook my head. Forrest
Treherne, I was thinking, nailed into a box, under six
feet of dirt. Finally.

A WEEK AFTER I had Forrest put in the ground,
Charles came to the front door. I had on an old housecoat and didn't even have my face paint on. When he
said, "You sure do make a pretty widow," I knew he was
lying.

"Where's your girl?" I asked him as he stepped in
without waiting for me to invite him. He looked over my
head, into the parlor, then took a step towards the kitchen.
From the hall, you could see the dishes piling up in the
sink and on the counter. When he quit looking, he slipped
his arm around my waist. "You're my only girl," he said.
"Fancy place you got here." He walked into the living

room, heavy steps leaving footprints on the rug, and picked up one of them glass figures that Forrest give me, a little horse with one leg lifted like it was prancing. "You got some pretty things in here. Forrest give you most of it?" The horse shattered when it hit the wall.

My words came out like somebody else was talking. "It's been too long. Go on back to your new girl."

"I know," he said, "it's been too long." He was standing behind me; I didn't even see him walk over. "That's why I'm here." Bending over me, he rubbed his hands on my stomach, kissed my neck.

"You ain't getting nothing," I told him, but I was starting to shake.

"Just let me warm you up," Charles says. He had his hands under my titties and was rubbing himself up against my backside. "Why don't you show me his room. Is it upstairs?"

"No." I couldn't quit shaking. I tried to pull him into the parlor, thinking we'd use the rug, but he was pulling me towards the stairs.

"I want to do it like a gentleman," he says, and laughs. "Trying to make me lie down on your floor. Is that any way to treat a guest?"

I got numb going up the stairs. "Is this it?" he asked, and opened the first door. Forrest's bed was made up, the blanket pulled taut. The only things on the dresser were his brush and comb set and a picture of me when I was young.

"Not in here; down the hall," I said, pulling on his hand, trying not to step through the door. I knew Forrest'd be waiting on me in the mirror, seeing everything I'd be doing.

Charles yanked me by the arm, then pushed me a little towards the bed, kicking the door closed with his boot. "I want to see what it's like being the man of the house."

Charles was still good looking. Wrinkles hadn't hurt his face none, just made him look rougher. His eyes were still green, like emeralds. The blanket smelled of Forrest.

"Just like old times," he said when we was through. He still hung over me, smiling, smoothing my hair back real gentle. "You sure are pretty."

I turned my face away. Before he left he said he'd be back tomorrow if I didn't mind him calling on me. Said it real formal as he was backing out the bedroom door, me still lying on the bed, half dressed. "I don't mind," I told him, like I was one of them puppets you pull the strings on. The whole house shook as he went down the steps.

I stayed on the bed, trying to think how I could get out of the room without looking in the mirror or the mirror looking at me. There was a wet spot on the blanket, and I thought how Forrest never would have allowed no stain on his bed.

I must have slept a good while, because when I woke, the room was dark. Sliding off the bed, I could feel Forrest everywhere. On the stairway I heard the snapping sound his guns made when he cleaned them. I looked at the rack. One of them had moved, like somebody'd taken it down, handled it, put it back so it wasn't exactly straight. Wind banged up against the kitchen windows, set them to rattling. I took out a can of something to heat up. Someone with heavy boots walked across the porch. Real quick, I switch on the light. Then I see it, through the windows, a carcass Forrest left me, hanging from a tree limb near the house. A huge carcass, maybe a deer or a bear. I saw how its blood must be staining the ground forever.

I went on the porch. The wind blew up and the thing shifted. That's when I seen it was just a shadow the wind was playing with. Didn't make Forrest's being there any less true, though.

I go back inside, eat my supper from the can, cold. I sleep on the rug in the living room. Make myself a bed with a few blankets near the door. The smell of the dishes piled high in the sink follows me. Pieces of glass from my horse lie on the rug. I won't clean any of it until Forrest leaves.

The next week, Charles stops by every afternoon just when the sun's getting warm. We try out doing it differ-ent places in the house — on the sofa bed in the parlor, on the new rug Forrest brought home last year for the dining room. Charles never lets me pull the curtains.

One afternoon just when I'm putting my slip back on, fixing my makeup, here comes Becky up the walk, car-rying a basket. She's wearing a skirt and blouse, white

socks, anklets, looks like the model schoolgirl. She ain't
been up to the house in years, maybe not since she was
little and rode with Rose the time the mill school got shut
down and I let them use my car to drive to the town
school.

She rings the bell. I slip on the long housecoat Forrest give me for Christmas, made of pink silk with a fur
collar. When I open the door she just stands there, staring.

"Well?" I ask her.

"I'm Becky. You know, Rose's youngest," she tells
me, like I don't know. Then she holds out the basket.
"It's meat loaf, green beans, and rolls. We made them in
Homemakers, and Mrs. Tribble said I could carry them
to you since Uncle Forrest passed away."

Homemakers. I can see her standing over a stove,
trying to look pert, a pressed little apron tied in a big
bow around her waist. I bet she puts on gloves to do the
dishes.

"We all feel bad about Uncle Forrest. We sure are
sorry," she says, waiting on me to take the basket.

A do-gooder. Goody-goody. I take the basket, invite
her in.

When I get back from calling to Charles, she's in the
parlor on her hands and knees, picking up the pieces of
glass from that damn horse Charles broke. "Don't touch
nothing," I tell her, and she jumps up, little slivers of
glass catching sunlight as they fall back to the rug.

"Sorry," she says, backing up. "I just thought I'd tidy
things up a bit for you."

Just then Charles walks up. He's got on the sweater I give Forrest for his birthday. It looks real good on him too. Picks up the green in his eyes. He says, "Nice to see you," settles himself in the armchair. Then he offers Becky one of the cigarettes in my thin gold case.

She giggles, shaking her head. "Mama would kill me," she says.

"Then she'd have someone else's soul to worry on," I mutter. "Might leave mine alone."

"To rot," says Charles, making me laugh so bad I got to sit down.

I look at Becky. She's got her hands in her lap but can't keep them still. I make my face get serious looking. "What did you think of the service I give Forrest?" I ask her. "Weren't the flowers pretty?"

"Yes, ma'am." She nods, looking around the room instead of at me. I got some real nice-looking furniture in the parlor, velvet.

"Tell your mama," I said, smiling at Charles, "that the preacher was here with me." I got up, and she followed me to the door.

"Come by again, sweetie," Charles calls after her. "I'll take you to the picture show. Right now I got to help your Aunt Lily get down on her knees."

And that's what he done too. Soon as she was gone.

A FEW DAYS LATER, when she comes back for the basket, me and Charles is on the porch. "Your mama know about you coming over?" I ask her. Rose don't allow none of hers in my house since way before Forrest died.

"No, ma'am," she tells me, standing on the porch step in her schoolgirl skirt and blouse, that hat on her head for some goody-goody school club. "She found out about Tuesday and me bringing the basket. Switched me with a willow branch like I was a little kid." She stuck out her lip. "Made me lift up my skirt."

"Let's see, honey," says Charles. "Show Uncle Charles how she made you lift it. Come on up on the porch and show me."

Becky turns red. She comes up on the porch, lifts her skirt a little.

"Come sit on my lap," says Charles. "Right here." He pats his lap. "Uncle Charles will make it better."

"Well." She smiles at him, getting real coy-like. "I come for the basket."

"Aunt Lily will get it." He glances at me. I'm gritting my teeth. "You sit here on the swing with me a minute." He's patting the place next to him now. "Looking at this here magazine is as good as going to the picture show." He opens the magazine as she sits down. It's got pictures of women in it. "These here are all the picture stars."

When I get back with the basket, she's telling him how she wants to be in the picture shows when she grows up. "My mama don't know it, but I saw *Enchantment* with a girlfriend," she says. I know the kind of picture star he's thinking on.

"You'd be beautiful," he tells her, "a beautiful star. Just like this one." He points at a girl got on one of them new two-piece bathing suits.

Yeah, Goody Two-Shoes, I'm thinking.

"Get home now," I tell Becky, holding out the basket. "Be quick about it."

She takes the basket, runs down the steps yelling "Bye," doesn't even look back.

Charles is laughing, a low sound coming deep in his throat. "Cute kid," he says.

"I'll have to send word round to Rose," I say. "Thank her for sending Becky over." I look at Charles. He's grinning up at me from the swing. "Hope she gets whooped good," I tell him.

He just starts laughing again, that warm low sound like water bubbling over me.

The next day, I put on one of the dresses I used to wear to town — deep green, little gathers at the waist, with a short hem, a low neckline that fits snug. I wanted Charles to see what I still got.

For more than two weeks he'd come by every afternoon. He made a game of doing our business in different rooms in the house, but his favorite was Forrest's. I was careful to smooth the blankets when we were done and kept the door closed when we weren't in there.

I had my stockings and dress on and was painting my lipstick, when I felt Forrest touch me. I couldn't see nothing in the mirror, but when I turned around real slow, the door to my room moved a little like it was opening. I got up, walked to the door, shut it, but it swayed open again. There was nothing I could do to get it to latch.

When I heard Charles drive up I ran downstairs and met him in the yard. He was driving my Mercury back and forth from his rooming house. It was a real warm day, leaves filling up the sky, shading the yard and house. Charles caught me up and hugged me. "You're looking real fine," he said as he kissed me.

"I been thinking," I said, laying my head on his shoulder. "Why don't you just bring your things on over. No reason for you to be paying to stay at the boarding-house when you're here every day. I been ordering my groceries from the company store. A boy brings them up, leaves them on the porch. I don't care about talk."

He gave me a little squeeze. "You sure do know how to figure things," he told me.

I sat on the porch while he drove back for his things. I could feel Forrest inside, waiting on me. Seems like sometimes his hitting me was the only way he knew. Maybe moving doors and leaving the smell of his after-shave in a room was just another way of wanting me.

When the Mercury loaded with Charles's things pulled up, I'd made up my mind to close Forrest's room, maybe nail the door so he wouldn't have to see what me and Charles did. It didn't take long to carry the piles of clothes and boxes to the house. "I thought we'd fix up the guest

room for you, or you could stay with me," I said, trying
to pull him towards my room. He was carrying a stack
of clothing.

"I'll set up right here." He pushed the door to Forrest's room open with his foot.

"My room's nicer." I wrapped myself around him.
"Let's just board this room up. No reason to let him bother
us."

Charles pushed away my hands and stepped into the
room. He emptied out a drawer and laid his clothes in it.
"I'll go through these things later. See what I can use,"
he said. "I might need some new things, now I'm man of
the house. And after all them years of me having to watch
you run home to Forrest." He hugged me tight around
the waist. "Why don't you go make me a little drink while
I finish unpacking."

Forrest had several bottles of liquor in a cabinet
downstairs. I'd took to drinking from them before I lay
down on my blankets in the living room and went to
sleep. I poured Charles a little whiskey and dropped in a
few ice cubes.

When I got back, Charles had filled the wastebasket
with Forrest's brush and comb set and the pens he always kept on the desk. There was a picture propped up
there, a small one. When I picked it up I saw it was of a
girl, younger than me, with pretty, long, dark hair and
friendly eyes. "Who is she?" I asked him.

"Just a friend," he said. "What you worried about?

You got me here." He grinned. I turned the picture down and went to him.

After we got done, I looked into the mirror and saw only myself with Charles lying down behind me. My hair was all mussed and my face was smeared looking. I closed my eyes. I couldn't feel Forrest anywhere.

Chapter 14

SILVIA'S STORY

IN EARLY MORNING, the field shimmers with water. If I took a comb through the grasses, it would be coated silver when I finished. Benjy won't play with me in the yard or near the house, but he follows me to secret places like this field where they used to grow cotton at the edge of town. The early sun spins webs in the stalks. Dew sitting on each blade, a little mirror.

Benjy follows me to the large tree in the middle of the field. We don't speak until we're leaning against its trunk. "I think Mama heard us leave," Benjy says. "Maybe we shouldn't stay long." He puts a blade of grass between his lips.

"Soon as we graduate, there'll be lots of places to go," I tell him. "We could go to Florida or California, where it's always sunny. We could go to Paris. Somewhere far away and new. I know a preacher in town who'd marry us. He wouldn't have to know anything. I'm adopted. It's not like we're really brother and sister."

Sliding over beside him, I try to take his hand, but he pulls it back, turns to lean over me, holding my shoulders against the trunk. "Stop," he says, but kisses me on the mouth until we are both out of breath.

I smile, fingering his dark hair. "You can do whatever you want here."

"Don't say that." He sits back, pushing me away. "Some days I wish you'd go out with one of the others, like Doug or Steven," he says, pulling a piece of bark from the trunk. "But then I can barely stand for them to watch you."

I pick up a stick and dig in the soft ground around the roots. When his hand slides down around mine, I tell him about the deer bones I found. "Over there where those trees are starting to grow," I say, pointing. "There's a skull still."

He grins. We're kids again, playing at being Japs or Indians. He takes off running and I'm behind him, our feet pounding the uneven ground. When we get to the field's edge we're both out of breath and laughing. I point at the bones lying between two small pines. "They're perfect," he calls, running towards them. "They haven't been touched."

The skeleton is complete. I run my fingers along the smooth white ribs, mirrored on the animal's other side. "Maybe we can take it apart, then set it up at home again," says Benjy. "It'd make a great science project." But after laying our hands on each bone, we leave it intact, another secret between us.

Each afternoon after the school bus lets us off, I try to walk with Benjy, but he runs ahead, calls to some boys to wait. Behind the slides in the playground, in the corner of the classroom, I hear the whispers about Benjy and his sister, how it will ruin her. "It's not natural. They grew up together, sleeping in the same bed." I don't let their voices touch me. One week I read *Moby Dick* or spend a whole afternoon tracing the flowers out of a botany book. Mr. Larkin says my drawings from the microscope are the best he's seen and hangs them on the wall. I close my eyes and wish myself to France, Germany, Australia, somewhere far away where nobody sounds like Ash Hill.

Then, just when I think Benjy has stopped talking to me, I feel him behind me. "Follow me." I hear the whisper as he steps in front of me, runs a little. Soon we're stumbling along the river's bank. I try to fit my feet into the smooth hollows made by the high water from the fall rains. The water's dragged down branches and limbs we have to step over, but Benjy moves swift. When he stoops to drink by the river's edge, I can just see his dark hair. He leads me up the bank, pointing. The water's dug a cave in the dirt. We crawl in, laughing because we can't help but touch here.

"I thought you'd like this," Benjy says. "I found it yesterday, walking."

"You said you were playing ball."

"Nah. I just told Mama that. Had to get away." He dug his feet into the dirt, and part of the wall crumbled on us.

"You had to get away from me, didn't you?" I ask.

He kicks down some more dirt, watches it fall from his shoes. "Some days I got to get away from everyone," he says.

The dirt is cool, moist. Curling closer, I make myself into a ball next to Benjy. "I need to get away too, but with you," I tell him.

Benjy takes a long time looking out the cave's hole. Sunlight, leaves, and wind make dancing shadows. "We're going to get found out someday," he says finally. "We ought to quit pretending. I'm almost done with high school and haven't had a girlfriend. Most everybody knows something's not right. Even with you being adopted, this town never will stand for us courting."

I tell him again how it will be once we get away from here, how no one will know us, how we can be whoever we want. "Remember the postcards I found from Aunt June?" I ask him. "The ones she sent from Florida with the ocean? We could go there." When I wrap my arms around his neck, he kisses me back. We stay curled around each other in the dirt cave until Benjy says it's near suppertime.

A few days later, Benjy's bent over the kitchen table, where his books are spread. "Come on," I call to him. "Mama and Daddy won't be back for an hour or two. I want to show you something." He starts to walk towards Becky's and my room. "No, not there. I want to show you in one of the secret places."

He walked towards me, set his pencil on the table. "It's cold outside, Silvia. No one's home. Show me here."

I lifted our jackets from the pegs, handed Benjy his. "Come on." I pulled him towards the door. "Listen. The ice is melting. Hear it dripping from the roof? It's warm with the sun shining on everything."

Thin sheets of ice covering the puddles cracked under our feet. Benjy dug his hands into his pockets. "This better be worth the walk," he told me. I ran on ahead and soon heard his steps quicken. In my pocket I held the small white box.

I followed the river upstream until we came to a tree trunk so wide that when we both sat together at its base we could only be seen from the river. Benjy sat on his heels. "The ground's wet." He rocked back, a little unsteadily. "Now what did you want to show me?"

I tossed a piece of bark in and watched it twirl round and round in the rough water.

"Silvia, it's cold and I've got lots of homework. Show me. I'm not going to stay here long." He worked his feet under him like he was about to stand.

"Okay," I said, not looking at him. "But now I almost don't want to give it to you."

"Give me what?"

I put the box in his hand and stood up, walked to the

river's edge. A headless plastic doll knocked back and forth between the rocks before getting dragged under. When the ice melts and the river runs faster, whatever falls in get lost. Benjy must have sat watching me a few minutes before he walked down. "Silvia," he said, putting his hand on my shoulder, "I can't keep this. Where did you get the money for it?" He tried to put the ring in my hand.

"I want you to have it," I said, closing his fingers around the ring. "Miss Ellis had some work in the school office she let me do last week after school. That's why I was late coming home. When she paid me, I thought about the class rings and how you wanted to order one but Mama didn't have the money. They had a few extras at the office, and this was your size." He was turning it over in his hand. I couldn't see his face. "I thought it would make a good present. I thought you'd be proud to have it."

"It's not that; it's just . . ." He sat down on the bank and looked up at me. "I ought to be buying you a ring. Seems like every time you get some money, you spend it on me. Just doesn't seem right. You should have got one for yourself."

I sat down but kept my back to him. "I wanted to get it for you." I could hardly say the words.

Benjy stood up, took a step towards the river. I heard the splash of something hitting the water and looked, but he still held the ring cupped loosely in his hand. When he turned back towards me, he bent over, tried to get me to take the ring. "You keep it," he said. "Wear it on a necklace."

I didn't tell him that the girls at school wore their boyfriends' rings like that to show they were going steady. Instead, I started to cry. Benjy walked on down the river. Didn't even tell me to hush and how everything would come out all right. I guess he had the ring in his pocket. He stood looking over the edge of the bank for a good while, then he walked back. "It isn't right for me to keep this ring, Silvia," he said. "What are we going to tell Mama and Daddy? They don't even know we go off together. And who knows what'll happen after we graduate?"

"Just throw it in the river." I lay on my stomach with my face against the wet moldy leaves.

"Look, Silvia," he said as he squatted down next to me. "I'll keep it. But I can't wear it. I'll carry it like this, in my pocket." He tried to get me to look. "But this is going too far. We've got to start thinking about what we'll do after graduation. It might not work for us to stay together."

I sat up, looked straight at him. "Why not?" I asked. "We always planned it that way." He was looking out over the river. Somehow, in the last few months, his face had gotten more grown-up looking.

"Let's wait," he said, like he was talking to the river instead of me. "Neither one of us have even gone out with anyone else, and high school's almost over. We better just wait and see what works out." He was sitting on the damp cold leaves, watching the river. I stood up. I couldn't think of a way to make him look at me.

As we walked back towards the house, I stopped only once, to pick up a stick, toss it towards the river. When it hit the water, it made a small splash. Benjy never even turned around.

ALL THE NEXT WEEK Benjy won't look at me. On the way home from school, he runs ahead and is off playing ball before we reach the house.

So when Annie asks if I'll baby-sit John Lee while she does her shopping, I say yes. I rock him and give him his bottle. I sing "Hush, Little Baby" even while he sleeps in my arms. I whisper the names of places I'll go to when I'm grown — Paris, California, Alaska, Brazil. The pictures I describe are from our geography book. "This is a white world. The man and woman dressed in furs live in a circle of ice. There are walruses and penguins and ice fishing. In Brazil there's an ocean, white sand, and forests, the dark green dripping with rain, huge red flowers. There are monkeys and parrots." John Lee sleeps.

When Annie gets home, she dumps the packages on the kitchen counter, turns to me, and shakes her head. "I bet you had him on your lap the whole time," she says.

I just smile. John Lee is warm and heavy, breathing slow, even sleep breaths.

"Why don't you come over to the house Saturday," she says. "Billy's got a friend coming. We'll sit on the porch, drink some Cokes."

I stand up slow as I can. John Lee keeps sleeping. When I get back from setting him in his baby bed, Annie's got most of the groceries put up. "Well?" she asks me, one hand on her hip like she knows what I'll answer.

"I don't know." I pick up my bag and sweater. "I got homework."

"Silvia," she says, and her hand's still on her hip, "you are going to turn into an old maid. Here it is your senior year, and you ain't never had a boyfriend. Billy and me were engaged by then."

I can't help the long sigh that comes out.

"And it ain't 'cause you're not pretty," she goes on. "Carol Anne says you're the prettiest girl at the high school. Most girls would kill for your thick blond hair. 'Like honey,' that's what Carol Anne says."

"Yeah." I can't help smiling. I can just see Carol Anne taking notes on what every girl in Ash Hill looks like. "Well, I got to go," I tell her, turning towards the door.

"I know why you ain't had a boyfriend and spend all your time with your books." She sets her lips in a thin line, like she's waiting on me to tell her. "It's Benjy," she says finally. "You always done for him. The two of you always together in the shed or down by the creek. Wouldn't let me come. Don't think I don't know why."

I tell my feet to walk out, but I'm standing still, my hand on the doorknob.

"Everybody in town knows but Mama and Daddy. I hear them whispering at church when you walk in. 'Pretty Silvia's got her brother all tied up in knots so he can't look at another girl.' That's what they say. But I know who's tied up in knots." There's a long minute where nobody's saying anything. "Loving your brother like that is worse than a sin. It's sick, Silvia," she says finally.

Then, before I have to say something back, her telephone rings. The mill put one in each house last year, and most of them are on one line. One of Annie's friends calls, and six or eight of them pick up. "Phone party," that's what Annie calls it.

"Jean Simpson. Well, hi. And is that Carol Anne's voice?" She cradles the receiver in her hand. "Yes, I just got back from the store." She doesn't look up when I pull the door closed behind me.

When I got home, Benjy wasn't back yet, but Becky was in the bedroom, smoothing out the skirt on a dress she'd sewn in Homemakers.

"Very nice," I told her as she did a turn in the middle of the room.

"I've still got to add the collar," she told me. "Think it'll win a place in the dress show?"

But my head was too full of what Annie'd said to answer.

"Where you been?" Becky asked.

"At Annie's. Baby-sitting John Lee."

"Oh. I thought you were watching Benjy play ball."

I gathered my books, that were spread across the bed. "I've got homework," I told her.

"Silvia." She sat on her bed, fingering the hem of her dress. "Why won't Mama let me and you cook stuff in the kitchen like Annie did? She let Annie make cookies, biscuits, and just about anything. And I know more about cooking and nutrition than Annie ever did."

"Annie's a lot like Mama," I told her. "She learned how to cook early, got married early and to a mill worker; she's already got a baby. I guess Mama figured Annie could just do like she wanted."

"Hm . . ." Becky shook her head. I didn't understand it either.

"Anybody can see how Annie's life will go. She'll stay right here in the mill town and grow old, just like Mama's done," I told her. "Not like me. I'd rather travel to a foreign country where nobody knows me than stay in Ash Hill and work at the mill or marry somebody that works there."

Becky smiled to herself. "I'm going to be a cheerleader when I get to high school." Becky can be sweet. She's always wanting to cut or curl my hair like a picture she sees in a magazine. But most of the time she's thinking about clubs she can join and all the friends she'll make. The girls at school look away and whisper to each other when I come into a room. My only friend is Benjy.

I stretch out, open my chemistry book. Becky's saying how she'll join some group this spring where they teach you different cheers so you can try out for the team the next fall. Soon enough her voice gets soft and I quit making out what she says.

THE NEXT DAY, when Mr. Hart called me down to his office, I was right in the middle of writing down a formula for my science lab. I sat down when he pointed to the wooden chair facing his desk. He wanted to know was I planning on college. I shook my head. "There's a scholarship given each year by the mill to the brightest graduating senior," he told me. "Now, usually it goes to a boy, and usually that boy is our valedictorian. But this year, you have the highest grades in your class. If your grades stay high this marking period, I'm going to recommend you for that scholarship."

I can't tell how long I sat there. "Don't you want to go to college?" he asked finally.

"I never thought about it. Just what would I do there?" I asked, but it was Benjy I was thinking of.

"Whatever you wanted. You're good in all subjects. You don't have to decide now. Wait until you get there. This is an opportunity to become whatever you want."

I didn't know what or who I wanted to be. The studying just kept my head full while Benjy was playing ball or out working on the house with Daddy.

Mr. Hart smiled as he stood up. "Here's some pamphlets about the universities you might start to consider. Take them home and talk to your parents about them."

I thanked him and put them in my notebook. As I walked back, I ran my fingers along the closed locker doors, just to fill the empty hall up with a sound. Become whatever I wanted . . . I could be anyone. I could go anywhere. I stopped and opened my notebook to tuck the pamphlets in a folder behind my history report.

When I opened the door to the classroom, I saw lab had started. Benjy tapped my shoulder as I walked by. "What'd the principal want?" he whispered.

"Nothing," I told him. "Just wanted to make sure I'd have that big history report done in time."

Benjy frowned, but that was the last he asked me of it.

That evening after supper, I slipped out the door and ran towards the river. When I turned around, I saw Benjy behind me, moving with my quickness, the quickness of an animal. We ran until we reached the river, Benjy calling to warn me the banks might be crumbling, with the river so high from the winter rains. Out of breath, we stood together, watching the water churn up leaves and branches. "Remember," I said to Benjy, "when we used to pretend we were rabbits or deer leaping over the high grass? I used to believe when we held hands and ran, we actually left the ground, like when we'd fly over the river on the rope swing."

A gray foam clung to some of the twigs. If the water got much higher the bank would disappear. "My favorite was when we were soldiers," Benjy said, part of the bank sliding out from under him and falling into the river as he sat down. "I still think about it."

"You think about us," I asked, sitting down beside him, my hand on the back of his neck, "and the games we played together?"

"Yeah, sometimes." He threw a chunk of dirt into the river. I saw how fast it was taken under by the current, lost. "I think about joining up." He turned to look at me. "You know, the service and all. Maybe the air force."

"I guess I could come with you," I said, trying to forget he had his own plans. "You might get sent to a foreign country."

He didn't answer, but when I wrapped my arms around his neck, he hugged me back. We fell to the ground, kissing and rolling together on the side of the river. When I'm with Benjy, the damp ground doesn't make me cold. Nothing matters but our bodies touching. It's like I've read about in novels, where the hero of the story wins the lady and you know they will always be warm and dry and safe and happy.

When we're in a hidden place and Benjy puts his arms around me, I forget Mama and Daddy and Annie and Becky and all of Ash Hill. Benjy says our being together is more special because it's a secret. When we're sitting at the table eating supper, he looks at me as if I'm just his adopted sister, and he's careful not to brush up against me if we pass each other in the halls at school. But at the river we're in love.

———

IT WAS A few weeks later when they called me to the office to say I would be the top person to graduate and would I give the speech for my class. "This is the first time we've given this honor to a girl," said Mr. Hart. "We're all proud of you."

I smiled and said, "Thank you." Then I added that I didn't think I could do the speech.

"Oh, of course you can," said Mr. Hart. When I didn't say anything, he asked me why not.

"She's shy," Miss Ellis whispered behind her hand, like I couldn't hear her. "She doesn't have many friends, never speaks up in class." She put her hand down and smiled at me.

"It doesn't have to be a long speech, Silvia," says Mr. Hart. "And Miss Ellis and I will help you with writing it. You could come up on Saturday mornings to practice saying it."

"That's a good idea," said Miss Ellis. I just nodded.

Then they explained about the scholarship, and how it would pay all my tuition so long as the school wasn't real expensive. He wanted to know had I talked to my parents yet.

"No, sir," I told him. Benjy hadn't said much about where we'd go after graduation, but I'd decided to take it on myself to tell Mama we planned to marry. If he enlisted, I'd be going with him.

"You need to think about all this and talk with your

parents, Silvia," Mr. Hart told me. "We could call them in and tell them for you if you're worried your father wouldn't want you to go. This is a great opportunity. We'd like to see you use it."

"I'll tell them," I said before I left. "You don't need to call them in." I walked home, through downtown Ash Hill, past the stores and to the other side, where the mill town was, past Annie's house and all the other small, neat square houses. The clotheslines were set up in the same spot in each yard. There was a little patch for a garden right behind all the houses. Most of them had the same chair, bought from the mill store, sitting on their porches. If Benjy didn't want to get married, I'd take the scholarship they offered me. I'd pick a school with a far-away name, and I wouldn't plan to come back.

When I got home, Benjy was sitting on the porch with a book. He looked up into my face, and for a second I could see how he wanted me. Then his face changed like when you stir the river with a stick and it clouds up so you can't make out the stones or leaves on the bottom anymore.

"How come you're late?" he said, looking down at his book again. "Didn't see you after school."

I smiled at him even though he was reading again. "Took the long way home." Maybe I wouldn't take the scholarship. Maybe if I made Mama understand that Benjy and me were right for one another, maybe then the water would clear and I could see through to Benjy again.

Chapter 15

ROSE'S STORY

THE MILL'S DECIDED not to rent out houses no more. Last week Joe Newton, one of the boss men, tells Edward that we got until the end of the summer to finish our house building and get moved if we don't want to buy the mill house we always lived in.

"I told him we'd be out by the end of next month," Edward tells me that evening. "We ain't going to live off borrowed time. If they don't want us here no longer, we ain't staying."

Everything's going all to pieces. The mill give Annie and Billy two more months in their house; then they got to say if they're going to buy or not. Most amount of house they can afford is a one-bedroom, not much bigger than a shed. Billy says how there's other mills providing for their workers. Annie says if he goes, she's staying put with John Lee. And Edward says Billy's took up liquor.

He gets home late, then comes to bed with his clothes on. Used to be, a family had trouble, the mill helped out, talked to a husband that took to drinking. The mill kept people straight. Way back, when they found out Charles was drinking, they give him a month to quit, and when he wouldn't and talked trash, they told him not to come back no more. Now they just look the other way.

Most every evening we go out to the house, trying to get it finished. If he has to, Edward says, he'll borrow the money we need to get all the walls up by next month. I hate to leave Helen and them, but there ain't much left to the mill town. And with them selling off the mill houses, lots of folks is leaving.

Yesterday evening Benjy and Becky rode out with us. Edward walked us through the house. "This will be the kitchen," he said, pointing at where the sink will go. "And this one here will be your room, Becky." He pointed to the first bedroom off the living room. "If Silvia stays you'll share it with her so Benjy can have a room." He pointed to the next room.

"I guess I'll be going somewhere after high school," Benjy said, standing at the doorway, looking into the empty room Edward pointed at. Him and Silvia, always talking about leaving Ash Hill, leaving home.

While Benjy helped Edward put in an overhead light, Becky and me walked into the living room. Paint cans were stacked in a corner. Sawdust was still scattered on the floor. I picked up a broom and started sweeping. "You need to get a new sofa and chairs for this room," says Becky. "You could put the sofa here." She pointed to the wall across from the picture window. "And a television. We got to get a television."

I shook my head. "New furniture costs too much. And a television? We don't need one of them things."

She went over to the window and stood while I finished my sweeping.

"What's the matter, Shortcake?" Edward asks her when he comes in and sees her staring sad like out the window at the field across the road.

"I was just wishing the new house was closer to town," she says. "Maybe in one of those newer sections where everything's so modern. I don't know if I'll like living on a farm."

Edward put his arm around her shoulders. I was sweeping my dust pile out the door. "This isn't a real farm," I heard him say. "We might put up a small barn next to a garage and keep a tractor for mowing in it. Your mama wants a vegetable garden." He glanced at me.

Benjy stands in the doorway, laughing. "Mama's idea of a vegetable garden will be that field." He pointed out the window.

"I won't have time to help much with planting and weeding," says Becky. "I got my clubs and maybe cheerleading next fall. This summer I'm going to do volunteer work with Julie at the hospital."

Edward gathered the drawings of the house. Benjy,

me, and Becky followed him out to the car. "You'll help out when you're needed" was all he said to Becky.

On the ride home, none of us said anything. I watched the houses and fields and pine trees fly past through the car's window. "Just like our lives," I told myself, "flying past every which way." Us moving out of the mill town, Silvia and Benjy both talking about leaving Ash Hill, Annie and them about to get thrown out of their house, and now little Becky saying she wants to live closer to town. Don't want what me and Edward been planning for all this time.

When we got to the mill town, Edward starts talking. "Me and your mama always wanted to live on a farm," he's telling Becky and Benjy. "I wish we could have raised you kids on a farm, where folks are independent and grow all the food they eat."

I turned around in my seat. Becky and Benjy was staring straight ahead, and I couldn't tell what they was thinking. Outside, the world flashed by, loose threads, bits and pieces that'd never stay together.

"Me and your mama," Edward tells them, "worked hard to build this house for our family. We bought the land before you was born. We been planning it ever since. It'll be a place you can come to whenever you need it, a place to bring your children."

We had pulled up to the old house. Edward turned off the car. Benjy and Becky run off real quick, but me and Edward sat there in the almost dark yard. "They're all leaving" was the sentence going through my head, and Edward didn't say nothing to change it.

Then Becky comes running out into the yard. "Julie's on the phone," she yells out. "She wants to know can I stay after school tomorrow to work on our dresses for Homemakers and then eat supper at her house."

Edward had planned on all of us going out to the house the next evening to help finish the painting that needed to be done.

"Yeah," I called to her, stepping out from the car. "You can go." I looked back at Edward, still sitting in the car, his hands resting on the wheel, and shrugged. But I couldn't ever tell if he seen me.

IT WAS A WEEK before Silvia and Benjy's graduation when I get a phone call from the school asking can I stop by their office. After work that evening, Edward drove me over. When we walked in, the principal shook our hands. I set down. "I have some good news for you," he said; then just stood there a minute like he forgot what news it was he had to tell us. When he started talking, he was smiling, leaning across the desk. "We're all real proud of Silvia," he said. "Now, she asked me not to tell you this, but I think you should know. Silvia's so quiet and shy. She just doesn't want anyone to make a fuss over her."

The principal looked out the window like he had to think on what he was saying. Then he looked back at us.

"Silvia is a smart girl, I'm sure you know that," he told us. "But you may not realize she's got the highest grades in her class." He rocked back in his chair. "She'll be making the graduation speech, and she's also won the college scholarship the mill gives each year to one grad-uating senior."

I heard Edward sit down behind me. "What does this mean," I ask the principal, "the scholarship and all?"

"Silvia can go to the college of her choice. The schol-arship will pay her tuition, room, and board. She needs to apply soon, though."

"I kind of hoped Silvia would get married, settle down around here like our Annabelle. I know she hasn't had a boyfriend, but she's pretty and all."

Folding his hands on his desktop, the principal smiled at us again. To him we was mill workers, with less edu-cation than any high school student. "She can still marry. And a husband who's gone to college will make a good living."

"If she goes off to college, she won't settle down around here," I said, but it was like I said it to myself.

Behind me, Edward stood up. "We'll tell her to go," he says. After all his preaching about school not being important, I couldn't turn to look at him. "Silvia's never been like us," he told the principal. "I guess you know we adopted her, so maybe it was bred into her. I can't see her working in the cotton mill. We'll do right and tell her she has to go."

"I'm so glad you agree," says the principal. I was turned around in my chair, trying to make Edward look at me. "I sent some catalogs from different schools home with Silvia," he said. "You'll need to go through them with her and help her pick one soon."

Edward said we would; then, without saying goodbye, he opened the door for me. Mixed in with the sound of it shutting behind us, I heard the principal's voice thanking us for coming.

When we got home Edward took Benjy and Becky on out to the house. Silvia stayed to help me with supper. Figuring this'd be the one time I had alone with her to talk, I told her while we was peeling potatoes; "We was at your school today. Principal called us down, to talk about you." She shut off the water, set the strainer full of wet potatoes on the counter. The peeler slipped through my fingers. I fumbled with the potato before I picked it up again and peeled back the thick skin. "Said you was smartest in your class, that you won a scholarship."

I could feel her sit down behind me, her head down, looking at her hands or maybe the shape her shoes made against the floor. "Don't know why you didn't say nothing. Me and your daddy's proud of you. We want you to go."

As I turned from the sink to look at her, the peeling dropped to the floor. She had her arms on the table now, her head cradled in them, like she was just a child. I set the peeled potato in the bowl. "We can help you with your speech. I know it'll make us all proud," I said before I picked up the peeling from the floor.

Silvia hid her face for a good while. When she looked up, whatever she was thinking was still hid. Finally she said, "I'm not going to college, Mama."

"Principal thinks you'll do real fine in college. You can go to one that's close by and come back to visit a lot," I said, thinking maybe she was scared of going off and making good. But somewhere in me I was still hoping she wanted to stay in Ash Hill near me and her daddy, get settled, raise a family.

She leaned back in her chair, watching me through the blond hair that fell in front of her face. Silvia's skin was always so smooth and her eyes blue as the sky on a clear day. She was pure looking. I always knew she kept part of herself real private, but I saw now by the way she watched me, like a cat trying to figure which way to run past a pack of dogs, that she could lie and there'd be nothing on her face to show it. I remembered all them times she left the house saying she needed to be alone for a while to think about a paper or read a book. The fear got in me so sudden I could hardly feel myself standing in the kitchen in front of a bowl of wet white potatoes. It took the peeler slicing my finger to bring me back.

"Ahh!" I yelled. Me and Silvia both jumped at the sound.

Silvia left the room, came back with a roll of gauze

and tape. She set them on the table, opened the drawer, took out the scissors. She hadn't said nothing. "That was stupid," I told her. "Haven't cut myself peeling potatoes since I was first married." I was washing my finger in the cold tap water to get the bleeding to stop.

"Just a scrape, really." I patted it with a towel. "Don't need nothing."

But she'd already cut the gauze to fit over it and began wrapping it real slow and tight, still saying nothing. When she got done she put the scissors in the drawer. I stood there, watching her. Didn't even think to go back to the supper I had to cook. When she turned around, the sun come through the window on her face so I couldn't see nothing but how lit up her hair got. "Mama," she said, and stopped for a minute like she had to think through all she was going to say first. "I've got other plans for after graduation. Me and Benjy, we both have plans. That is, we want to be together." I was blinded by the sun on her hair. All I kept thinking was she looked like an angel standing there, all light and radiance. "We want to get married. If he joins up with the air force, I'll be going with him." I was so blinded I almost didn't hear her.

"Married?" I repeated, stepping backwards. The sun wasn't between us no more. I could see how she was watching me, catlike again, but now the cat was being patient, waiting.

"We've loved each other a long time, Mama. And with me being adopted, I don't see that it would matter if we married. We both plan to leave Ash Hill. We'll be living somewhere new, where no one knows us."

She sat down again, looking at the floor, but still seeing me out of the corner of her eyes.

I thought how when Edward got back, I'd tell him to take Benjy outside, beat some sense into him. I hadn't used a switch on Silvia in a long time, but I seen then how I should have made her mind more, the way I did Annie. "You're going to college," I told her. "After graduation. You and Benjy ain't seeing each other again. Not long as I'm living." I turned to the sink, picked up a potato, and pulled off the peel in thick slabs.

Silvia was so quiet I didn't hear her stand up, but I could feel everything she done. And I'd been worried about her not marrying an Ash Hill boy. "Mama, would it really be so awful if we did marry? Think about it some more. We know each other real well, we love each other, and we're not blood related."

The peeler clanged against the sink. I was seeing her and Benjy coming through the kitchen door together like they did so many evenings, with flushed faces, saying they been at a neighbor's house. I wondered how many seen them. All Ash Hill must have known but me and Edward. And I could see how my lie led to all her lies, how the lies had piled on top of each other until Silvia was black with them. Black with sin, our sins — mine, James's, James's mother's.

Silvia was watching me again. She'd pushed her hair

back from her face, and even after what she'd done, I could see how her eyes were still pure looking as a young child's. "I got to tell you something, honey." I sat down next to her. "All this ain't your fault, the way it seems." I couldn't tell how to say it best, so I told her straight off. "You and Benjy are blood related; you're cousins."

I tried to reach for her hands, but she pulled them back, her eyes turning bigger. Her face was whiter. "No," she said. "I don't believe you. I would have heard it if that were true. You're just saying that so we won't marry." She hid her hands in the folds of her skirt like I might try to hold them again. "You told me my parents were probably dead."

"That's what seemed best to say at the time." I stared at my hands; they were raw looking, the bandage already wet from the potatoes and the blood. "You are adopted. But you're June's." My fingers curled around the bandage. "We took you in when you were just a baby and they sent her off to Columbia. People talked at first. But as you got older, I made them hush."

When I looked up she was shaking her head like that would make it not true, her hair flying in front of her face so I couldn't make her out. She stopped to look at me, the hair still hiding her eyes. "Why was she sent to Columbia?"

I couldn't hardly swallow; I thought the answer'd choke me. And I knew finally that's why I'd lied, to keep from having to say this.

"Why was she sent?" she asked again, pushing the hair from her eyes. They were a hard, bright blue, like pieces of turquoise or glass might look under water.

"June was out of her mind after she had you." I was looking into her eyes like she had me under some kind of spell and I couldn't look away, couldn't stop until I said it. "She had a hard time birthing you. It was the coldest part of winter." I picked at the bandage. "Your father weren't much help to her afterwards, I guess. You was just a couple of months old" — the gauze unraveled — "when he come home to find June about to put you in a pot full of boiling hot water." Silvia's look didn't change none when I said this, but seemed like her eyes got clearer, more blue. "She didn't mean to kill you or nothing, I feel certain. Just wasn't in her right mind. Your father drove her to Columbia that night, signed the papers on her. He brought you by, just squalling, in the morning. You was so hungry, seemed like after that you never could get filled up, sucking down bottles of milk quick as I'd warm them."

"So my father gave me to you?"

I took a breath, looked at my ate-up fingers playing with the hem on my apron. I knew I had to say it all now, that the lying couldn't keep up, even part way. "He and his mother came out. Said they were getting the marriage annulled. Didn't want it to hurt his position none. He was well off. Since our folks was poor, his mother never did like June. He wouldn't claim you."

"Who was he?" Maybe it was the sun coming through the window again; her eyes kept going lighter.

"James Cutler. He runs the bank in town now. Remember when I took you by to see him?"

She stared off into the sun coming through the window. If I wasn't a Christian woman I would have cursed James for not claiming her. I got up to finish my potatoes, the wet gauze hanging from my finger. When I turned back to her, the sun came in just right and I couldn't see her face, only a lit place in the kitchen. "One thing more I got to say and you'll know it all. When James took her down there, he signed some papers that said you were dead, that she'd killed her baby. She still thinks she killed you." I pulled the peeling from the last potato. "I almost told her who you was when she was here. You was ten years old then; she figured I'd named one of mine after her dead baby. I was afraid for you knowing the truth. I should have been afraid for you not knowing it."

I put the potatoes in a pot and lit the stove burner under it. The way the roast I was cooking smelled, I knew the potatoes wouldn't be done in time. I went to Silvia. The light wasn't on her no more, and she looked like Silvia again, her hair a little darker than the color of field corn. She was bent over the table like she might be crying. I put my hands on her shoulders, but she inched forward, trying to get out from under them. "Don't," she said, and I backed away. I checked the roast and warmed a jar of green beans. Before I went to sit on the porch and watch for Edward, I pulled the wet, bloodied gauze off my finger.

Later, as I was doing the dishes, I decided to wait on telling Benjy, maybe break it to him casual that she was his cousin, let her tell him what she wanted. I kept what she told me about her and Benjy from everybody but Edward, kept it hid inside me, where I'd kept the rest of it all them years.

THE NEXT WEEK Silvia stood up on the platform in her graduation dress, her hair wavy from the curls I put in it, looking real pretty. She even wore lipstick. With the wind blowing up I couldn't hear all her speech, but she'd read it to us the night before. It said how they was proud to be from Ash Hill and proud of the education they'd been given. "I hope each one of us can make something of himself," she said at the end. After all she'd been through, to come out on top. Sitting on the hard wooden bench with the wind and sun in my face, I had to wipe the tears out of my eyes.

Afterwards, when we all came back to the house for dinner, Annie and Billy came with us. I kept John Lee in my lap when he'd sit still. He ate the meat off a drumstick and had more mashed potatoes with gravy than me. "He's got himself an appetite," I told his daddy, who wouldn't hardly talk to none of us but sat in his chair and watched while we ate.

"Don't you want your dinner?" Becky asked him. The food was going cold.

He picked at the mashed potatoes with his fork. "Maybe he's not feeling too good, Becky," I said, to get her to hush.

Benjy didn't hardly eat either. We was talking about how good Silvia done with her speech and getting the scholarship. I guess we forgot it was Benjy's graduation too. And then Annie kept asking was he going to get a job at the mill, until Billy told her to keep quiet.

After dinner, when I was drying out my pots, Annie said to me, "What's Silvia think she'll do now? Being smart won't help much now she's not in school. It won't help with getting a husband."

The men were outside, and Becky had John Lee in the other room. Silvia'd been in her room since she cleared the table for me. Before I tried to answer, I put away my pots. "Silvia's always been different," I told her. "Maybe she'll find what she needs at college. Some days I hope none of mine will work in the mill." My legs were hurting most all the time now from walking the hard floors up and down the rows of turning spindles. Pulling out a chair, I sat at the table and waited on what Annie'd say. She was crying, trying to hide her face by staring out the window.

"What is it?" I asked finally. I hadn't seen Annie cry since she was a little girl and hurt herself or got a whipping. Even after John Lee was born she got out of bed the next day to cook a big dinner for Billy. I figured she was too strong to carry on like this.

"Me and Billy, we're just all the time on each other's nerves." She wouldn't turn around. It was like she was talking out the window to somebody. "If it weren't for John Lee, I guess there wouldn't be much between us."

I might have said something about how the Lord says we got to be patient. I wanted to tell her that she and Billy ought to go to the same church together, even if he is Baptist, but John Lee was fussing and she ran off to tend to him.

At the meeting room by the mill, they were having desserts and punch for the ones that graduated. I thought we'd all walk down, but Billy told Annie they needed to go on home. Annie said she'd see us in church.

I wrapped up the coconut cake I'd made, and the rest of us went on down. When Silvia walked in, everybody clapped. Becky got so excited she couldn't stop hugging on Silvia, but Benjy walked right over to Sue Shelby, whose mama used to work next to me. All evening he carried her punch and desserts. When we were getting ready to go home, Silvia called to him. He shook his head, said he'd be seeing Sue home first.

As we walked home I kept thinking that somehow all mine grew up. All except Becky, who was trying to get Silvia to race her and asking could she try on Silvia's gown when they got back. The sun was real low. The houses looked smaller than ever, like the blocks we'd been stacking for John Lee to knock over. Edward took my hand and said he was proud of Silvia.

"I told her about June," I said. "I told her everything."

Edward put our hands in his pocket. We were walking faster as we got closer to home.

"Silvia and Benjy" — my breath caught on what I had to say — "they were real close."

"Benjy's joining up with the air force." He said it without even looking at me. "I guess he meant to tell you. I told him it could be a hard time to sign up, the fighting in Korea and all, but he's made up his mind."

"Korea," I said. "I don't want him over there."

Edward squeezed my hand. "Maybe he won't get sent."

I took my hand from Edward's pocket and watched as he hurried on up to the house. I was standing in the middle of the road, fading like the houses in the evening light. In a few more weeks we'd be leaving the mill town. I looked up at the home we'd lived in all these years, ever since Edward and me married. When Annie was a little girl, she'd play at a friend's down the road and sometimes get lost coming home and go to the wrong door. I hung a red doily paper on our door so she'd know which one to come to. Now this house couldn't be anybody's but ours. It held the smell of the dinners we'd eaten. In the closet there was Benjy's old ball, his play soldiers, a doll house Edward made for the girls one Christmas. Edward's gruff complaining and his laughter, the cries of my babies, even Silvia and Benjy's whispering and June's moans when she had to give up her baby — they all lived in that house.

It was almost dark. Somebody lit the lamps in the front room. Many times I'd told Edward how much I wanted our own house, outside of the mill town, a house big enough that we could get off by ourselves when the children were there and with enough rooms for every one of them. I wanted a kitchen I could turn around in, and I wanted pretty cabinets in it and nice linoleum on the floor. Now that it would finally be finished, there'd be only me and Edward and Becky to fill it.

WHEN SILVIA TOLD ME she was going to a big university in Florida, I started to cry. I was standing at the sink, steam rising up to my face, so it took a minute for her to see the tears running down to my chin. "What is it, Mama?" she asked me, and I heard the fear in her voice. She hadn't seen me cry like that since the night they took June and Silvia sat with me on the porch until late. What was strange — I couldn't say why I was crying. "I'll come back to see you," Silvia kept saying, but that was just part of it. I was seeing how maybe Silvia had paid enough, in the Lord's eyes, for all of our lying and how maybe there were no more sins of ours to be laid on her. If she could get out of Ash Hill and finish college, that might set her free of the knots we'd all tied. Finally she'd be living her own life and not paying for ours.

Why all that made me cry, I still got no idea. I turned

around to hug Silvia. "I'm glad for you," I said to her. I'd been taking her to prayer meeting once every week, and each time we got close to the church door I'd pull her aside. "I'll be praying for you," I'd tell her. "Pray for God to deliver you from all that's happened. He can still save you." She never said nothing to me. When I asked could she feel the Lord's spirit moving in her, she said she didn't know. I quit asking. Each person's got to find Him in their own time.

Just when I was going to tell her that the Lord works in mysterious ways and her going to college might be part of His work, Benjy came into the house. He's been helping his daddy all he could before leaving for the service. When he sat down at the table with a few cookies, Silvia disappeared. I wiped at my face, but Benjy was too busy eating to see. I never did worry about him. Boys are all the time getting mixed up wrong with a girl, and I could see how his part was natural. He got up to pour himself a glass of milk. "Dad and me are driving out to the new house. Be back soon, I guess," he said as he was going out.

I stopped by Silvia's room just so she could see I weren't all tied up about her leaving. "We'll have to pick you out a few dresses to take with you," I said as I walked in. Silvia was looking at what she had hanging in the closet. Most of her school clothes were rubbed almost bare at the elbows and held together by my mending, but she never had complained.

"If she belonged to Homemakers, she could sew herself something." Becky doesn't look up from the hem she is making to tell me this. I forget how she's getting grown too. All mine are real different — Annie just a mill wife like me, then Silvia, who could be anything after going to college, and Becky, who already thinks she knows the best way to sew and such on them machines.

Silvia had quit looking and shut the closet door. "Maybe Saturday I can take you shopping, get you a few new things," I told her.

"That's okay," Silvia said. "What I got will last."

"Don't argue none." I was stepping out the door. "We got money enough, and I want you looking like somebody when you go down to that college."

I heard her soft "Yes, Mama" as the door latched shut.

EDWARD DID THE LAST of the painting and finished the plumbing, so we moved into the new house we built. Each day I find myself listening in the early morning and evening for the whistle. Like I told Annie and Helen Harper, who always did live next door to us, I have to get used to how quiet it is in the evening without hearing porch doors slam and somebody yelling for their children to come in to supper. Having Benjy and Silvia gone will make it even more quiet. I let Becky make all the noise she can in the kitchen, even let her stir up recipes. I have to fill that house with something. Then, after we been out here a few weeks, Edward wants

to get him some dogs to hunt with. He says he'll keep
them in a pen, where we'll hear them barking as we drive
up the road to our house each evening. Feeding and
training them dogs will keep us all busy. When Edward
gives me a little money for spending, I'll buy a nice lamp
or a fancy pillow for the living room. I'll ask Helen and
her husband and her boy to come out, and I'll show off
all we got.

Working at the mill wears me out. Edward says soon
as we get our bills paid I can quit and his check will be
enough. The spinning room's got these new red lights on
the machines, and every time one comes on I have to lift
out the full spindle and put in an empty one. Just when
I seen how the lights would make it easier, they give me
another row to work. Now I got to walk up and down
two rows looking for lights, and that's not counting the
threads that break. Some days seems like the buzzing
gets in my head so bad Edward has to say things two or
three times before I hear him. My ankles get swollen up
until I'm ashamed to wear skirts and dresses. Ain't nobody I can talk to on break about all this or even brag
to about my new house. Them girls in the spinning room
must live like trash, the way they talk about going out on
their husbands. One of them leaves her babies in the house
while she works.

Now that they're selling the mill houses off and won't
rent them to workers no more, seems like they just don't
care about how we live. The nursery's closed. There's

talk about selling the meeting house and the company store. Annie says they shut down the doctor's office and now everybody has to pay regular in town if they get sick. Next thing they'll stop giving the barbecue every summer.

Edward says we did right moving out. If things get bad, he says, we can always get us some chickens and pigs and plant a big garden. It's them like Annie who don't have enough saved up that's got to worry. If they stay on in Ash Hill, looks like they'll have to buy one of them tiny mill houses, just a two-room shack, really. By the time you hang a curtain to make a bedroom, you ain't got much living space. And when the mill put plumbing in, they just boarded off part of the room instead of adding on. I told her we'd give her what we could, but Edward says Billy don't work hard enough to get him a good-paying job. "They ain't going to put somebody who's slow and don't have his mind on things in the dyeing room," Edward told me. "He'll need more than a special course before they'll let him run those machines."

Some nights when the buzzing gets out of my head I like to sit on the porch swing and let the cricket noise fill me up. When they get quiet, there's nothing. It's like I'm living in the space between the threads. Knots might be all around me, but none of them touch me. Edward comes out to sit next to me. Most nights he just takes my hand. Out here, there's nothing we need to say to each other.

Chapter 16

SILVIA'S STORY

THE LAST WEEK of school, I told Benjy to meet me under the stands by the football field when classes let out. When I got there, he was waiting, peering between the bleachers, making sure we weren't seen.

"What'd you want?" he asked, shuffling his feet. The shadows from the bleachers stood like bars around us.

"I just had to tell you something."

"Silvia, couldn't this wait until we got home? Why did you have to meet me here?"

"I don't want to tell you at home," I said. "I wanted to tell you down by the river, but last time I asked you to meet me there, you never came." I turned away. "You act like you don't like me anymore."

He reached out, pulled me around. A shadow fell across his face, but I could still see the lines on his forehead. "You know that's not true. It's just here, everybody watches. So long as we stay in this town, we'll always be brother and sister." He fingered my hair, then let it go. "Tell me what you wanted to say." He smiled, like the Benjy who used to let me help shoot Japs.

"Mama told me who my parents are." It won't matter, I told myself. Once we moved away from here, being cousins wouldn't matter. "Aunt June was married before she got sent off. I guess she went crazy after having a baby." I touched his arm. "Her husband had her committed."

"You're Aunt June's child?" His mouth hung open. "We're cousins." He spat out the words as he turned away.

"Benjy, it's not as bad as it sounds." I was reaching out, trying to touch his shoulder, but he took a step away from me. He was gripping the edge of the seat above him. "We can still go away. No one will have to know. Cousins isn't the same as brother and sister."

He took a few steps past me, his hand out so he could push me aside if I tried to get in his way. "How long have you known this?" He turned to look at me.

"Not long," I said, the words sticking in my throat. "Maybe two weeks."

"I got to go." His face was down. I couldn't see if he was scared or sick from knowing it.

"I still love you," I told him. "This doesn't change anything."

He was walking, and I barely heard the words. "It changes everything."

I crouched under the stands, thinking I'd stay there, watch the darkness come through the horizontal bars made by the bleachers, let the dark come inside me. It was the first time I could cry since Mama told me it all. I said "Benjy" over and over under my breath, but I knew I was crying for more than that. I was remembering how Aunt June let me touch her stomach the summer she visited us. Under my hand I'd felt the baby she was carrying. I had felt it turn and kick. I'd felt how alive it was. Aunt June loved the baby before it was ever born. She used to sit in the rocker humming songs to it. When she thought no one was looking, she'd pat her stomach and say she couldn't wait to hold it in her arms.

When I got done crying, the sun was coming in under the bleachers, heating everything up. My dress was wrinkled and smeared with dirt. I got my books together and stepped out.

The sky was clear, the sun lower on the horizon. I walked the six blocks to the bank and got there just as a dark-haired woman wearing a neatly pressed gray suit was locking the door from the inside. When I knocked on the door, she cracked it open, stuck her head through the opening, said they were closed. "I need to see Mr. James Cutler," I told her.

"We're closed," she repeated and started to pull the door again. I slipped my foot into the opening.

"I need to see him now," I told her. "It's about his daughter."

She stepped back from the door reluctantly and led me to my father's office. The door was open.

"This girl says she need to speak with you," she said, "about your daughter."

James looked up from the papers spread across his desk. I watched the words he meant to say fall out of his mouth. "I don't know you," he said finally. "There must be some mistake."

"That's what I was afraid of," the woman behind me said sharply, her hand on my shoulder.

I shook my head. "You know me. I came here once with my mother, a long time ago. You gave me some candy."

"It's alright, Mrs. White," he told her smiling, like I had thanked him. His face changed into the nice-to-children-and-old-ladies businessman smile. "We do what we can for the children in this town. They can even open their own accounts, get a booklet and a free pen." He gestured toward Mrs. White and I felt her leave.

I closed the door and stepped towards his desk. "I know that you're my father," I told him, and watched his face go blank. "Rose told me everything. I know that you were married to June, that you had her locked away after what she tried to do to me."

I felt like I was floating, like there was no floor under me. "It's fear," I told myself. "I can't feel anything under me because I'm so afraid."

He stood up, shuffled a few papers, and slipped them into his briefcase. The clasp on it had a metal catch, and

I heard it snap when he closed it. "How do you know what she told you is true?" he asked. "Think about it. Why haven't we met before if I'm your real father? Go to the county courthouse, check the records. I've been married once."

I can't remember how I left his office, but when I got home Rose scolded at me for being so late. I didn't tell anyone where I'd been.

I NEVER DID SAY goodbye to Benjy before Daddy drove me to the train station. A few nights before I left, I'd followed him and Sue outside during a church dance and watched him give her the class ring I'd bought him. They tried to find a finger on Sue's hand that it would stay on. "That's okay," I heard her tell him, wrapping the ring in a hankie. "I've got a real pretty chain at home. I'll wear it around my neck and never take it off." She tucked the hankie away in her pocket and reached up to kiss Benjy. I even heard the sounds they made.

There was a dorm room ready for me at Florida State, and I would be able to take a summer course there that wasn't offered at our high school. The principal and teachers had made me a present of a pen set before I left, and Mama had packed two new dresses in my trunk.

Ash Hill disappeared quickly through the train window, mill houses and town houses both flashing by so fast I could barely make them out. I was relieved by the rush of images, glad for the speed.

In my purse I had a smooth rib bone I'd taken from

the deer skeleton Benjy and me had found. When I'd gone back to see it, the few bones left were scattered and bleached from the sun. The other thing in my purse, besides my new wallet and the pen set, was a box of brand-new hankies that Mama'd bought for me to give to Aunt June. "The train makes a stop in Columbia," she'd told me. "Take a few hours and go visit her. Tell her who you are." But I wanted more than anything for her to still be just the aunt who told stories of banana trees and parrots and let me feel the baby that moved inside her. As much as I could, I made myself forget the rest.

Part 4

1 9 6 5

Chapter 17

ℛ OSE'S STORY

WHEN MR. GREEN called me to his office, I got so nervous I almost tripped going up the stairs. The week before, they'd given one of my rows of spindles to a younger girl when they seen I wasn't keeping up. They were just letting me stay on because of Edward. "I'm all right," I hollered when Mr. Green's secretary started to come down the stairs after me. I had a hard time walking up the steps to his office; how could I tell Mr. Green I was fit to work?

He was sitting at his desk, didn't even stand when I come in. "I need my job," I told him, still holding on to the door.

"You get your husband's check. When you retire, you'll get yours too." He loosened his tie. "With two social security checks, you'll have plenty to live off of."

I closed the door, then took a step towards his desk.

"My two sisters live with me. I got to have enough to pay for them too."

"Mrs. Treherne gets a pension, a good one."

I'd never seen much of Lily's money. "I need to keep working," I said, taking another step towards his desk.

He stood up, pointing to a chair. "Sit down, Mrs. Watson." We both sat down, him leaning back far as he could in his chair. "We've tried to be good to you since Edward's accident, even though we have no written obligations. We felt we owed you. But most of our workers retire before they're sixty." He leaned forward again in his chair, tapped his pencil on the desk. "We just can't afford to keep you in the spinning room any longer."

"Just give me two more years," I said. "I'll have everything paid off then." I told how I'd borrowed against the house to help Becky out with school. Now that she was working, I kept meaning to get her to help out with the payments, but she was saving for a place of her own.

He rustled a few papers, then leaned back in his chair again. His glasses made him look official. "I can put you in the finishing room, marking cloth for flaws." He took too long watching me. "That's the best I can give you."

"How much does it pay?" I felt myself lean forward.

"My secretary will write it out for you," he said, standing up, but when I stayed in my chair, he said, "It'll pay less than you're making now. You can keep the job for two years, and after that we'll retire you." I didn't move. "That's the best I can offer."

That evening I stumbled into the kitchen, loaded down with grocery bags. "Let me get those," June says, meeting me at the door, and sets them on the counter. She's wearing a plain dress and a sweater, but with the little bit of color she's put in her short curly hair, she looks real pretty. As I set down to take off my shoes, she tucks some money under my purse. "Marvin Schuler came by for a painting this morning." Every time she gets any money, she gives it to me right off. "I might lose it," she says. "And you know what to spend it on better than me." Once she told me she didn't want anything for her paintings, just to know they was making somebody's life a little cheerier.

I rubbed my feet a little. "Get that milk and butter in the refrigerator, would you?" I asked June. The TV filled the house. I'd got so used to noise I didn't much notice it. When night came I'd lie awake in the dark quiet, listening. "Did Lily's check come?" I asked June as she opened the refrigerator.

"I don't know." She filled the bread drawer, careful not to look at me. "She got to the mailbox first again."

I put my feet back in my shoes, began lacing them up. "We have got to get that check. I found out at the mill they are sending it." Inside the shoes, my feet throbbed. June was setting the bread in its drawer. "June." I tried to get her to look, but she wouldn't. "You're the only other one who's here during the day. You've got to get to it first. I asked the mailman would he deliver it to you or me personally, but he said opening someone else's mail is against the law. Maybe Lily got to him first."

She closed the drawer, began folding the grocery bags. "I'll try," she whispered.

"Where's Becky?" I made myself walk to the stove. "Would you get those chicken pieces for me?"

"They're watching one of those stories," she said when she set the chicken on the counter. *The Edge of Town,* I think it's called."

I had to call Becky three times to get her to come. She was still wearing her uniform.

"You didn't start supper cooking?" I asked, pulling out my big cast-iron fryer.

"I was watching a show with Aunt Lily, Mama." She sat on the edge of the countertop. "I got to work in the operating room this morning after Carley took sick. And you know that new doctor I told you about, the one who's single?"

I rinsed my chicken pieces and scooped a little flour into a paper bag. I always get them coated with flour and a little salt and pepper before I cook them.

"Dr. Martin," says June when I don't answer.

"That's him," says Becky, tapping me on the arm as I shake salt into the bag. "Now, Mama, pay attention." I got me a little pepper, then set two chicken pieces in the bag. "All the while we're operating, he's smiling at me from under the mask." She reached over, stuck her finger in the cornmeal batter I'd got June to mix up. The whole time she's talking, I'm shaking the bag of chicken pieces. Couldn't hardly hear her. "Then, just as we're closing up, he says, 'You didn't leave any sponges in there, did you?' 'If I did, you'd be the first one I'd tell,' I said." She grabbed ahold of my arm to get me to stop my shaking. "He winked at me, right there where anyone could see."

"Oh, Becky," June says, forgetting to grease the skillet she was pouring the batter into. "That would be so exciting if you married one of those doctors."

"Scoot." I pushed Becky off the counter so I could lay my floured chicken pieces in the pan. "You tell them doctors they have to come by and meet your mama before they can take you out," I said, but I was hoping they would ask her.

"What vegetable are you cooking?" Becky opened the refrigerator.

"Thought I'd heat up a jar of beans."

"We had them last night." She opened the freezer. "I'll fix some frozen corn."

"Is it creamed corn?" asks June. She was sitting in a chair, with her hands in her lap. I have to ask to get her to do anything, even set the table.

"No, Aunt June." Becky handed me a pan. "It's frozen." Then Lily's coughing got so bad we just stopped and looked at each other.

"Speaking of doctors," I said to Becky when Lily finally quit. "What do you think's wrong with Lily? I can't talk her into seeing a doctor."

"Not much," Becky said, walking towards the doorway. "Maybe a cold. She sits too much. The TV will be the death of her."

"It's the only thing keeping her alive," I whispered, then said out loud that the chicken and corn bread would be another forty minutes. "Why don't you get yourself changed, Becky. I think I'll turn up the heat in the parlor. Sit by the window a spell."

When June followed me, I sent her back to the kitchen for two cold drinks. Curled up on the couch, we took a long time sipping them. I didn't need to say nothing, and June was happy looking at the sun make colors in the clouds. "Maybe I'll paint a sunset someday. It'll be special, to hang in your room," she said.

Edward used to like to sit and look way off. "It helps to make my mind empty," he'd say. Remembering little things like that makes me miss him. But he never would have stood for Lily or June moving in, and I like having my sisters with me, even Lily, who is such a worry. I let myself go loose and forgetful as the wind that tossed the dried-up grass and weeds in the field across the road. The sky colors got in my head. Even Lily's cough and not having enough money didn't mean nothing to me. If Becky hadn't set the food on the table, I would have forgotten supper.

————

THE NEXT MORNING I start looking for flaws. The cloth flows in front of me all day, and I stop it to mark with a chalk the places that are torn or crossed up or got a thread missing. They give me a stool to sit on. Then about noon the other women turn off their machines and tell me we get a half hour for lunch. I'm in the weaving building again, and Annie's downstairs working the looms. She's tying on a warp when I come down to see does she want to take her break with me. "Lunch!" she yells above all the noise. "I don't get no lunch." She pulls the threads into place as I stand there not knowing what to say. "Maybe in the spinning room they eat lunch, but I haven't been caught up enough to sit down and pee since I started this job."

I wanted to tell her I weren't in the spinning room no more, but the way she spat them words at me made me go all hot. I found Helen's daughter, Tracy, and sat with her. But all afternoon I'm hearing Annie's words and thinking it's the mill's made her sound so mean and look old when she's still young. "My head's like a shuttle," she told me one day, "shooting back and forth, just because somebody made it go that way."

Then there's Billy. A few years back when he quit drinking for a spell she decides to get pregnant again. John Danson, who's a loom fixer like Edward was, got Billy going to these meetings, and he got sober enough to work regular. They got a used Chevy to drive John Lee to his ball games and go to town in. Billy was talking

that he'd get him a better job dyeing cloth like he learned
to do way back when John Lee was a baby.

Annie starts looking almost pretty again. Her cheeks
get pink and her eyes laugh when she talks. "We're gonna
buy us a bigger house," she tells me, "one of those nice
ones with a sitting room and two bedrooms like they got
on South Street."

I didn't say nothing. Maybe, I was thinking, maybe
their luck's gonna change.

But soon as she had Marty, a dark-headed little thing,
he starts to drinking again. It was me drove Annie and
the baby home. He comes in the kitchen, where she's got
a baby bed set up, just smelling of it. "Don't you touch
that baby," she yells when he bends over the bed to get
a look. He takes that empty liquor bottle, smashes it into
the wall, and John Lee standing in the doorway watching all this. Annie runs out after him, crying, and I'm
picking glass out of the baby's bed. Marty never cried,
just watched me with big round eyes.

When the baby turned six months and Billy weren't
getting up in time for work but two or three days a week,
Annie got a sitter and went back to weaving and hiding
her checks.

"Why don't you come for the Thursday social this
week?" I asked when she called last week.

"Yeah, sure," she said. "What time do I got between
working all day, caring for Marty, running John Lee over
to his ball games, and keeping house for Billy?"

When I don't say nothing she tells me how Billy falls asleep on the couch with his clothes on every night and how she sleeps in the bed with Marty. "When Marty wets the bed, I'm too tired to get up and change things," she says.

Working at the mill gets me all tired. I sit watching the cloth unroll and can't hardly get myself to lift my arm and stop the machine when there's a thread missing. I told Annie to come to church more often and pray, how the Lord helps them that help themselves, but she turns away like that don't mean nothing to her.

The cloth never quits unrolling. When the whistle blows for second shift, Grace Mannings, who's old as me and has grandkids she pays for since their daddy run off, shows up to take over. "I ain't seen no flaws for the past hour," I tell her. "My eyes get tired. Might be I missed one."

Grace clicks them new false teeth she's got. Her hands look worse than mine — all swollen up with arthritis. "They'll be sure to tell you if you did," she says.

On the way out, I stop to walk with Annie. "Got me a new job," I tell her when we get outside and the noise from the machines quits.

"Doing what?" she asks, but don't look up from the sidewalk she's watching.

"I'm upstairs from you, checking cloth for flaws." The wind's up. Far off, I hear thunder rumbling, a deeper sound than the rattling in my head.

"So they took you out of the spinning room finally." She shakes her head, laughs. We're near the parking lot where I got my car. "You're lucky they didn't dump you altogether for not keeping up."

"What you talking?" I ask her. We're standing by the gate. There's others walking by us, and Annie waves to them.

"Carol Anne lost her job last week. They been timing everybody. If you're slow, you're out." She steps closer. "See that woman?" She points. "Name's Claire Little. She's always trying to beat me out. If she can get quicker than me, she'll get some of my looms. Then they cut back on my pay, maybe tell me I ain't got a job no more."

"No." I shake my head at her. When I worked the looms, we helped each other out, finished somebody's row if they got behind so the boss man wouldn't know. When I was still learning the batteries, Helen used to get some of my spools for me so we could take a break together in the water room.

"Ain't like when you was working here," Annie says, like she's reading my mind.

"You want a ride?" I ask her.

But she starts walking. "I got to pick up Marty at the sitter's."

"I can stop by there," I call out. But it's like she ain't heard me. "Maybe she's like me," I tell myself so I won't get to feeling bad. "Head too full of the mill sounds to hear anything else."

When I got home, there's a postcard from Silvia. It says Brazil on the back and shows a picture of a pink bird in a tree. She's doing what she calls "research" for this magazine she writes for. Always going somewhere. Ain't been back to Ash Hill but once for a visit since she left to go to that college.

Becky comes out to the porch. "Sit down," she says, pulling on me until I'm sitting with her on the swing. "Let me tell you what happened today." I pull my coat closed against the damp chill.

"I worked all morning with Dr. Martin in the operating room," she says. "He's the one looks like Dr. Kildare. Now, the whole time he's cutting into this lady to take out her kidney that went bad, he's telling this story about a doctor who was so lazy he married a pregnant woman. I told him he always keeps me in stitches, and then we're all laughing."

"You better talk nice," I tell her, since I can't make out her jokes.

"Laughed so hard I dropped a pair of scissors. Then got so busy I forgot and put them back on the tray. Penny seen me do it, but she said she wouldn't tell nobody. Anyways, Dr. Martin, who's so cute, says how I'm right on time with everything."

"I got to get dinner," I tell her, and stand up. Sometimes I can't tell what she means.

"Maybe he's the one," she says. "I heard he told another doctor that he thinks I'm cute. We could buy a house in town, and I'd work for him at his office until I had our first child."

"Don't count your chickens before they're hatched," I tell her. "There ain't no way for you to know when Mr. Right's coming along."

"Mama, you're so old-fashioned," she says, following me into the kitchen. "Nowadays a girl's got to pay attention and make sure, when Mr. Right does come along, he stops to notice."

I take down my cooking pans, and pretty soon I'm not hearing what she says. "I'll ask Annie and her kids over for dinner," I tell myself. "See if I can't set her life straight."

But it's a Saturday two weeks later before they can come. "Billy's gone out but at least he left the car," Annie tells me on the phone. "We been fighting all morning. John Lee took Marty outside when we started to yelling and Billy's throwing things. She don't even hide her face. Just stares at us like she can't figure out none of it. The bank's gonna throw us out if we don't make the payments on time, and Billy out spending all we got."

"I got some you can have," I tell her. "You and John Lee and Marty come over for dinner."

When they get to the house, me and June got dinner made and keeping warm in the oven. John Lee goes outside to play with the little dog I keep. "Where's Becky?" Annie asks.

I kneel down to take off Marty's jacket. "Had a boyfriend take her to the pictures."

"A doctor?" she asks. Becky's all the time talking about them doctors.

"Nah," I tell her, pulling the jacket off. "Studying to be one."

"Give your granny a kiss," Annie tells Marty, and the child leans over to me, nice and gentle.

"Let's see what I got for a little girl," I say, taking her by the hand. "How about a new dress for your baby doll?"

I open my sewing basket and take out the dress I sewed last night from a mill scrap. It has a bit of lace for a collar. Marty holds it up against her own dress.

"It's for your doll," I tell her.

Marty holds on to my hand until dinner, her quiet little face watching everything I do. When we sit down to eat, June says, "My turn," and puts Marty up on her lap. "You are the prettiest little girl I ever seen," she says, and makes a game of rubbing noses.

Lily won't come to the table for dinner, even when we got company. I have to carry it to her in the living room on a tray. Me and June and Annie can hardly hear each other talk with the TV going and her coughing. "Lily doesn't like to miss her shows," I tell Annie as I pass the roast. "She watches movies on Saturday. I don't care for them, but since Forrest died and she lost everything, I guess TV stories are all she's got." Then I gave the blessing.

June fixes a plate for Marty, picking out the potatoes with the most butter and a thin slice of meat. "I always wanted a little girl just like you," she says, giving Marty a squeeze. "I used to ask God for one."

"Hand her over here," I keep asking, but June won't give her up.

I put more meat on John Lee's plate. Now he's bigger, he don't talk much. "Are you playing ball this year?" I ask him.

"Yes, ma'am," he says, piling canned corn on his plate. "We start practicing in another month."

"How are your school grades?" I make him take more bread.

"They're almost all A's," says Annie, bragging on him. "The teachers all think he's real smart. One of them said — "

"Mom," John Lee says, red-faced, "I'm trying to eat."

Annie sets down her fork and smiles. "He's bashful about it," she tells me.

After dinner June piles a double helping of ice cream on Marty and John Lee's pie. While me and Annie clean the kitchen, June's got Marty in the rocker, telling her a made-up story about the one bluebird that grew up with a flock of starlings. By the time we get the dishes put up, Marty's asleep. Annie stands in the doorway watching me and June carry her off to bed. "We'll put her in my room, where it's warmest," I whisper.

When we get back, Annie's on the porch watching John Lee play stick with the dog. I put my arm around her. "Don't you worry none about them kids," I tell her.

"Anything happens, me and June will help raise them."
I was thinking about Billy, how anytime he might run
off. As it turned out, I got no idea what would happen.

I WAS ON MY LUNCH BREAK when Nelly came
to tell me. "Your Annie's been hit by a loose shuttle."

"Where is she?" I ask, standing up.

"They took her to the hospital. It's bad. Got her in
the face." Nelly must have seen what was going through
my head, because she took my hands, said, "It'll be all
right. She didn't get knocked unconscious or nothing."

I was hearing what they said when they come to tell
me Edward got hurt. It was Edward's boss man come
over to the spinning room to find me. "Come on," he
said. "I'll take you over to the hospital. Edward's hurt
bad." He'd gotten hit in the head when the belt on a
pulley broke. "Snapped right back. He didn't have a
chance to move." It was the first time I heard of a loom
fixer getting hit that way, but I always knew it could
happen.

By the time his boss man got me to the hospital, Edward was dead. Broke his neck, they told me. Probably
dead before the ambulance drivers laid him on the
stretcher. I never could forget what he looked like laying
on the table down there, his head twisted a little to one
side, but otherwise he could have been sleeping. I wanted
to take him home with me, do the washing myself, dress
him in his suit, but the boss man wouldn't hear of it. He

told them to take Edward to the funeral home and send the bill to his office. It weren't until later I thought to say no to him.

They had Annie in a hospital bed with her jaw wired up, face swollen. Her mouth hung open, to show the hole where her two front teeth were missing. I stood by her bed, not knowing what to say. "The nurse says you can go on home soon, maybe tomorrow," I told her finally. "You want me to pick up Marty, take her home with me tonight?"

She set there staring at the wall. "Where's Billy?" I ask her.

"Mother, she can't talk," says Becky as she steps into the room, pushing a metal cart filled with little cups and pills. "If she moves her mouth too much, them stitches will come loose." As I watched her walk over to Annie's bed, I was proud to see her in her uniform. "I told them to bring you a TV so you can watch stories," she told Annie.

Annie wouldn't look at her neither.

"It'll be fun, Annie," Becky tells her. "Something to do."

But Annie shut her eyes, her mouth still hanging open. Becky shook her head. "Well, be that way and I'll tell them not to bring it." She tucked the blanket in between the mattresses so it was pulled tight. "You could show some appreciation," she said, leaning close to Annie's head.

"Leave her be," I said, soft as I could. "She's too tired to watch TV."

Becky stuck her hands in the pockets on her uniform and walked towards the door. "I had to ask special for that TV. They were gonna bring it up here as a favor to me," she said before she left.

Annie was laying back against the pillow with her eyes closed. "I guess I'll go too," I said. "I'll pick up Marty. Billy's mama called, said they'd get John Lee."

She didn't open her eyes when I left.

IT WAS THE NEXT WEEK when Annie came back to work. All that morning, the cloth stretched out in front of me, rolling from one bolt to another — fine, finished cloth. The threads were still. Its whiteness got in my eyes until it all looked perfect and I wouldn't see the places a thread got loose or broke. Months from now another woman might be pulling it tight across a bed.

Watching the moving cloth gives me time to think. Sometimes I'm seeing Edward, how things would be if he would have gone on living, but mostly I think on all the lives that are still crossed up. Seems like I been doing this all my life. I thought everything would be fine when June and Lily moved in, what with Silvia and Benjy gone and Becky working her job at the hospital, but I didn't see how broken Lily was, like a split thread nobody can find the other end to. Now Annie done got hurt, and everybody's talking how one of the boss men says it's on account of her not watching and being careless and how she should lose her job.

The cloth slips through my hands, smooth and cool.

When I see a flaw, I stop the machine with the pedal my foot rests on and mark the cloth. Just after Marty was born, Annie stopped me after church to say Billy was drinking regular again. "A Christian wife should keep her husband on the straight path," I said. That made her eyes turn cold when she looked at me. Grace got word from her son that Billy don't hardly show up to move spools anymore and that when he does, they tell him they don't have the work for him that day.

So when I hear that Annie come in to work this morning, her mouth still bandaged up, I know they need the money. Worse, so does everybody else. "Boss man told her to take more time off, that's a fact," says Helen when she sees me. "Coming back early won't help her keep her job. You need to talk to Cassy about that son of hers." Billy's mama still lives in the mill town. I see her at Senior Citizens when I go.

"Won't do much good," I told her. I was fastening the cloth to the rollers. "I just wish I knew what to say to Annie. She's got those two kids to raise. And the compensation paid her hospital bill but won't pay to get her teeth fixed. If she loses her job I don't know what she'll do."

Helen shook her head. "Ain't much she can do."

The next weekend the mill has a spring picnic, first one in more than ten years. The way everything had gone to pieces in the mill town, I was surprised when I seen the signs they put up telling about a picnic after all the

time of not having one. The mill didn't help no more by
giving people houses, and most all the people worked there
were spread out, living all over town. The company store
been closed a long time, and they'd boarded up the windows. What with people losing their jobs if they didn't
work quick enough, none of us had time for the kind of
fun we used to have with telling stories on each other
and hiding a bobbin or greasing a shuttle. It was mostly
old workers at the picnic, and the boss men that did come
all sat at one table, didn't try to talk to none of us.

We was still keeping Marty for Annie. When we got
to the picnic, I gave her to June to take care of and
walked Lily to a dogwood tree just starting to blossom
that was set back away from things. Lily's grabbing at
everybody who passes her, telling stories to anyone who'll
listen. I opened up the chairs we'd brought and told her
to stay put. I'd used three safety pins to fasten her dress
together in the back. The day before the picnic, while I
was busy with my baking, June found her strutting down
the road in just her slip.

"Should have left her on her own to rot after her
boyfriend skipped out with all her money," says Becky.
"Next we'll find her dancing to town half dressed."

Before bringing her to the picnic, I made sure there
was no way she could get out of her clothes.

Helen, Matty, and me sat near Lily and ate the plate
dinner together. June had her paintings lined up on folding chairs. Two of them were of birds and the rest of

flowers, all done on black velvet. My favorite was one of sky-blue Canterbury bells. June hardly had time to join us between selling paintings and talking to the men folk. "She gets prettier every day," says Helen as June goes off with Mr. Midkiff to get more lemonade. "I just get older." Not one of us can explain it.

Marty ran with the other young'uns, sitting on my lap just long enough to eat the biscuit or bites of chicken I put in her mouth. "She's a smart little thing," says Matty when Marty stands still to sing her ABC's. John Lee said hello, then went to eat with his daddy's family. One of his cousins is just his age, and they spend all their time together, playing ball. Billy was nowhere to be seen, and it weren't until they announced they were judging desserts and I walked over to the tent that I seen Annie.

Like always, I entered my chocolate cake, since it was Edward's favorite. Matty always takes the cake prize, so I weren't expecting much. "I got two pies up there," says Annie. "Can't wait to see who wins." Whenever she said anything, them spaces where her teeth was knocked out made her mouth look all black. Like the darkness get in there and never get out again.

"How much does the dentist ask to do your teeth?" I ask her.

Annie shook her head, grinned. "Don't know." She patted my arm, touched me like she ain't done in a long time. "It don't matter" was all she said.

That's when Helen comes over. "They're judging the

pies now," she says. It was a few minutes later when they announced the winners, saying Annie got first place for her lemon cream. I was still standing there, not believing my ears, when Annie walked right up and took that ribbon they handed her. When she comes back with it, everybody could see her smile. After I got done being embarrassed for her with that big black hole showing, I got proud. "Ain't that something," I said when she handed me the ribbon. It weren't her being able to bake a good pie but that she baked them and entered them even though she was beat up still from the spindle and even though her husband was always drunk somewhere else and they were in debt. I could feel myself smiling with how proud I was when I tried to give it back. "No, Mama," she says, pushing my hand away. "You keep it for me."

Marty was pulling at her skirt, begging her to play. "I can hold it for you while you play with Marty if you want," I said, laying the ribbon careful-like in my purse.

"No," she said, looking straight into my face. "I mean for you to have it." Before I got a chance to argue, she let Marty pull her away. They run in circles until they fell on top of each other.

Marty reached up to Annie's face and put a finger on the mark that was left alongside her mama's mouth. "What is it?" I heard her ask.

"It's a sign from God," Annie says, smiling. "A sign telling me what to do with my life."

I turned away so Annie wouldn't know I heard. Marty

was touching the mark again. "Does it tickle?" she was asking. I heard Annie's laugh and Marty's high-pitched giggle.

It weren't until later 'when I was sitting on the porch swing with the sun going down that I saw how mysterious the work of the Lord had been. Annie'd accepted the ways of things. It'd taken getting hit with a shuttle for her to see she had to keep going no matter how much suffering there was in her life. Now all I could hope was she'd get through to Billy.

When June opened the door, I could hear the show Lily was watching. "I made almost two hundred dollars," she told me. "That's the most I've got yet."

"Maybe we could give something to Annie — you know, help out with her dentist bills," I said, moving over on the swing seat to make room.

"You do whatever's best," June said, and tucked the money in my hand as she sat down. "I love it out here, Rose. Especially on a quiet evening with the sun going down."

Leaning back in the swing, I closed my eyes. Whenever I'm on the swing with my eyes closed, I can feel Edward next to me, the way he'd rest his arm on the swing's back, the way he'd sway towards me. I can hear him saying how proud he is of Annie and how we got to help her all we can. And I can hear him saying how we got to send June back to Columbia and put Lily in a home somewhere, how there ain't no other way. I want to tell him that everybody sees things different and how June making up stories and painting all day maybe isn't crazy for June. And how Lily undressing all the time and acting mean is just her way of not giving up after she lost everything she had. I thought this way a good long while, until I seen how even Edward's death might be the Lord's hand letting me do right by my sisters.

"There's a moon tonight," June said. Sometimes her talking voice sounds like she's singing.

"I wish Edward could have been there," I said, "to see Annie win that first prize. He'd a been proud." I opened my eyes. Sure enough a big red harvest moon was rising. "Not just because of her baking, but everything. How she come back since the accident." I set the swing to rocking. "I believe she might help Billy get straight now."

June fastened her sweater around her shoulders and settled back into the swing. "Even with her teeth missing, she has a beautiful smile."

"It's the Lord shining through her," I said, patting June's arm. "She's found the path of God."

$\mathcal{L}$ILY'S STORY

IF KIMBERLY MARRIES Steven, I might have to switch stories. I can't stand weddings. Then I'll have to fight Becky, who gets *Dr. Kildare* mixed up with the one in town. "Which one is your life?" I ask her.

"I'm not the one who's confused, Aunt Lily," she tells me. "I get up and leave the house to go to work every morning. I have a life away from the TV screen," she says, walking towards her room.

I light up a cigarette.

"That isn't going to help your cough any," she stops at her door to tell me.

I take a long drag, let the smoke out slow. "Did I ask for a doctor's report?"

She shrugs, goes into her room, shouting back that if I want her to drive me into town for my hair appointment, I better act nice. Truth is, I'd rather stay here with my shows than go into town with her, but Becky says she won't let me get that run down. "You used to be pretty, Aunt Lily," she says. "How can you let yourself go this way?" Someday I'll make sure all them old pictures Forrest took of me get put in the trash.

Once a month on her day off, she drives me to town. Since Charles stole my old Mercury when he run off, I have to ride with her. She tells the woman to put a dark rinse in my hair before curling it. I'm quiet the whole time they're gabbing.

Once that woman said something bad about Cheryl on *Edge of Night*. "Don't go talking her down," I said, starting to get out of my chair, curlers and all. "She don't need no husband. She can get what she wants without one." I sat back down so she could finish putting curlers in. She didn't say nothing about Cheryl again.

After I get my hair fixed up, I put a dress on, even paint my face. I sit at the supper table until late. Nobody but Rose and June and Becky sees me. I don't bother to wash the face paint off until the next morning. For the rest of the week, I wear my housecoat.

The next morning it ain't even ten o'clock before the doorbell's ringing. A gust of cold air blows into the house as June stands with the door open, waving one of her boyfriends into the house.

Dried-up lizards, they come calling, hoping they'll find enough juice to keep them alive. June has them sit at the table and drink coffee. She tells them they are "clever" or "sincere" or "sensitive." They want to touch her. A little blond rinse, and she still looks thirty. On her dressing table there's just one bottle of face cream; she doesn't even color her lips. Every day I shrink. My dresses fit like sacks.

"Mr. Schuler," she's crying out. "It's so good to see you. Sit right down." Don't matter that I'm still drinking my coffee. I picked up the cup and went into the living room, turned on the TV, *All My Children*. I still heard every word they said.

"Are all your paintings on black velvet?" he asks her. She's busy spreading them out on the table. They buy her paintings so she can call herself an artist instead of a whore.

"Oh, yes," she chirps back. "The colors show up so well on it."

"Yes, yes," he's clucking. "I think I'll buy another of your bird pictures. I just love the one with the wild geese. It's hanging over my sofa."

"The birds are my favorite too." Last week it was flowers. I seen her with her tracing paper and the way she copies from a picture. "I love these tanagers. They're flying. Just like we would be if we could. Nothing but velvet to keep their wings from touching the sky." On my TV story Jenny's in love with Steve, but he wants Karla.

"You are an extraordinary woman," Mr. Schuler says. "May I call you June?"

"Of course, Mr. Schuler."

"Please, call me Marvin." Listening to them could get better than the story I'm watching.

"Would you like some coffee?" Her voice is drenched in sweetness.

"Oh, that would be nice. And I'll pay you for the painting." I can see his skinny sparrow hands fumbling with his wallet.

"You can set it on the table," she says, and I hear the sound of her pouring out coffee. "I get twenty dollars for that size."

"It gives me great pleasure to support a local artist," he says, making loud sipping noises with his thin lips. I know what else he'd like to be giving her.

My favorite commercial comes on — dishwashing liquid for the hands — and I got to turn up the sound. "Please excuse my sister," June says above the noise. "She's had a difficult time, and I try to ignore her bad habits."

"You are such a good person, June." Voice heavy with sap. "A real Christian lady."

"You're a real gentleman yourself." The click of the TV breaks up the sugar in her voice. "That's strange. Lily usually keeps it going all day."

"Wanted to see what you brought in out of the cold," I say, pushing the door open. My worn-out housecoat's open to the waist. Each morning June gets up early, irons a dress, puts on stockings. "Well, you caught a live one," I say, plucking at his shirt sleeve, "a real live man." Mr. Marvin turns red. "What'd you use for bait?" I ask June.

June stands straight up. "Lily," she tells me, "you sit

down and be good if you want to stay in here." She pulls out a chair on her side of the table, but I sit down next to Mr. Marvin. "And fasten that housecoat," she says. "You look a sight."

"A sight for sore eyes." I grin at Mr. Marvin and lick my lips. "I bet your friend wouldn't mind seeing more." June kicks my shin with her pointed-toe shoe before I get to open my housecoat all the way.

"Mr. Schuler doesn't want to look inside your robe, Lily," she says. "He's a Christian man."

Mr. Schuler's nodding his head, up and down, a wooden bird like in a cuckoo clock. I know better. "Ah-oh," I screech. "I've met some Christian men before. I know what they like." I hold my hand out to him, friendly like. "Mr. Schuler, I'm glad to meet you," I say. "I'm Lily, June's sister."

He nods, can't take his eyes off my hand.

"Care for cream and sugar?" June passes him the little tray Rose keeps on the table.

"No, thank you," he says, his eyes still on me, traveling up my housecoat to where it gapes. "This coffee is delicious just as it is. I don't believe I've ever had coffee quite so good."

When I stood up, my titties showed, all shrunk and wrinkled. "I'll leave you two lovebirds," I say, pulling the door closed behind me.

There's another story on the TV. Marcia and Julie are fighting over a boyfriend. "He's planning to marry me," hisses Marcia, her hand stiff like she'll slap Julie's face. Then I hear Mr. Marvin, his voice a whisper under Julie's. "I just can't believe you two are sisters. You are such a pretty woman. You don't look a bit like Lily."

"Poor Lily," says June, and I can see her shaking her head. "She has this awful cough. Sometimes it keeps us up all night. Rose keeps telling her to get to a doctor."

I light a cigarette, let the smoke choke me, hear how quiet they get. Finally Mr. Marvin whispers, "Won't she go?"

June's whisper is like an insect beating against a door, harsh, slight. "She thinks they're after her money, thinks everybody is. She gets a check every month from the mill. Rose and me never see it." Her voice gets almost squeaky, and I have to forget Marcia and Julie to hear it. "She either hides it or loses it. When we ask about it, she accuses us of stealing it."

I laugh loud as I can, and a commercial selling laundry detergent blares out.

Mr. Marvin mumbles something, then I hear June under the TV song. "Sad part about it is, when she coughs, she sounds near dead. She must be all ate up inside."

"Makes me shaky just to think about it," says Marvin, skinny little sparrow of a man.

And I can just see June's hands on him, patting. "That's how sensitive you are. I knew it before when you said you had a feeling for my birds."

"You are full of sympathy for others." He's kissing

her hands. David comes on the TV, all dark and handsome, eyes like a cat. "So few people understand what it's like to be sensitive."

"I know just what you mean," squeaks June. "Believe me, if I didn't have my birds . . ."

Another commercial, breakfast cereal. The porch door closes. "Enjoy your painting," June was calling to him.

"I'll take good care of it." His voice was little, narrow, even when he hollered back.

LATER THAT SAME MORNING her real boyfriend comes calling. Thomas Midkiff has hair white as ash and eyes a pale green. He wears hunting shirts like Forrest and smells of the woods.

Whenever June sees his car, she gets out the leftovers from supper, warms them in the oven. She starts a fresh pot of coffee.

"You take care of me just like a wife," Thomas says when she sits him down at the table.

"You need taking care of." She's fussing with the napkin she's tucked in his collar, piling his plate high with chicken, corn, and canned green beans.

I step through the doorway, got my housecoat opened most of the way. I'm leaning against the kitchen counter, blowing smoke.

"Boo!" he says. "You can't scare me."

I can't help laughing.

He smiles at me over his coffee cup. "I don't care if

you want to catch your death walking around that way," he tells me. "But personally I like a woman that's dressed up. Adds a little romance."

I grin back at him, my face stretching wide like a cat's. "Anything for you," I say, and slink out the doorway to change.

I'm rustling through my closet, taking out dresses, the ones I used to wear to town, low-cut with tight waistbands, when I hear their love talk.

"It's you I'm interested in," he says. "We could get married, but I guess I like having you for my girl too much."

June giggles. "I had a husband. And he died true to me. I'll never marry again."

Yeah, I'm thinking. Her fairy tales are more real than what happened by now. She's told them too many times.

Next he's telling her what a great artist she is. She's brought out the painting of his dog she's made him. "A true artist. Looks real enough to start barking." Copied it off a slide he took.

"I won't take a cent for it," she says. "That's what art's for, to make people like us love being alive."

The dress I took out hangs in my hand. I hear the noise of their smooching.

"That's what you've done for me," he whispers, a husky, dry sound. "Whenever I see you I thank God I'm still alive, even if I do have a little arthritis."

I can see them in my head, how she's rubbing his

shoulders and him turning his head to kiss her arm. "You're so good to me," he says.

She smooths her hands down his shirtfront. "We're so good to each other."

IT'S THE NEXT AFTERNOON when a shiny Cadillac drives up to the house. June's outside hanging laundry, got on a new dress and a hand-knit sweater. The man who gets out of the Cadillac has thin gray hair, wears glasses and a suit. June's got a sign up by the main road to lure them in.

She takes him around to the front porch, where she's got the "artwork" set up. "These are really very good." There's surprise in his voice. Tracing paper, bright paints, and cloth.

"I have a few more of cats inside," she tells him. "Mostly I do flowers and birds. I think the birds are best, personally, but some like the flowers better."

He doesn't say nothing. She asks does he want coffee.

"I'll just get a painting and be on my way," he says. "My wife is very ill. Cancer, for three years now. She won't last much longer." Just the kind June likes. She can pat his hand and cluck over him.

"I'll take this one of the two snowbirds," he says. "How much is it?"

"Twenty-five, since it's a large one." She sells them like they were meat, by the pound.

I hear the rustle of bills in his wallet. "Keep the change," he says.

"Oh, I can't." She's all flustered. "It's too much." I try to guess the amount — fifty, a hundred? I'll dig it out of her drawer later. "At least pick a second one," she's saying. "Another large one."

"This is the only one I want," he tells her. "And it's worth at least fifty dollars." A fifty. "I'll promise to come back and get another one, but you know, these are worth more. You really should think about changing your prices."

They're walking off the porch, June's light step, his shuffle. "I call this one *Lovebirds*," she says. "Maybe it will help your wife get through her last days, I mean looking at the birds. Whenever I feel sad, that's what I do, find some birds to watch."

I go to the kitchen, open the window to hear them. "By the way, my name's June Reynolds," June tells him. "In case no one told you my name."

He takes too long to answer. "I'm James. James Cutler."

I'm turning the name through my head, letting its sounds twist and pull a long time after the sound of his car gets far off, a long time before I can place it. But when I finally do, it sticks like a thin, shiny needle in my head.

"WELL, LOOK HERE," I said, waltzing through the door a few days later, my hand over my mouth like I was surprised. Twenty years ago I knew he'd be back.

"Do you know Mr. Cutler?" June spilled the milk she was pouring into her cup.

I sat down next to James. "Maybe next time I come to the bank you won't be so rude," I said, eyeing him, my blouse undone partway, hanging open.

"I'm sure I don't know what you mean." He stirred sugar into his coffee. "We haven't met."

"I never have forgot a face, Mr. Cutler," I said, leaning towards him. "Especially when it belongs to a relative." I licked my lips.

With one swallow, he drank his coffee, and it was steaming too. "I'd better be going," he said, standing up. "It's my opinion your sister needs professional care."

June followed him to the door, muttering, "Oh, yes," as many times as she could.

"Thank you for the lovely painting," he tells her.

"Of course, of course," she says. I may be drying up inside my clothes, but at least I still got my backbone.

After he leaves she sits at the table and pouts. "You did that on purpose," she tells me. "And Mr. Cutler may lose his wife soon too. You're jealous because they come to see me."

I get up, pour myself some coffee. "You don't know the favor I done you," I tell her with my back turned. "He's the one messed you up for life." When I turn around, I seen how blank her face is, like a piece of white paper. "He's your husband, for Christ's sake. The one that got you locked up all them years."

She stood up, carried her cup to the sink. It didn't even rattle in the saucer. "I'll have to tell Rose what you

said," she tells me, turning around. "We don't want to
have to put you away, but if you keep making up stories
we might have to. Now." She sits down next to me and
holds my hands. Her fingers are cold. "You know that
my husband died in the war nearly twenty years ago.
Since then I've had the attention of several gentlemen,
but none of them have moved my heart." She smiled like
I was a child. "You've got to stop confusing what really
happened with all those stories you watch on TV."

"Only difference between me and you," I told her
before I got up and walked out, "is I watch my stories,
you live yours."

I'm like Christine on *Edge of Night,* who has to leave
town because she can't forget; only, my car and all my
money got stolen, so I'm stuck here. I know what a fool
everyone in this town sees me for. There weren't even
enough to pay the back taxes when Charles drove off
with that little whore he kept just outside town sitting
next to him, his pockets full of my money. Him living
like a rich man in my house. And knowing about the girl,
I cleaned for him and cooked those fancy meals served
off china like he wanted.

Rose thinks I watch TV to forget. But it's just something to do until night comes and I get to go blank for a
while or maybe dream I'm pretty Lily, White Lily, Lily
of the Valley, a young girl again tying up loose threads,
keeping the spindles turning, waiting for my chance.

That evening when Rose come in, she switched the

TV off. "I'm right in the middle of my story," I told her, standing up.

"Sit down," she says. "It stays off until we get done talking."

It was in my head to push her out of the way, but then I turn around and see June standing in the doorway. "What you want?" We both sat down.

"You're not to chase Mr. Schuler or Mr. Cutler or any of June's customers from the house anymore by walking in half dressed and talking trash." Her eyes are like stones.

"Just being friendly," I tell her. I'm like the woman on *Edge of Night* who is so pretty her own sisters turn against her.

"It's disgraceful and you know it. I won't have you acting this way in my house."

I sit back against the couch. My laugh is real soft. "I guess I know what they come here for, but seems like you think they just want it from June."

Rose leaned towards me, slapped me across the face before I could think to pull back. "Don't you ever talk that way about June again," she says. "The money from her paintings buys the food you put in your mouth. Since you moved in, the money you get ain't paid for one meal." I was shaking my head. "Don't you shake your head at me. I know for a fact you're getting checks from the mill, and I know how much."

I stuck my hands in my pockets. The check was gone.

"What you done with it?" I had my hands on her arms. If I wanted I could shake it out of her. "Where's my money?" I screamed at her.

"Get your hands off me." Her voice was low, like an animal makes when it's real still. I felt June move up behind me. "No one has your money," Rose says when I let go of her. "You're the one gets the mail. June and me never see your checks." I leaned back against the sofa again. I'd remembered where I had them hid. "Now look." June came over to stand next to Rose. "If you can't start behaving yourself, we're going to have to find a home to put you in."

"We love you, Lily," June says, shaking her head, "but it's just getting impossible — "

"Shut up," I told her. Just then the door banged shut. First thing Becky did when she walked in was turn the TV on.

"What's this doing off?" she says, pushing past Rose and June. "I got to get out of this uniform and put on some comfortable shoes." After she left the living room, we could hear the door to her bedroom open and close.

Rose looked at me. "No more trouble," she says, and walks to the kitchen with June right behind her.

I go to my room. Under my fancy underthings and nighties, the whole pile is wrapped up with a rubber band. Some are unopened. There's a knock. I put them away quick and shut the drawer.

"Aunt Lily," Becky says as she pushes my door open.

"You got to tell me what happened on *Edge of Night*, since I had to work late." She's still buttoning her shirt.

I nod and light up a cigarette for my nerves. Soon as I take a puff, the coughing starts. "That cigarette isn't helping you any," says Becky. I gather up my cigarettes and lighter before closing the door behind me.

THE NEXT AFTERNOON I can't listen to June's sweet talk no more. I get dressed up in my sleeveless silk blouse, a skirt I cut off short, and a pair of high heels. I walk to town. It's a damp spring day and the wind's up, but the cold can't touch me.

About halfway there, I'm on the main road, cars honking. I decide to take off my blouse. Give me something to wave in the air, maybe catch me a ride with a fellow. That's when Becky pulls over.

"Come on, Aunt Lily," she yells. "I'll give you a ride."

"Are you going to town?" I ask her, trying to see in through her window.

"Sure am." She opened the door. "Come on and get in."

Some man was honking his horn. I waved, friendly like. "Are you going to the picture show?"

"Sure. Get in, Aunt Lily."

Before I even get settled on the seat, she's reaching over me, slamming the door shut, snapping the lock. The car pulls out onto the road. "Get your blouse hooked up," she bosses me. "And where'd you get those beads?"

I spied them on her dressertop when I was leaving. "My husband give them to me," I said, rubbing a bead between my fingers. "He's always giving me pretty things."

She's shaking her head, turning the car down a side street that heads towards the house. "Where we going?" I hollered. When she don't answer, I try the lock. "Let me out! I'm going to the picture show."

She reached over and pushed on the lock until it clicked again, and I'm swinging my arms at her. Then she pulls off the road and cuts off the motor. Slaps my face again and again, but I can't feel nothing. "Sit back on the car seat and don't move until we get home, or I'll quit driving you to town for your hair appointments," she hissed at me when she got done. She starts to drive again. "If you ever try to walk to town like that again, Mama will put you in a nursing home so quick you won't have a chance to throw a fit." She give me a long sharp stare. "And they ain't got TVs in nursing homes. You'd lie in a bed all day, just the window to look out of. In a nursing home they tie up people like you."

That's when I started shivering, the noise of my teeth knocking together filling the car. "If you don't catch pneumonia, it'll be a miracle," says Becky as she's pulling into the driveway. But I couldn't make myself quit. "People who do stupid things like you just done end up in the hospital, dying."

When June sees me she brings me inside, runs a hot bath, even takes off my clothes and helps me step in. The hot water touches my skin, it gets inside me and turns me all sleepy and warm. I'm cussing at myself for letting it inside and for feeling good when June washes me with a soapy cloth.

"There, there," she's saying like I'm a child. "Step out and let June wrap you up in a warm, dry towel."

I stand limp while she dresses me, then wraps me in my housecoat and buttons a sweater over it.

My feet move on their own. I go out to the living room and curl up in the armchair like a cat. "I want to watch my story," I told Becky, who's got the TV going.

"This is your story," she snaps back. "There's a commercial on."

When Rose gets home, Becky runs right out to the kitchen to tell her what I done. June's whining about how sorry she is, how she was with a "gentleman friend, having coffee," and I must have gone out the front door.

"She needs to be in a home, Mama," says Becky. "She's too much for Aunt June to handle. I know one that'd take her."

June's saying, "Don't send her to a home. I'll watch her better, really I will."

I'm trying to hear my story.

Then Rose speaks up. "Nobody's sending anybody to a home. Now, maybe one of you can set the table and the other one can make a salad. There's plenty of mayonnaise for a dressing."

When the food's ready, I come in to sit at the table

before Rose can bring me a tray. They're all real quiet until I tell how our Uncle Clyde used to make corn liquor in a still up in the woods. "He used to like to do a little corn licking as well as lady licking up behind them trees," I tell them. "Daddy found him once, his mouth full of both." June just smiles and nods her head, so I know she don't get it. But Rose is laughing too hard to swallow her mashed potatoes, and Becky's choking.

"Hush, hush," Rose tells me, but we all joke and smile right through supper and into dessert.

Chapter 19

Silvia's Story

THE CAR'S LIGHTS stretched out into the darkness, two circular beams taking me home. It was almost three when the rain started, quiet dark drops that streamed down the windshield. The swish-swishing of the wipers nearly put me to sleep. Mama'd told me to wait until morning to make the drive, but I hadn't had an assignment in over a week, and the urge to be moving was in me.

The funeral would be Friday morning, to give Benjy and his family time to get there. They lived at the base in Charleston, just a day's drive, but the earliest he could leave was Thursday morning. There wouldn't be a viewing. Mama said the body was too mangled; they wouldn't even let her see it. "A horrible accident." Her voice kept fading into the phone. "Marty was staying the night at our house. All I can figure, she was trying to drive out here and forgot about that train crossing. Those trains fly when they come down that hill from the mill. The state said they'll put up a crossing bar. Too late for our Annie."

I'd last seen Annie when I went home for a visit after graduating from college. Her house wasn't much bigger than my apartment. She had a cot near the stove for John Lee, and a sheet hung in the doorway to hers and Billy's room. There was a dresser Mama'd given them that had a few knobs missing, which Annie said Billy was going to fix. The paint was peeling off it. On the couch near John Lee's cot, Billy lay asleep. I could smell the liquor on him when I'd walked into the house. It was a Saturday morning. "He had to work the third last night," Annie said, pointing at him. Even Marty, pulling a lamp off the table next to the couch, didn't wake Billy up.

I never did feel like a sister to Annie, and as I drove up for her funeral I told myself I was going out of guilt. The doll I'd bought for Marty and the new baseball glove I got for John Lee weren't penance enough. That last afternoon of my visit when I stopped by with the gifts and saw all they'd had for supper was rice and what looked like a few little pieces of ham cut up and cooked with it, I told myself it wasn't my fault I'd got out of Ash Hill and she'd stayed. Annie had gotten exactly the life she'd always wanted.

We hadn't had much to say to each other. She never asked about the job I was starting with the travel magazine, and I heard her tell a friend over the phone that I wore blue jeans and dressed like a hippie. Still, when I said goodbye, she hugged me and said, "Sisters should visit more often," and that maybe I'd move back someday. After I stepped through her doorway, I didn't think about her again until Rose called.

That was the only visit I made to Ash Hill since I left for college. I stayed a week and Rose had made an event of each meal — serving dishes piled high with fried chicken, mashed potatoes, corn, okra, squash. Then, the day I'd flown back to Florida, she left early for work without telling me goodbye. I hadn't gone back for Benjy's wedding or for Daddy's funeral.

By the time I drove into Ash Hill, everything had turned gray. Maybe, I thought, the sun will come out later and the world will turn washed and new. But Ash Hill was unchanged. The mill section where I'd grown up only looked more run down. Ever since high school, I'd told myself I'd get as far away as I could. Right after college I'd taken the job with the travel magazine, even though it didn't pay much and all I got to write were glossy travel pieces. Almost six months of each year I spent in places like the Caribbean. I'd been to Greece once, and the next fall I was scheduled to go to England.

As I pulled into Rose's driveway, rain pelted the car. It wasn't quite five, but there was a light on in the kitchen. I must have sat in the car for several minutes, peering through the rain, before I could make out the form in the window. I knew it wasn't Rose's thick figure, but June's name didn't immediately occur to me. When it did, I knew why I had come — not out of guilt towards Annie but because June would be here.

She answered my knock, smelling of talcum powder, and when she hugged me, I barely felt her arms.

"I was just heating some water for coffee. Won't you have some with me?" I nodded and sat down at the table. She set out two cups. "I woke up and couldn't get back to sleep. Your mama's been so nervous over all this." The countertops were wiped clean. Mama had had the cabinets built specially when she first moved in. They still looked new. "We didn't expect you until this afternoon," June said as she poured the coffee into my cup. In its darkness I saw myself, murky, unformed.

I took a slow sip. The warmth of the coffee made me sleepy all over. "I thought I'd drive in early, when there was no traffic. I wanted to get here."

June nodded. She had her hands folded on the table, small, bone-thin hands. The last time I'd seen her she was still living in Columbia, in a large old house for people recently released from the mental hospital. She spent most of her days cleaning a rich woman's home, but in the evenings she worked to create the beautiful flower beds in back of the house she lived in. Vibrant mums, delicate lilies, but her favorites were the bright orange poppies. I sat in a lawn chair, watching her pull weeds. She wore a neatly pressed dress, a straw hat, and gardening gloves. She looked like the type of woman who attended PTA meetings and belonged to the gardening club. She looked like she could be anyone's mother.

"Your own sister," she said now. "It must be a shock. Your mother won't talk about it, but I know she's suffering." Her eyes were bright turquoise. She had hardly a wrinkle on her face.

"Annie wasn't my real sister," I heard myself say, and told myself it was being up all night and the coffee that made me say it. "Rose told me years ago." June and I looked at each other, but neither one of us saw the other. "I'm your child, the one they said you killed," I told her, and knew saying this was the reason I'd come. "I didn't die."

I picked up my coffee cup. It was hot, but I wrapped my fingers around it. "No, dear," I heard June say. I took a long drink of coffee, felt my insides on fire. "I don't know where you heard that, but I'm childless."

"I'm your daughter," I said, and when the cup fell from my hands, hot coffee splattered against my legs. I felt its warmth through the denim of my jeans. "The one you named Silvia." June scrambled to the floor and began picking up the cup's fragments. "The one you started to put in the pot of boiling water. It's me, Silvia. I'm alive."

"Ouch!" she cried. She knelt on the floor, so close that I could have reached down and pounded the truth from her. "Now you've made me cut myself." She put

the porcelain pieces on the table, then wrapped her finger in the dish towel she'd been carrying. "And look at
this mess."

Next to my chair, the coffee pooled on the linoleum.
I reached down and grabbed her thin shoulders. Under
my hands, I could feel her bones. Her face was inches
from mine. "My father had you locked up for years in
that hospital in Columbia for what you tried to do to me.
He told them I was dead. But I'm alive." She pulled away
so suddenly my glasses fell. "Don't you remember? You're
my mother," I heard myself whisper. The cry, a long thin
animal noise, caught in my throat.

June had stood up. She turned away from the table.
"I'll just get a little glue," she said. I watched her take
the few steps to the cabinet over the sink, reach up to
open it. From the back, with her hair colored blond, she
looked young enough to be the mother of a small child,
young enough to be my sister. When she turned towards
me, the glue was in her hands. Broken porcelain was still
scattered on the floor by my feet. I made no move to pick
it up. "I'll just glue it together," she said, trying to smile.
"You shouldn't say those things to me." She sat at the
table and tried to fit together the few pieces she'd picked
up from the floor.

"You're my mother," I whispered, and I remembered
watching her pull the thin pieces of grass from between
the poppies and wishing the garden was our garden behind a neat, comfortable house and that she was asking

me about the courses I would take at college and saying that she and James would miss me at the supper table but of course I would come and visit every chance I got. I had wanted her so badly that day to pull me from the lawn chair and hug me, to stand like that in the garden until the sun disappeared and I could imagine James was waiting for us inside the house.

"You have always been my favorite of Rose's children," she said as she picked up another piece. "Now just look at what you've done."

"You're my mother." I looked at the cup's broken pieces on the floor and tried to see a pattern, how they might have fit together, but it had shattered into too many pieces.

"I know you hear some strange things, traveling all over the way you do." She shook her head, smiling. "But my life's been very normal."

"June." I looked at her. "The reason I chose the school in Florida was because of all you told me about it — white beaches, trees dripping with moss, banana trees. Remember the banana trees?"

"I don't know what you're talking about. All these stories you've made up." Her hands shook as she squeezed a bead of glue onto the cup's handle. "And I don't know why you said those things. You're trying to hurt me." When she looked up, her eyes were filmed with tears. "I would never try to kill anyone, especially a baby. How could you tell such a thing?"

"I thought you'd want to know I lived," I said, standing up and leaning across the table. She was looking at the pieces in her hands. "I thought you'd want me for a daughter."

She looked up, her eyes the hard blue of marbles. "If you ever say these things again, I'll tell your mother." Her voice was low, steady. "She'll see to it you leave your poor aunt alone."

I turned, suddenly, to leave. "I'll never mention it again, Aunt June." The sarcasm in my voice hovered over the table as I turned to leave. "I'm going to get some sleep." June began to wipe up the spilled coffee with her dish towel. I left the pieces of china for her to throw away.

I didn't wake again until early that afternoon. As soon as Rose saw me she took me to her bedroom, locked the door. I was sure she'd talked with June, but she never mentioned it. Instead, she handed me a letter that Annie'd left. It took me a while to read it; Annie's writing was never very good. "Who else has seen this?" I asked her when I got finished.

"No one," she told me, squeezing her hands together. "I couldn't even make most of it out." She went pale and sat on the bed. "It says she done it to herself, don't it?"

I walked to the window, folding the letter, running my finger along the crease line. Storm clouds filled the sky. A steady rain fell.

"Why did she do it, Silvia?"

"The letter doesn't say," I said finally. The storm's darkness coated the window, pressed in on us. I turned to Rose. "It says the insurance money will be split between John Lee and Marty. It's written in her policy that way. She says Billy's family will probably want to raise John Lee. She wants you to raise Marty."

Rose fell back on the bed, gasping, "Oh, Lord."

I sat down next to her.

"She did it for the money." Rose tried to sit up. "Annie did it for the insurance."

I pushed her back. "Mama, lie down. I should get Becky."

"No." She pulled at the quilt as I wrapped her in it. "I don't want anyone but you to know."

I couldn't help grimacing. Annie and I had never been close. Now I would be the only one besides Rose to know her darkest secret. If Rose were gone, I would be the only one to know. I looked down at her. She breathed easier. "Do you want some water?" I asked.

She shook her head. "Why? Why do you think she done it?"

I wanted to take her head onto my lap, smooth back the wavy gray hair. "She must have done it for her kids, for John Lee and Marty. I guess she just couldn't see any other way," I told her.

"You know, at the picnic," Rose whispered, "she was so happy. I thought sure it was an act of God and she'd found the faith to see her through."

I looked into the darkening window and forgot Mama's unshaken belief in the scriptures. "Maybe Annie had found faith," I said, "the faith to do what she believed she had to do. Maybe she was at peace."

Rose snapped upright and tears filled her eyes. "That kind of talk will take you straight to the devil," she told me.

"Mama," I sighed. A heavy tiredness filled me.

"Annie's in hell," she whispered. "Trying to get the money to raise her two kids got her to hell. That's where that train took her." She shut her eyes. "I could have given her some money."

"No, Mama." I tried to hold her hands. "It wouldn't have mattered. Billy would have spent that much more on drinking."

She pulled her hands from mine. "From the time Annie was little, she wanted to stay in the mill town, marry a mill worker. But everything's different here now, gone to pieces." She turned her head, and light from the lamp by her bed fell across her face. I could see for the first time how thick her skin was with wrinkles.

"I guess she couldn't see past her own life to find a way to change things," I said, letting my eyes close.

"We're all stuck now," Rose said, "working at the mill. There ain't nowhere to go. Like threads caught behind a beater. Last night," she whispered, "I lay awake in the dark, trying to see if Annie was burning. Seems like I'd know if one of mine was suffering worse than death. But nothing came. Maybe there is mercy."

There was a long time when we both were quiet. "I guess Benjy will be here soon," she said finally.

I hadn't seen Benjy since before I left for college. "And his wife and child," I added.

When I opened my eyes, Rose was watching me. "You need to make your peace with him. This family's lost too much."

BENJY AND HIS WIFE and son arrived that evening, the evening before Annie's funeral. As I watched him walk through the yard I kept waiting for a rush of feeling — anger, hurt, a sense of longing. His body was thicker and bent over with carrying their suitcases. Except for the set jaw, his face was still that of a young Benjy — wide open, as if everything he saw was new to him. I'd had one boyfriend after another since leaving Ash Hill, and I'd left them all the same way I'd left Benjy — never saying goodbye. When I'd been engaged two years ago, I hadn't even sent back the ring, just gone away on a long assignment and changed apartments when I returned.

Benjy and his family entered the house in a flurry. "You must be Silvia," his wife said, embracing me before Benjy was able to give me a quick kiss on the cheek. "I've said to Ben so many times, 'When will I get to meet Silvia?' but it never seemed the right time. And to be brought together by this." She turned to hug Rose. "A tragedy. I am so sorry."

Rachel was a plain-looking woman with long dark hair. Her bangs almost covered her large brown eyes. "This must be your son?" I asked her.

Nodding, she drew the boy out of the doorway and into the room. "This is our Nathan." He was small for a five-year-old, with the same quiet, knowing face Benjy had always had. Rachel pulled me aside. "I'm expecting again, this winter." Benjy had disappeared with their suitcases. "Last month they made Ben crew chief."

"That's nice," I told her.

"He works on all those planes they're sending to 'Nam. I thank God he hasn't had to go."

"Let's all sit down and eat. I know you're hungry," said Rose. It took a while for everyone to find their places and then for Rose to say grace. She never mentioned Annie, just said she was thankful to have us all around one table.

Throughout dinner Aunt Lily told jokes about trains and people leaving town by trains, while Rose served the fried chicken and passed the mashed potatoes and greens around. The rest of us were quiet. "You know what a man likes best about a woman?" Lily asked, and when nobody stopped eating to guess, she told us. "If she moans real sweet, just like a train's whistle coming from far off." She leaned over the table so we could all see down into her loosely fastened blouse. Her skin was wrinkled and gray. "That's why I was so popular." When she started telling stories about June's boyfriends, Mama asked Becky to take her back to her room and get her ready for bed.

"See if you can get her to watch her programs," Mama said as Becky steered her from the room.

"So nice to have dined with you on this memorable occasion," Lily said, turning around to flash a grin before Becky pulled her through the doorway. Rachel stared after them, open-mouthed.

After supper Mama helped Rachel and Benjy get settled in her room. She'd borrowed two rollaways from a friend. She was sleeping on one she'd set up in Lily and June's room. I was sleeping in Becky's room. Marty slept on a cot next to me. I hadn't seen her cry since I got there. She sat in June or Rose's lap constantly, and big as she was, they sometimes carried her with them when they went into another room. Whenever anyone else tried to talk to her, she hid her face in June's skirt and didn't say a word.

It wasn't until late that night that I had a chance to talk with Benjy. Rachel and Nathan went to bed early. Mama tried to stay awake until one or the other of us went to bed, but she fell asleep on the couch. When Benjy went outside, I followed him.

A horde of insects clustered around the porch light. He was sitting on the steps, looking out across the yard. "I can remember when Mama and Daddy were building this house," he said, turning to look at me. "Daddy let me think I put up some of those walls." He moved over on the step so I could sit next to him. "But he was the one out here every spare minute, making sure it all got done right." He blew smoke in a long stream out into the night.

"When did you start smoking?" I asked.

"After I joined up. Seemed like most of the boys were." He gave me a playful nudge. "When did you get those glasses?" I shrugged. "And that short hair-cut." He put out his cigarette, shaking his head. "You sure do look different," he said, turning to look straight at me.

"A lot's changed."

"Yeah, a lot of water under the bridge, or a lot of cloth rolled onto the rollers, as Mama'd say. She always did have some crazy sayings."

"Are you happy?" I asked him. We were both look-ing out into the yard. A dented tricycle lay overturned near the house. Its wheels spun whenever the breeze picked up.

"Sure," he said, as if it meant nothing. "Rachel's a good wife. Nathan's growing up. He starts school in the fall. I guess Rachel told you we got another one on the way." I nodded when he turned his head to look at me. "The air force is a good life."

"A good life, huh?" I laughed. "Do you ever get to fly any of those planes you work on?"

He tapped the ashes from his cigarette. "Don't want to."

"You used to. Used to be, that's all you talked about." Smoke rose up between us.

"And your life's been so wonderful," he said, putting the cigarette between his lips, watching me from the corner of his eyes as he blew out the smoke. "Puerto Rico, the Caribbean, Brazil — Mama's shown me the postcards. Been so busy you only got back once for a visit. Didn't even make it for Daddy's funeral."

I stood up and took a few steps into the night before facing him. "Yeah," I told him. "Well, it's always been hard for me to come back." And I don't know why I bothered to say the rest, except that I'd said everything I could to June and she'd refused to hear me. "Remember how we were in high school?" I asked him. "Remember when we met by the river, all those hours we spent? We were close, Benjy, real close."

His cigarette fell to the ground, and he stood to stomp it out. "You got to quit making stuff like that up," he said, digging in his jacket pocket. "I guess there's always been trouble with some of you women folk on Mom's side of the family. You got to straighten up, get yourself together." He sat down on the step, lit another cigarette with his air force lighter. "Rachel's the only girl I've ever been close to."

I could see him coming home to supper every night, pecking Rachel's cheek, drinking a Coke while he watched the news or read the paper. A marriage made in fantasy land. "You and your mousy wife," I said. "Don't you remember all our plans?"

"Your plans," he said, digging the toe of his boot in the dirt. "We were kids then, pretending." He stood up, ground the cigarette he'd just lit into the concrete step. "It was all play." He stepped up on the porch. "All of it."

He stood in the doorway for a moment, framed by the light. He'd gained too much weight. The lean look he used to have in his face was gone. But his eyes were the same, quiet and open.

When the door closed behind him I looked inside myself for the Silvia who was just seventeen. I saw the trees in the field we used to run through and heard the muddy river rushing back behind our old house. But whatever it was that pulled me to spend hours there with Benjy's taste all through me was gone.

I looked up into the sky. Stars covered the darkness, a milky whiteness of light. Later that night, before I felt Marty crawl into bed with me, I lay awake hearing in the back of my mind the list of places I used to recite: San Francisco, New York, Paris . . . I'd lost that too, my sense of discovery. Traveling to tourist spots had become a routine of escape. But that night before going inside I had stood in the yard, marveling at the tapestry of darkness and light.

Chapter 20

L I L Y ' S   S T O R Y

ROSE CAME into my room just when I had picked out the dress I was gonna wear. I'd bought it way back, on sale. Charles used to say it showed off my hips. "No," says Rose right off, and snatched up the dress from where I'd left it lying on the bed and hung it in the back of the closet.

"I had that picked out special," I told her, walking to the closet. "You shouldn't have put it back. It's dark colored. Just right for a funeral."

She put her arms out so I couldn't get by. "Sit down, Lily," she says, like I'm just a kid. "I'll find a dress for you." Then she pulls out a shapeless dark brown dress she bought for me last year that I ain't ever worn. It's got full-length sleeves and a collar. In May.

"Brown ain't my color," I tell her. "Besides, I'll roast in that big old thing."

"I can get a neighbor to come stay with you," she says, folding her arms across her chest. She looks like a cow that won't be milked. There's a minute where we're both eyeing the other one down.

"All right," I tell her, getting off the bed and walking to my dresser. "I'll wear it." I dig out my makeup bag with the little mirror and start coloring my eyes.

"This is a funeral you're going to," says Rose, "not a party. You don't need none of that."

"No reason not to look my best." I lay my powder, rouge, and eye pencil on the dresser. "I looked good for Forrest's, and at Edward's I stood in the back real proper like in my wide-brimmed hat, you remember? I wish I still had that hat."

She was laying out a slip with the dress and didn't say nothing.

"I like to look good for the dead."

"Stop it." In my mirror I saw her stand up, glaring at the back of my head. "I won't have your blasphemy at my daughter's funeral. It was bad enough you acting that way at your own husband's. I still think . . ." She quit talking and went to digging through my closet.

"You still think what?" I asked, and drew two perfect lines over my eyes, waiting on her answer. "You think I done it, don't you?" I said when she kept still. "You think I killed him."

She was kneeling on the closet floor, her back to me. She'd picked up a pair of shoes.

"Would have been easier if he'd been dead when I found him, like one of them animals he strung up on the porch rail. If he'd died sooner, I wouldn't a had nothing to look back and worry on."

"Oh, God," she whispers, still kneeling, like she was praying.

"What's your God got to say about that?" I asked, sick of her prayers, sick of her clean life. When she took me in after Charles left, she did it to be charitable, like heaven was waiting on those that help their families. "I saw him stumble out of the woods and into the yard," I said, watching her lips move in the mirror, pleading with her Lord to strike me mute. "I let him lie where he fell, just watched from the window until I thought it was over." The rouge I rubbed on my cheeks was a deep red. I smiled into the mirror, hoping she'd see me.

"When I got to him I seen he was still breathing. 'Lily,' he says, 'I got shot. Call a doctor.' I sat down just close enough so we could see each other." I waited for Rose to look up before putting the lipstick to my mouth, but her eyes were empty as she went back to mumbling at the floor, like she hadn't noticed nothing.

"When he seen I weren't moving, his face got hateful," I told her, turning in my chair. "You ever seen somebody look at you like they'd kill you if they got half a chance?" When she quit praying, I went back to my mirror.

"Only asked me once to do something for him, turn

him on his side when the blood started choking him. 'I can't stand to die choking,' he said." I coughed a few times for effect. "When I bent down to turn him, he smiled. 'We could have had something,' he says right before he died. I said, 'Yeah, maybe we could have.'"

"Oh, God," Rose says again, her mouth hanging open like an unhinged door. I pinched my cheeks for the final effect before standing up.

"When I seen he was dead, I went on back to the house, scrubbed the kitchen, then called for the sheriff. I knew Forrest wouldn't want the law coming out with the place dirty. I would have cleaned up Forrest too. Seemed only right since I cleaned all them animals he shot. But the sheriff said not to move him."

I stood in front of Rose, waiting for her to get up. "Charles always said there was only one thing to do on your knees," I told her, "and it wasn't praying or scrubbing floors."

She stood real slow, rubbing her knees. Her shoulders were slumped. "Don't you feel no guilt?" she asked, turning around, my dark brown shoes in her hand.

Walking back to my dressing table, I picked up my gold-plated brush, one of the only things Charles hadn't sold or given to his whore. Maybe if I had told him what I'd just told Rose he wouldn't have done me the way he did, driving off with that whore and all my money. I pulled the brush through my hair, light as I could so not much would fall out. Rose seemed far off and it was just me standing in the room. "I never quit seeing him. I tried everything, even Charles, to keep him away. I still smell his cigars when I wake up. June can believe all the stories she makes up about her life. I never been able to forget nothing." I took off my housecoat. My stomach stuck out like I was pregnant. Everywhere else I was skinny. "So don't think I don't know about dying and funerals." I pulled the slip over my head, careful not to smear my makeup. "Just because I try to look my best at them."

Right then June comes to the door, says she's got Marty dressed. "Do you need any help?" she asks Rose. Rose shakes her head, says to see about the flowers.

When June closes the door, Rose says, "All you done, and I never quit claiming you. I just wish you'd say you're sorry."

I had the dress on. She buttoned it in the back. "Don't change nothing if I am."

"Might change how I felt," she said, slipping the hook into the eye. But I wouldn't say it.

Chapter 21

SILVIA'S STORY

Rose's parlor was filled with flowers the morning of the funeral — tulips, irises, roses — most of them cut fresh from mill workers' yards. My head buzzed with their thick scent. It was just eight-thirty, but Benjy was in the kitchen, already dressed in his uniform, shoveling down scrambled eggs between the orders he gave to Rachel and Nathan. "We got to straighten up here and get over to the church for Mama," he told me, but I found a cereal bowl and spoon, sat down slow as I could, smiled at Rachel.

"So," I said, turning to Benjy. "You think you'll get to go to Vietnam?"

Benjy glanced across the table at me. "I'll go if they send me," he said. "I'll go gladly."

"But Ben—" Rachel's eyes were round with panic. "They're not sending many mechanics over, are they?"

"If they need me, I'll go," he repeated, the heat rising

in his face as it set into hard lines. I wanted to see him this way—Ben Watson, member of the armed forces, not the Benjy I knew. "I'd be proud to go over there and fight," he told us both.

I poured in cereal and milk, spoke at my bowl. "Must have been rough when you didn't get to go to Korea."

Benjy set his fork on the table and left the room. Rachel was crying because she "couldn't stand it if Ben had to go to war." I ate my cereal.

The service was short, the preacher lamenting that Annie was "cut down in the prime of life." At the graveside I spotted Billy, dressed in a poorly fitted new suit, standing with his brother's family and John Lee. According to Rose, John Lee was staying with his uncle until he finished high school. They were putting away the insurance money to pay for college. None of us spoke to Billy, but he and his family and John Lee followed us over to Rose's house after the ceremony.

As we walked to the car, June stopped to speak with an older man wearing an expensive suit, standing apart from everyone else. "Who is that?" I asked Mama, pointing.

Mama just shook her head and climbed into the car next to Aunt Lily. It wasn't until I was seated and had the key in the ignition that Aunt June got in next to me, waving, the man in the well-made suit nodding slightly towards her. "Who is he?" I asked when she'd slid in beside me and closed the door.

"One of her boyfriends," Lily grumbled from the back seat. "I need a smoke." I heard her open her handbag, coughing. "Who took my smokes?" she demanded between coughs. "Somebody's been stealing from me." No one bothered to answer.

"What's his name?" I asked June.

"Mr. Cutler," she replied, looking out the window at the crowd of people climbing into their cars to follow us to Rose's house. "He likes my paintings, calls me a real artist. He's bought three, all of them birds. It was so thoughtful of him to come today."

"James Cutler," I said out loud. "He's changed a lot. What was he doing at the funeral?" Mama's face went white in the rearview mirror.

"Oh," said June, "he's such a gentleman. Poor thing, lost his wife recently." She pulled out a hankie and dabbed her eyes. "That was a beautiful service, Rose, just lovely."

Mama nodded mechanically.

"Does he still work at the First National Bank?" I asked.

"No," Mama said real quick. "This is a different — "

But before she could finish, June said, "Yes, I believe he still does. . . ." Her voice made her sound far away. She was fingering the edges of her hankie.

"He does more than work at the First National," says Lily all of a sudden. "He owns that bank. And years ago — "

But Mama made her hush. "Annie just dead and hardly

buried any time. I'm ashamed of all this talk." The rest
of the drive, no one spoke.

Later that afternoon at the house, as I finished telling
Mr. Hart about my work with the travel magazine, I saw
Mr. Cutler standing in the doorway. Our eyes met, but
he quickly turned to June. "I just stopped by to pay my
respects," he said, stepping outside.

I reached his car before he got in. His face was smooth.
There was no hint he knew. "You must be Rose's girl,"
he said, his hand resting on the car's door. It was a dark
Cadillac.

"Yes." I looked into his eyes; nothing. He didn't seem
at all nervous. "She brought me up."

"Oh, yes." The recognition was false. "The one who
lives in Florida and writes for a travel magazine. Rose
and June are both so proud of you."

I looked for a crack, a thin split like a thread missing.
There was none. "You know who I am," I said finally.

He pulled the car door open, but I put my arm across
it, blocking his way. For a while we just looked at each
other. The mask had slipped off, and I watched as he put
it on again, slowly, the smile coming back to his mouth,
the smoothness returning to his eyes. "What do you want?"
he asked. "Money?"

After Rose first told me that James had my mother
put away, she refused to talk about it. No matter how
many times I called to ask what happened, she said she
didn't know. I'd waited for years to hear the truth.

"I want to hear you say what happened," I told him. "I want to hear from you why you had her locked up for years."

He looked at the ground, shook his head. "You know, I didn't mean for it to happen that way."

"You think because you buy her paintings now and sit down at a table with her over coffee like old friends that changes everything. You think it erases the past." I tried to make him look at me. "All through high school the only boy I got to know was my brother. The other kids teased me about being a bastard. First Rose tells me my parents are dead; then I find out my own father didn't want me enough to claim me."

He looked into my face. "I'm sorry." When he reached out to touch my shoulder, I jumped. "But things do change," he said. "I know I can't erase the past, but I need to see June now, even if she doesn't seem to know who I am. I love her paintings. They make me feel happy, and it makes her happy when I buy them. What's the harm in that?"

I made him wait for my answer. "It's a lie," I told him. "That's the harm. You're living a lie. You had her locked away. You ruined her life. Then you pretended I didn't exist. You even told the hospital I was dead. At the bank, both times, you acted like you didn't know me. What would it have cost you to call and ask how I was once in a while, to have admitted you were my father at the bank that day? You erased me."

His cold thin fingers circled my arm. "You don't understand. All those years, I worried about you. But I didn't want to confuse you once you were older by telling you I was your father. When you came to the bank that afternoon, I was just too startled. I couldn't think straight." His eyes searched my face. "Do you understand me?"

I said nothing.

"Look," he said, shaking his head, his eyes on the ground. "You need to put all this behind you." He forced a laugh. "You turned out better than the daughter I raised. She's living on some commune. And after all I spent on that private college she went to."

I'd started writing to Janet after I left Ash Hill for college. I'd told her we were half-sisters and she'd written back, saying she felt like she didn't have James for a father either and how he was always at the bank. We'd kept in touch while she was at Bennington and later when she worked in an art museum in Washington, D.C. I'd visited the farm she lived on in Maryland when I was writing a tour brochure on that part of the East Coast. A dozen or more people lived there with her. They were raising their own food and pounding out plant hooks in a metal shop they'd set up in an old chicken coop. Their idea was to be self-sufficient.

She was worried about her mother, who had recently become sick with cancer, and for the first time she spoke candidly about her parents' relationship. There was little love between them, she told me. Her mother had been wrapped up in her club work for years, and James lived for the bank. They hadn't shared a bedroom since Janet could remember.

"Do you think he loved my mother," I asked her, "and never got over her?"

Janet shrugged. She said she couldn't imagine him in love with anyone.

She seemed so clear about her past; she seemed free of it. I envied her for that and for the complete physical abandon with which she threw herself into her work. I watched her feed the goats they kept, stuffing hay into the feeders, scooping out grain for their buckets, stroking each one behind the ears as it nuzzled against her. I could feel how much she was herself and not James's daughter. And I saw how in not claiming me he had determined my life more than hers. The man on the farm whom she shared her life with was a gentle carpenter who was turning the smaller barn and outbuildings into homes for the people living there. I always got involved with men who were remote, and my longest relationship had lasted nine months. I couldn't believe anyone could want me.

James was watching me intently, as if there might be a space somewhere in my silence that he could step into. "If you need any money," he said finally, "I'll give it to you. I'd like to help you." He held out his hands like he had something to offer me. I clenched the edge of the car door and shook my head. "Don't tell June," his voice was pleading. "Just don't tell June. I need her. I need to come here and see her. It's helped me. It's helped change the past so I can live with it."

He looked at the ground. I wanted him to cry. "I want to change things with you, Silvia," he said. "I'd like to offer you something — money, whatever you want. . . ."

"What you did was wrong; your whole life — wrong." I let go of the car door. "I want nothing from you." I turned and walked towards the house.

It wasn't until I had nearly reached the front porch, until after he drove away, that I felt the tears. I couldn't stop them from coming. I couldn't wipe them away, not even when I saw June hurrying towards me. "Poor thing," she said, patting me as if I were a small child. "You just let it out. Crying's the best thing when someone's died." And burying my face in her bosom, I wept.

When June led me back to the house, Rose hugged me, sat me down in a chair on the porch where there was a breeze, and fixed me a plate of ham slices, bread, and coleslaw. "There's dessert inside," she told me. "Now eat up. It'll make you feel better."

June reached over to pat my knee. "That Mr. Cutler is so nice," she said.

I glanced up at Rose. "Oh, yes," she agreed, nodding. "He sent a beautiful flower arrangement of white lilies. It's in the parlor."

Several of Rose's and Annie's friends from the mill sat on the porch, eating. Their conversations spun around me. I wanted to shout at Rose and June, "Don't you remember what he did thirty years ago? How can you say he's 'so nice'?" But I sat there staring into my coleslaw.

Just then Marty ran out onto the porch. "Where's my mommy?" she asked Rose.

"She's in heaven, baby," Rose told her. Annie's letter was hidden away by now or destroyed. I knew Marty would grow up believing her mother was killed in an accident. No telling what story Rose would make herself believe. She and June took Marty's hands and led her inside.

As soon as the door shut behind them, Aunt Lily, who sat in a rocker with a plate full of cake, cackled. "All this time worrying about which side of the tracks we were living on, and if we'd just got on the tracks we'd a been in heaven."

An older mill worker, who was too small for his suit, tapped a spoon against his chair and said, "Yep, you got a point there."

"Reckon," said Lily, "if I were to lie down on that track, the train'd pull out of Ash Hill, taking me to heaven?"

No one said anything.

"It'd pull me sixty feet this side of town and leave me for the birds to find." She was smoking a cigarette and had to bend over to grind it out on the concrete floor. "That's all I'd be — meat for birds or maybe a pack of wild dogs."

Rose stood in the doorway. As everyone stood to go

inside or walk in the yard, she told Lily to hush through the screen. "There's a God of justice and mercy, and you know it. Annie lived a pure life. She's in heaven right now, watching over us."

Everyone still standing on the porch nodded, but I stared at the screen door, now empty, in amazement. I saw how Lily, June, and Rose had all created their own worlds, and although they lived together and had shared much of what had happened in their lives, each one still held on to a separate way of seeing those events. Even though their lives might intersect one another, they'd all lived apart, alone. No one knew anymore what had really happened. And it didn't matter.

And I knew then, sitting on Rose's porch, touched by a slight breeze in the afternoon heat, that I created my world also. My own mother and father might have tried to erase my existence, but I could create myself now; I could let myself, Silvia, daughter of June and James Cutler, daughter also to Rose and Edward, live.

On the quiet porch, I ate the food Rose had brought me. As it turned out, traveling to faraway places had not helped me to leave Ash Hill. I'd had to come back to put Ash Hill behind me.

Chapter 22

ROSE'S STORY

SOON AFTER Annie's death, Becky moved out. I had just got home with the groceries and was standing in front of the refrigerator with a bottle of ketchup in my hand when she told me. "Penny needs a roommate," she said. "The apartment's all furnished and real modern, with a kitchen range and a dishwasher." A dishwasher. I couldn't imagine how a machine could do that. I like to feel my plates and glasses all soapy and warm, then watch them shine under the rinse water.

"When you moving?" I asked her.

"Next week." She opened a box of cookies I'd set on the counter.

"Well" — I shrugged — "be out on your own, I guess. That's what you been wanting." I was thinking on them doctors she goes out with and how it'd look with her living at her own place.

"I'll still come by," she said, taking the cookies she wanted from the box, "to drive Lily to her hair appointments and all."

After she got moved I put Marty in her old room. When I'm at work, Marty stays with June and Lily. June lets Marty paint on sheets of paper she gets from the butcher, while she's making her pictures on black velvet. When I get home Marty tells me all she done, as I make supper. Some evenings Cassy brings John Lee out for a visit. He throws ball with Marty, and Cassy shows us all the marks he makes in school. He wants to go on to college like Silvia did.

This morning it's Saturday and so bright and clear we tell Lily to turn off her programs and come outside. She won't listen until Marty begs her. She lets the child pull her to her feet and out the door. A child's love can work miracles, I think, watching how Marty gets Lily to carry her baby doll for her as she chases Lily around the yard. Marty is such a happy child. She asks for her mama still, which is only natural, and asks God to "keep Mama in heaven" when she says her prayers. But she shows love to me and June, and last night I found her curled up asleep on the couch next to Lily.

"Just leave the baby awhile," says Lily when I went to carry her to bed. It was ten o'clock before Lily'd let me take her.

"I can't run no more," Lily shouts, and nearly falls down next to me. She's coughing so hard I'm afraid she won't be able to quit. Marty races to the shed and pulls out an old wagon. "That child can run," Lily says between coughs.

"You better sit down and rest yourself," I tell Lily, and lead her to the porch. I get her in a chair and go in for a glass of water. When I bring it out for her, she's pointing at Marty.

"Look at that." She laughs. "Marty's telling the little dog from up the road how to pull the wagon." June's digging in her garden. Lily sips her water, and the cough stops. "Having Marty here makes me think I might not be an old woman yet," says Lily. "Sometimes it seems like she belongs to us."

"She does," I say, settling back in my chair. "Now that her mama's died and gone to heaven."

"Heaven," she says. Lily coughs again and spits over the porch rail. "I couldn't have no children. Forrest always wanted them. I never let on to him, even after the doctor told me my womb was all tore up."

"I never knew that," I say. "Was it sickness?"

Her laugh is so loud Marty squints in the bright air to see us. "Do you want your baby doll?" I call to her, and run to take it from the porch and put it in the wagon.

"Go for a ride, baby," I hear her say as I walk back.

"I was always healthy as a horse," Lily says when I sit down again. "You know that. Never had to miss a day of work. But even after the divorce was final, I kept on seeing Charles. Forrest was courting me when I knew I was pregnant, carrying Charles's bastard. As it was, I had to do some sweet talking to get Forrest to take an interest in me, me being divorced and all. Once he seen I was pregnant, I wouldn't have had a chance."

Lily will drive me to my grave with her stories. I can't see how she lives with them, but I nod my head.

"There was a doctor in town, or at least I heard he was a doctor. I had to go to a house after dark. He made me lay on a bed with my feet in the air. I passed out. When I woke up my clothes and the sheets were soaked with blood. There was a woman telling me to get up, that I had to leave. The bleeding had stopped, but I was so faint I nearly crawled on the sidewalk."

"Marty," I call out, to hear the sound of my voice. But she is too busy trying to pull the wagon over the grass to look up. If Lily's mind goes anymore, we'll have to find a home for her, like Becky says.

"Charles's room was right down the road," she goes on. "The boardinghouse lady comes to the door when I knocked. It was still dark. I was lying on the step. 'Get your trash out of here,' she says to Charles after dragging him out. He carried me to his bed. When I told him what I done, he kisses me real gentle over and over, whispering that we'll get married again and we can have another one. I let him say it. He took care of me for three days, until I got better." She takes to coughing and has to drink her water. "Never could have children after that. Thing is, I did it for Forrest, and then we get married and the one thing he wants from me is a baby. Didn't care much about lovemaking, even though I was good." She winks, grinning, just like we was girls again. Then the coughing starts up.

"Now, Lily," I tell her, "you hush awhile. Telling those stories aggravates your throat. I don't know where you get those wild tales, but I hope you have sense not to tell them when Marty's around."

"Wild tales. I've had me some wild tails," Lily says, trying to laugh between coughs. But just then Marty climbs up on the porch, which hushes her.

"Would you help me get on the swing, Granny?" she says, sweet as can be.

"Of course, baby." I follow her to the tire Benjy hung from the tree while he was here for the funeral and lift her so she can put her legs through. "Hold on," I tell her, and give her a push.

That afternoon me and June sit on the porch. Thomas Midkiff, who's come calling, is in the yard teaching Marty how to throw a ball. "Silvia called," I say, sitting on the swing next to June. "She's moving to California."

June smiles. "I loved California. Palm trees, sandy beaches . . ."

"That was Florida," I tell her.

She looks at me, surprised. "Well, their climates are similar," she says finally.

"She leaves the end of the summer," I say, watching

Marty jump to try and catch the ball. Thomas was throwing it too high. "She wants to go to graduate school there."

"Well, that's good." June leans back in the swing, smiling.

"Annie left a bag filled with patches, little squares she must have cut from old mill scraps," I tell June. "They're the perfect size for quilting. Cassy had it sent over to me at the mill yesterday."

June claps her hands together like a child. "We can sew them into a quilt, Rose. Just like the one Mama made before she died." This is the first thing June has remembered of our childhood since she went to Columbia. "It'd have some of Annie in it," she goes on. "We could give it to Marty when she's grown."

"I've got lots of mill scraps I've been saving, packed in grocery sacks in my closet," I tell June. Soon I'll have to quit the mill. And with all mine gone, and Silvia moved to California, where I'll never see her, I'll need something to keep me busy. "I still can't get over Silvia moving," I say to June.

June turns to me and smiles. "She should do what she wants with her life."

"You know, you're right." I smile back at her, patting her knee. "I was thinking she was just running off to get far away as she could, but she's doing what she wants, weaving her own cloth. None of us ever did."

"You can't always tell what makes things come out a

certain way. I never thought my husband would die so young, before we had a chance to have children. We do what we can."

I don't try to tell June her life is any different than the way she remembers it.

Part 5

---

1 9 8 1

Chapter 23

SILVIA'S STORY

IT WAS A FIVE-HOUR DRIVE from Ash Hill to the college in North Carolina that Marty was attending. She'd taken the bus down for Rose's funeral, but I'd promised I'd drive her back in the rental car. It would mean an extra day before I got back to San Francisco, and I'd be rushed to complete my article, but I needed the morning drive with Marty, who was the closest I'd ever come to having a daughter and my link to Rose and June.

We spent the day before the drive cleaning out Rose's house so I could lock it up while Becky, Benjy, and I decided how to sell it. Marty carefully unpinned her posters and the postcards I'd sent her from the piece of cork that covered one wall of her room. Several were from my trip to Europe when I wrote an article on Berlin for a news journal a few years ago. When I had stayed

in Paris, I called Marty. She wanted to know everything — what the French were wearing, the color of the
Seine, the sounds of the city at night.

Next to the postcards was a world map with bright
thumbtacks stuck into the countries I'd traveled to. "You
should save the map too," I told her. "Someday it'll be
covered with tacks showing the places you've been to."
Later I found it, folded on top of the postcards, the tacks
in a glass jar beside it.

In another bag, she placed the small ceramic figures
I'd sent Rose from Peru. I'd been there three months,
and when I returned it was with Brad, who'd been doing
agricultural research there. We were married a few months
later. "Do you mind if I take this too?" Marty asked. It
was a small pillow Rose had sewn from a piece of em-
broidered cloth I'd bought from a woman in one of the
villages.

"Go ahead," I called. "Get everything you want now,
before the house gets sold. All I want are the set of tea-
cups with the hand-painted flowers and the quilt Granny
made for her years ago. You should keep the one Rose
and June made from mill scraps when you were little."
Rose had kept all her important papers in a shoe box in
a cabinet over the kitchen sink. In it, I guessed, were
June's release papers from the hospital in Columbia and
a record of the agency that had handled the adoption of
June's second child. Shortly after I moved to California,
I wrote letters and made phone calls trying to locate my

half-sister, but none of the agencies I contacted listed the name Reynolds. Then a few years ago, after June's death, Rose told me she had papers documenting June's release and stating the name of the adoption agency, but she refused to look for them. Now I couldn't find the box.

As we were loading our bags into the car, Becky drove up in her freshly waxed cream-colored Buick. "Get everything you wanted?" she called out as she slammed the car door. She wore a lime-green dress with matching shoes and a jacket. The dress fit snugly across the thickness of her hips.

I nodded. "How about you?" I asked, knowing she'd come over before the funeral to get the china set she wanted.

"Oh, yeah. Wasn't much I did want." Marty carried a box from the porch. Like me, she wore blue jeans and a sweater. Becky took a few steps towards us. "Come have supper at my house tonight. At six. Marty knows where the house is." It was a new house, built a few years ago by her husband, a pharmaceutical salesman. "Too bad John Lee had to rush back to Atlanta. We could have had a regular get-together," she added. "But at least you two can come." John Lee worked in Atlanta as an engineer. He had driven down for the funeral but had to get back that same evening to his wife and little girl.

"Thanks, but we've got to get an early start." I slammed the door to the trunk. "It's a five-hour drive, and I have to be in San Francisco by Wednesday morning." I wanted to spend the entire evening at Rose's house, just sit on the porch and watch the sun drop into the mountains.

"Nonsense," she called, walking back to her car. "I'll see you at six."

Marty smiled as the car drove off. "I think she wants you to see her new house."

"I know she wants me to see her new house." I grinned. "Is it expensive looking? Is it elegant?"

She laughed. "The rooms look like they were set up for a photographer that never came. If you move a chair or pick up a magazine, she sets it back exactly as it was. The kitchen is so clean I doubt she's ever cooked in it. It's got four big bedrooms — two are for guests, or maybe she just shows them to guests."

"Let's finish," I said, smoothing back Marty's long light brown hair. "I want to sit on the porch awhile one last time. Do you know how often Aunt June and your grandma sat on that swing?" As I pointed, the swing swayed slightly, creaking in the breeze. Most of the white paint had peeled off, but the surface was rubbed smooth.

"About every night," said Marty as we carried the last paper sacks to the car. "Grandma used to sit on that swing by herself after Aunt June died."

"Let's wait to lock up," I said as we walked back to the house. "We can do it in the morning." I motioned for her to sit next to me on the swing. We'd cleaned out the kitchen and swept the floors, but I put off locking the windows and doors. There was too much of Rose and June left.

"Do you think they're still here, in the house?" Marty shivered. Her long legs dangled from the swing.

"Not like ghosts or anything," I told her, "but look at all they made here, like that clump of tulips starting to bud. Can't you just see June over there, kneeling next to them, coaxing them open?"

I felt Marty nod. "You know, Grandma called a few days before she had the stroke. She asked what I planned to do after I graduated, and I told her I wanted to write, like you, or maybe study law. I told her about your offer to come and live in San Francisco and work for your newsmagazine while I decide."

I turned to look at her. Marty's eyes had always been the softest shade of gray. Without them, she wouldn't have been pretty. Her face was plain, and she had Annie and Rose's nose. "What did she have to say? Did she like the idea?"

"I think she did. She said that California was a far-away place and she might not see me again, but that she'd be at peace if she knew I'd be happy. She made me promise never to work in the mills. I guess because of what happened to my mother."

I had to smile.

"Grandma worked in the mills most of her life and she did all right." Marty glanced at me. "She always seemed happy with the way her life turned out."

"Your grandmother would have enjoyed anything she

did. She used to sing hymns while she scrubbed our clothes in an old galvanized tub. During the Depression, when we were little, she found time to grow a big garden so we'd have fresh vegetables all summer. And she'd can what was left over."

"I heard what you said at the funeral to that man who used to be her boss, about how she didn't get to be a fine strong woman from working at the mills but she was born that way, and how he was lucky to have Grandma work for him." Marty glanced at me, then stretched her feet out in front of her and studied her worn sneakers. "I know what you meant. They shouldn't take the credit. She made herself that way."

I nodded. Rose had left a large metal watering can next to a thin dogwood she'd recently planted. I could see her lugging the full can to the tree, cold water splashing her legs and feet, then tilting it slowly while the water sprinkled around the tree's roots.

Marty looked out into the yard also. "You know, when Aunt Lily died, I was still pretty young, and that fall I got all worried about her and where she was. I used to ask Grandma if she was in heaven and how could that be if we'd buried her. Grandma told me the dead take care of themselves and I better start worrying about my schoolwork and passing my math test. I guess that's how she always was. I think she knew she was going to die when she called me. She was worrying about how I'd live my life."

I put my arm around Marty and gave her a squeeze.

It crossed my mind that perhaps this perceptive young woman deserved to know the truth about her mother's death, but I saw that Marty was content with what she knew. She'd seen both parents buried before she was twelve. Lily had died of emphysema when Marty was eight, and June had died six years later. This was the fifth family funeral she'd been to.

The sun had slipped towards earth. The edges of the clouds turned pink. "I guess we better go," I said to Marty. "Your Aunt Becky will be waiting."

"We don't want to get there until she's thrown out the evidence." Marty laughed. "Whenever she's had Grandma and me over, she cooks frozen dinners in her microwave, arranges the food on plates, and throws away the boxes. Grandma found out when Aunt Becky forgot and left a box on the counter. Sometimes the meat's still cold in the middle."

We both laughed. "I can't wait. You know, it's been too long since I came for a visit. How old is Becky's daughter?"

"Diane? She's in high school. I used to see her at the pool when Aunt Becky would take Grandma and me. Her mother thinks Diane is real active in the clubs after school, but I bet she stays late so she can get high."

"What does Aunt Becky spend her day doing?" I asked. "Watching soaps?"

"Yeah, and making sure her house is ready in case the photographers from *Better Homes and Gardens* arrive to take pictures."

I shook my head and let my laughter rise up out of me so that Rose and June would hear. "Come on," I nearly shouted. "Let's go." And I pulled Marty from the swing. In the morning we'd have to shut the house up, but tonight the wind could come through the screens, sweeping away all that had happened, until the house, like us, let go of the dead.

WHEN I DROVE Marty back to college the next morning, I said goodbye to Ash Hill. Since I wasn't close to Becky anymore, there wouldn't be much reason for me to go back. The leaving wasn't hard, with a bright morning drive through the mountains ahead of us and our voices slowly filling the car. I described for Marty the house Brad and I had recently built outside San Francisco and Brad's two sons, who were also in college and spent some of the summers and holidays with us. "You'll love it," I kept assuring her. "I'll have a room fixed up for you when you get there." I promised to hang lots of plants in the window and buy a bright woven blanket for her bed.

Marty reminded me of the trip we'd all taken to California when she was a young girl. I had flown back for Aunt Lily's funeral and afterwards had insisted they all drive back with me in a rented car. I'd promised to get them home by the end of the summer. Rose and June got up the next morning, and the car was loaded with their things. Marty'd stayed up late helping me pack the clothes and food they needed for the trip. They had no choice but to go. The drive out there was as memorable as the two-month visit. Rose surprised us all by taking the wheel most of the time and driving seventy. "Get this car on down the road," she'd mutter when I slowed to let another car pass us. June talked nonstop about tropical fruit and how she'd lived in a house right on the prettiest beach in all of California just after she was married. She ate a mango every morning of the visit.

Since then I'd only come back for short visits, but I wrote to Marty often. And since she turned nine, she has written to me, long letters filled with everything she saw as she rode her bike around town, and she sometimes recorded the stories June or Rose told about the past. When June started talking out loud to God all the time before she died, and Marty was scared, I came and stayed for a week, then took Marty for another week to Atlanta with me. And when I found out Rose needed more money to send Marty to college, I was glad I could afford to send it.

"If I can, I'll fly out for your graduation," I tell her as we drive through the mountains. "Maybe we can take a trip to Mexico later this summer, after you move to California."

Marty turns to smile at me, and behind that smile I see Annie, Rose, and even June. When she laughs I hear their voices ring out. Outside the car's window, branches cross one on top of another, the dark limbs and pale green buds layered with light. We disappear into the pattern.